10.24

MW00464271

Mike Grist is the British/American author of the Chris Wren and Girl Zero thrillers. Born and brought up in the UK, he has lived and worked in the USA, Japan and Korea as a teacher, photographer and writer. He enjoys Ultimate Frisbee, 5k runs and spending time with his wife and son.

Christopher Wren (thrillers)
Saint Justice

No Mercy

Make Them Pay

False Flag

Firestorm

Enemy of the People

Backlash

Never Forgive

War of Choice

Hammer of God

Girl Zero (thrillers)
Girl Zero

Zero Day

Kill Zero

The Last Mayor (post-apocalypse)
The Last

The Lost

The Least

The Loss

The List
The Laws
The Lash
The Lies
The Light

NO MERCY

A CHRISTOPHER WREN THRILLER

MIKE GRIST

SHOTGUN
BOOKS

SHOTGUN BOOKS

www.shotgunbooks.com

Copyright © Mike Grist 2019

Mike Grist asserts the moral right to be identified as the author of this book. All rights reserved.

No part of this publication may be reproduced, stored in a retrieval system, or transmitted, in any form or by any means without the prior written permission of the author.

This book is a work of fiction, and except in the case of historical fact, any resemblance to actual persons, living or dead, is purely coincidental.

Paperback ISBN - 9781739951122

1

MINSK

C hristopher Wren laid out flat atop a snow-capped roof somewhere on the outskirts of Minsk, Belarus. Through the scope of his Barrett M82 sniper rifle, he watched a building three hundred yards away, praying this would be the raid that finally made his family safe.

In the tawny dusk light, the building looked like nothing special. Just another communist-era construction, a brutalist block of thin concrete slabs held together with propaganda postings, like the gravestone for a dying ideology. Wren picked out scraps of communist-red clenched-fist posters, overlaid atop Lenin's jutting arm and the old and gold hammer and sickle. Breaking the ramshackle effect were several newer, metal-barred windows on each of the building's seven floors, with a single steel door at ground floor opening onto a snow-frosted sidewalk.

Wren switched to his Thor infrared scope. Heat-mapped, the building was alive with processing power. The outlines of hundreds of computer server racks across all seven stories blazed like a hellish scaffold, glowing brightest at the top. Thick data lines burned hot down the building's exterior, venting heat before they plunged through holes drilled to the sewers, each laundering vast quantities of dark Internet data out to the open digital ocean.

This had to be it.

For six months Wren had been hunting the mythical Blue Fairy.

She flitted through the dark Internet's hidden trunk lines like a ghost, leaving only her stylized, child-like image as a calling card on the vilest chat boards. She was a signal to the world's most depraved men, promising services they couldn't get anywhere else.

Drugs. Sex. Weapons.

Kids.

Six months ago, the names of Wren's own children had been unearthed in the papers of the Saints, marked with the Blue Fairy symbol, just when he'd been ready to quit the black ops life for good.

Now he was here.

He redoubled his focus on the building ahead.

Five bright orange figures were on guard on the ground floor near the entrance. A few stood scattered across the levels, two patrolled the roof, and three were seated on the seventh floor; their faint haloes outlined within the white-hot heat of the servers, searing through the thin walls.

These had to be Blue Fairy cyber traffickers, hard at work managing the ceaseless flow of criminal data; every byte another slice of human misery. It would be better to take them alive if he could, gather every possible shred of evidence, but the real prize was the building itself. The data flowing through its hundreds of servers, kept invisible by Belarus' dictator-sanctioned haven status, should be enough to bring the Blue Fairy and its wider network down.

"In position, Commander," came a voice in Wren's earpiece. This was his Interpol captain, Isa Rashidi, a 6' 5" Ukrainian special forces soldier.

Wren swung the scope over and down to a dark alley at the building's side. Rashidi stood in front of the glowing yellow engine of their bullet-shaped UAZ-452 insertion van; a Russian Military Police vehicle that looked like a VW camper van. Plenty of them around in Belarus, easy to blend in. Around it stood Rashidi's five-strong Interpol IRT Incident Report Troop.

Rashidi was a man Wren trusted implicitly. He'd been instrumental in one of Wren's biggest black-ops stings on the Belarusian regime, toppling an underground railroad in trafficked humans several years back. Wren pulled back from the scope to bare-eye the alley, but the troop were wholly invisible in their gray urban camo gear.

"You have eyes on the power line?" Wren asked, switching back to the scope.

"Yes, Commander." Rashidi opened the rear doors of the van. "Under the chassis, beneath a grating. It looks like two-inch reinforced copper sheaths. We will burn the grate, then my team blow the lines on a ten-second fuse. All the lights will go out."

Not all the lights. Wren swept his gaze up to the seventh floor, where the lone dark block in the superheated space marked out the building's backup generator. Taking that out fell to Wren. He scanned up to the roof, where the guards patrolled. They didn't seem to have noticed a thing. Wren's CIA overwatch team had already digitally looped their CCTV remotely. If only it was as simple a thing to hack their darknet.

"You're screened from above?"

"Yes, under the UAZ. We are ready to cut the grating for access. Two blowtorches, two minutes."

Two minutes. Six months of prep.

"Cut it."

Wren caught the flare of the blowtorches igniting

underneath the van. He checked again on the two men on the rooftop through the scope, but there was no response. No line of sight, with the van in the way. He shuffled his grip on the M82's stock, then checked his chamber; loaded with .50 caliber Browning Machine Gun rounds, able to make mincemeat of a wall even ten inches thick. With the rifle on semi-automatic, he could put a dozen shots from the box magazine through the wall in ten seconds flat.

He'd need them all. Turn the backup generator to slag, and no one else Wren trusted to make the shot. Miss it, or the traffickers if they ran, and the warning signal would go out. The darknet would know a hit was underway, and any trace of the Blue Fairy would flush from their servers as if they'd never been there at all.

Six months' worth of intelligence capture and asset risk lost in a flash.

"Explosives placed," came Rashidi's voice in Wren's headset. "Standing ready."

Wren took one last breath, looking out over the city. The faintest glow of a cold, dreary day died out in a rust-red line across the western horizon. Some four thousand miles further on, his kids would still be asleep in their Delaware duplex with no idea of the threat hanging over their heads.

Wren intended to keep it that way.

A wind gusted, pulling him back to the moment. Maybe minus ten degrees out now, and seemed fresh snow was in the offing. He adjusted the scope's reticle to the wind, took a steadying breath. The air tasted of diesel fumes and raw onion, stinging down his lungs.

He wasn't a fan of Minsk.

"Blow it."

"Fuse is lit," answered Rashidi. Wren refocused his scope on the backup generator, nestled between two of the traffickers on the seventh floor. At the same time he watched

4

with his off-eye as Rashidi led his IRT troops toward the building's front, readying a portable ram. Five seconds, three, then came the firework flash from under the van, the firecracker snap as the blast reached Wren, and he was firing.

The first shot burrowed dust from the wall dead-on, the second hit three inches over, the third tore a divot and the next five .50 cal slugs tunneled wider through crumbling concrete to rupture anything on the other side. Metal, plastic, wiring, bodies.

"Power's out on the ground floor," came Rashidi's voice in his ear, accompanied by the muted barks of rifle fire. "Two down so far. We're seeing heavy-gauge server stacks, computers are all dark."

Exactly as planned. Wren scanned the guys on the seventh floor. One of them was down and motionless already, might have caught a ricochet or shrapnel, another was balled-up under his desk, but then Wren caught a shadow of the third, running west toward the core server racks.

Either making a break to escape, or toward a kill switch to fry every computer on the grid. Every darknet hub he'd come across had a self-destruct plan of some kind: one pull to self-combust the servers, sending the evidence Wren needed up in digital smoke.

He couldn't take that chance, and fired three times through the wall. The guy's orange silhouette collapsed. Maybe going for the door, but equal chance he was going for an explosive breaker.

He swung back to the two other guys, saw the one lying flat was now moving at a crawl. Wren put a shot through his chest to be sure. No loss. The balled-up one hadn't budged. All the better to keep at least one alive. He could help them open Pandora's Box.

"Ground floor clear," Rashidi said in his earpiece. "Five hostiles down. We're heading up."

"Proceed with caution," Wren said, and reached out a hand to his loader, who dropped a fresh box of BMGs into it. Took three seconds to eject the old box and insert the new, then he swung the scope up to the roof.

The two guys there looked to be panicking, dithering at the edge. Their heat signatures came in crystal-clear compared to the diffused blue of the others, seen through the building's tissue-thin walls. Wren pinged them both with chest shots then strafed the scope down to scan Rashidi's path, catching movement on the third floor. It didn't look like armed response, someone running in the wrong direction to flee, but maybe headed for the trip switch.

Wren fired five times, and the figure collapsed.

"Second floor looks clear," Rashidi said.

"Two down on the seventh, two on the roof, one on the third," Wren answered. "Entering overwatch."

"Appreciate it, Commander."

Wren scrolled the building, tracking ahead of the IRT as Rashidi led them higher. In back of the squad a figure silhouetted itself briefly, maybe bobbing out of the elevator shaft before dropping back in.

Wren fired without thinking, the rest of the mag and clipped the guy's arm through concrete as he ducked back into shelter.

"Your floor, man winged behind the elevator," he reported.

"I see him," said Rashidi, sent his troops flanking. More rifle fire erupted then died away.

"Second floor clear, continuing the ascent."

Wren's heart pounded. He reached out a hand and received another reload, another three seconds to switch out. It took his eye off the scope for a heartbeat, and when he looked again the trafficker on the seventh floor was in motion. Heading the same way as the first, west to the server racks.

Wren cursed and fired every round from the box, sawing a line through the wall to cut the guy down like a felled tree. He dropped.

Wren let a breath. "All three on the seventh are down."

"I heard that. They ran?"

"They ran."

"It's a pity. Third floor's clear. Anything else in store?"

Wren reloaded again, sweating now despite the cold. "I think you're clear."

The building looked quiet except for the IRT methodically clearing room by room. The building didn't have a big footprint. He swept the building again, saw nothing, then pulled out from the scope and blinked once long and slow before casting his eyes over the street.

Hot afterimages popped across the dark road. About time reinforcements appeared.

"We have incoming," came another voice in his ear, this one belonging to Sally Rogers, his CIA lieutenant poached from a rival department, and a brilliant field analyst. She was a hard charger, aiming for Director-level before she was forty. Brought up as a military brat, dragged halfway around the world by two Army parents until her mom was killed in Afghanistan, she burned with a need for revenge.

Wren liked that about her. You couldn't fake drive.

She was operating remotely out of Texas, with eyes in the sky via a LUNA surveillance drone at ten thousand feet. "Looks like two trucks inbound, they're big, eight-wheelers, maybe MKZT-6002 by the profiles. Military bearing, five men apiece."

Wren cursed under his breath. The MKZT-6002 was a beast, looked like the flatbed for a tower construction crane, but no crane attached. Squat and solid as a double-length Humvee, and not commonplace on the streets at all.

But they were ready for this.

"Activate the second squad."

Somewhere below a second IRT squad fired up their UAZ van, ready to ram the inbound trucks. It'd barely make a dent on the eight-wheelers, though.

"Coming out of the northeast, boss," Rogers said.

Wren swung the scope over the building one more time, saw Rashidi on the fourth floor and advancing unopposed, then trained in on the road coming in from the north. No sign of the massive MKZTs yet.

"Estimate fifteen seconds 'til you have visibility."

They'd prepared for something like this. Not coming so fast, or with as much mass behind them, but he had redundancies in place. A Lada saloon below waiting to ferry Wren closer to any action, a second UAZ van weighted down with plate metal, ready to act as a ram or blockade a road.

"I'll take their engine blocks if I can," he said. "Get the ram vehicle ready to intercept."

"Boss."

Three seconds left, then the first of the squared-off MKZT-6002s came into sight, as big as a squashed garbage truck and racing at forty miles an hour. Easily three times the mass of his UAZ backup van, even loaded down with metal. Most likely it would be shredded by the bigger MKZTs.

Wren unloaded with the M82 rifle. He hit the glass windshield but sparked off, had to be triple-layer reinforced. He tagged the front grille but it was armored and didn't do a thing to slow the truck's momentum.

"Unable," he barked, reloading as the truck plowed on, chased by the second. "Hit it with the UAZ!"

Two blocks over, the UAZ rocketed out of a side street at

the perfect ninety-degree vector, making up with velocity what it lacked in mass. The hit came with a delayed crunch, just enough mass to jog the massive military vehicle to the side and send it careening up the curb to bury itself in a shuttered storefront.

Wren drilled twelve more shots through the windshield, digging enough holes to take out the driver and passenger and maybe coring the engine from above.

"Boss!" called Rogers.

He swung as he reloaded, watched the second MKZT-6002 closing on the building. He didn't have the angle now, it was almost directly below his vantage point. He fired shots that sparked off its roof and bodywork, then it stopped at the front of the server building, shielding the entrance with its bulk.

"You have incoming, Rashidi!" He shouted down the line. "Rogers, give us a count of how many enter the building."

A second passed, and Wren stood, lifting the M82 off its tripod prongs to a shoulder lock, trying to get an angle. Via the thermal scope he picked out six figures inside the truck, but they weren't moving.

"I'm seeing no movement," Rogers said. "Boss, do you think-"

The truck started up. Wren's eyes flared. Not a single man had exited.

He scanned the building again, saw Rashidi on the sixth floor, almost to the core servers, and made the only leap possible as the MKZT raced away.

"Bomb, Rashidi! Get your men out!"

He barely heard the response. Dropped his M82 and snatched up the waiting fast rope, tossed it off the roof then threw himself after it.

Three big bounces carried him down six stories in seven

seconds flat, then he was on the frosted sidewalk and unclipping. The Lada was right there as planned, door open, and he dropped into the passenger side.

"Go!" The car took off. Up ahead came the clanging crash of gunfire, the moonlight splash of glass breaking as the IRT squad broke a way through and tossed fast ropes of their own.

"Exiting," came Rashidi's urgent voice as the Lada strained for velocity. Only two blocks away now and the driver breezed through a red light. Maybe there were figures rappelling fast down the building's side now, hard to tell.

Wren drew his Sig Sauer P320, .45 ACP eight-shell mag at the ready. There were barely two hundred yards left to cover with the MKZT charging west.

"Get out!" he shouted, looking up at the foreboding building as figures raced down the side like evacuating data trails. Nothing came back but whistling wind and the urgency of movement until-

"Team clearing the building, Commander," shouted Rashidi, with Wren maybe a hundred yards out. "I have-"

Then the building exploded.

Blasts rippled up from its base to its tip like a shockwave, dozens of fiery eruptions ripping through the structure like a vertical field of flowers blooming in dizzying fast-forward, each blowing out jets of cement dust and shrapnel.

The Lada skidded. The feed in Wren's earpiece roared to static. A second of crazy weightlessness followed as gravity took charge of the building, then it began to collapse, some two-hundred-fifty standing feet of ancient Russian engineering crashing down into a falling storm of masonry debris.

The Lada braked hard into a sudden bank of brick dust, striking the windshield like a tidal wave as the building vented its insides out. Shrapnel smashed spidery trails across the glass, a chunk of rock punched through and knocked out the rearview mirror. Dust puffed through the busted ventilation system, the brakes backwashed burning rubber, the Lada's momentum died out and Wren rocked back against the seat.

"Rashidi!" he shouted, already kicking his door open and charging ahead.

No answer came.

The earth shook like it had been hit by Lucifer's hammer, smoke and tumbling debris spinning through the dark. Ten yards on Wren stumbled on a chunk of concrete twisted with rebar but kept on, entering an avalanche of sloping rubble as the destroyed building found its new equilibrium.

"Rashidi!" he called, reached what had to be the curb, now buried some ten feet deep beneath the fresh flow of wreckage. A gusting wind pulled ribbony openings through the dust, giving Wren interlacing sight-lines across the block where the building had stood.

All gone. A giant, groaning heap of broken concrete, hissing with ruptured gas lines and spurting water mains, all muted by the swaddling dust. Sirens pierced the shifting stillness, but distantly. Wren's heart pounded. He spun, trying to get a sense of where the team had exited, where they might have reached.

"Rogers!" he shouted. "Give me something."

"Winding back the footage," she answered. "Here, looks like they all made it out but got swallowed up by the rubble wave. Your five o'clock boss."

He staggered backward down the ruins. "Tell me!"

"Ten yards," she answered.

He reached the point, picked up a chunk of masonry and tossed it away, calling Rashidi's name.

Maybe some of them were alive. Some of them had to be alive.

Into the night he worked. Barely thinking about what had

happened, about how the Blue Fairy had been more ready than he'd imagined, with a trip switch big enough to bring the entire building down. Scale, size, intensity, resources. The darknet was a trillion-dollar industry.

He kept working as fire crews filed up, police secured the area, earth-moving equipment was brought in to clear the roads and allow better access. Right alongside the emergency services he labored, accepting gloves and a mask when they were handed to him, swinging a pick when it was given, periodically calling Rashidi's name.

By the dawn it was done.

Five members of the IRT were alive. Dug out bleeding at the fringe of the wreckage, suffering from smoke inhalation and a dozen other injuries. Bloodshot eyes, dust plastered to their skin with cold sweat, but alive.

All except Rashidi. They found him last, closest to the building, where he'd been ensuring the safety of his team. His cold gaze burned into Wren's heart.

The Blue Fairy was going to pay for this.

Rashidi was laid on a gurney and carried away. Wren was left standing as they unearthed the dead traffickers. There was nothing to say. Smoke steadily rose, bulging out in a column that blocked the dawn light, and Wren's rage only grew with it.

They'd known. They'd been waiting for him.

His phone chimed in his pocket. He brought it up, found dozens of messages were waiting, all come in while he'd been digging. All of them images. He tapped one and it full-screened.

A stylized image of the Blue Fairy, black silhouette on a blue background, with twin children standing either side of her, holding her hands. Above their heads were his children's names.

Jake. Quinn.

Text ran along the bottom in block capitals.

SUFFER THE LITTLE CHILDREN, CHRISTOPHER WREN

2

_____

LORALEI

Thirteen hours, two flights and a dozen calls later, Wren stood on a suburban Delaware street in mid-afternoon, striding toward the duplex where his wife and kids had started their new life without him.

For six months he'd let his wife dictate terms. Loralei. She had cause to be angry with him. He'd kept his double life as a black-ops CIA agent secret from her. He'd quit the CIA to spend more time with his family, but it had come too late.

She'd found out, taken the kids and fled their New York apartment, leaving him out in the cold. She'd wanted to get away, and he'd largely respected her wishes.

This was different.

This was a genuine threat against his family. He'd already sent Sally Rogers out to find and secure them, set up some kind of witness protection, and Loralei's response had been clear and absolute.

No.

Now he strode up the drive, muscles working under his jaw. He saw his son Jake's bike by the garage, a small red BMX with the training wheels on, and it broke his heart. Knocked on the door and stood with his pulse thumping upward. Instantly he was transported back to their New York apartment, when he'd been carrying a bottle of wine and cakes for the kids, freshly out of the CIA and hoping everything was going to change.

How wrong he'd been.

Footsteps sounded closer. The door unlatched and swung open.

It was a guy.

Wren blinked.

He was almost half Wren's size, wore glasses, a sweater vest, khaki pants and loafers. He looked like the kind of guy who came out to fix your cables when the Wi-Fi was down. Maybe he was.

"Yes?"

"I'm here to see Loralei Wren. My name's Christopher Wren. I'm her husband."

It took a second, then the guy's expression soured slightly. Not to fear, surprisingly, but to anger. To Wren's surprise, the guy actually stepped forward, pulling the door half-closed behind him.

"You shouldn't be here. She doesn't want to see you."

If Wren weren't so wired, he would have laughed. One slap and the guy would go cartwheeling down the yard. But he wasn't here for that. Rather, Wren lifted him gently under the arms the same way you'd lift a toddler, deposited him to the side and pushed through the door.

The guy barked something behind him, but Wren paid him no mind, then he was in the kitchen, and so was she.

Loralei. She was standing at the counter chopping cucumbers. The smell of bacon sizzled in the air, smoke rising from a griddle. Two plates were laid out with bread, cilantro and salsa. Loralei's infamous 'Mexican' BLTs. Not bad for a Brit from East London. There was a jar of mayonnaise with a butter knife sticking out. The guy jogged around to stand in front of Wren.

"I tried to stop him," he started, but Wren just laid a hand on his shoulder, barely even needed to squeeze to shut him up.

Loralei stared daggers. Wren tried to read her. It had been five months since he'd seen her, and she was as beautiful as ever. Dark strands of hair hanging down from a slack ponytail, dressed in snug jeans and a check shirt. Sweet lips spreading to an angry O, those wide-set green eyes flaring, her hairpin brows glowering like tiny thunderheads.

"Chris," she said.

"Loralei."

A heavy moment passed, then she pointed the kitchen knife at him. "You can't be here. I said that to your people. I'm saying it to you. Witness protection? I'm not interested. This afternoon I applied for a restraining order."

That was news to him. "Against me? Why?"

She laughed. "Why? You're kidding me, right?"

Nothing to say to that. He looked around, saw pictures drawn by his kids on the fridge, toys strewn in the den, signs of a normal family life. Everything he'd lost. "Where are Jake and Quinn?"

"With their aunt. Now let James go."

Wren looked at 'James'. He looked to be in pain, wincing away from Wren's glove-like hand on his shoulder. He hadn't realized he was squeezing hard and let go. The guy whimpered.

"Give us a minute, James," Wren said.

Loralei reached for a phone. "You haven't changed. This is his house, Chris. You need to get out or I'm calling the police."

He hadn't expected that either. "His house?"

Loralei just stared. Holding up the phone, ready to dial.

"Listen," he said. "I'm sorry, Loralei. For everything. Maybe sometime soon we can talk about all that, but it's not why I'm here now. I'm here about the threat to our family. Our kids." He paused a second. "You know this. Why are you rejecting protection?"

Her eyes flickered slightly, a hint of tenderness, though that was swiftly replaced by anger.

"You don't get it. Any threat to the kids, it's because of you. Because of the choices you keep making. Now you just pull us back into your orbit, into your 'protection', like our lives don't matter at all?"

"I'm trying to keep you alive."

Loralei shook her head. "Listen to what I'm saying, Chris. You really don't get it. There's more to life than just being alive. We-"

"So I'll have nothing to do with the protection detail," he interrupted. "It's why I didn't come myself at first. But I can't live with the kids in danger, Lor. I don't even need to know where you are. I-"

"Like you didn't know where we are now?" That shut him up. Loralei pressed on. "I didn't tell anyone. Only my Dad and my sister, and I know they didn't tell you. So you used some shady back channels to find us, and that can't be legal. Now you want us even closer, in the palm of your hand?"

Wren flinched. "It's not like that. I-"

Now her eyes burned. "It's exactly like that. You want to protect us, you do it the way you always did. Somewhere far away, your CIA bullshit, way out of our lives. I am not moving the kids again. I will not make them into refugees. You want to be their father? Then clean up the mess you made!"

She was almost shouting. Wren recalculated fast. If she wasn't on board, witness protection wouldn't work.

"At least let us have a presence here. Rotate security, keep eyes on, we can-"

"No." She came around the counter, holding the knife up now, eyes flaming. "I want you gone. 'Saint Justice' they call you, right? 'Black-ops'? Once I found out, did you really think there was any coming back from that?"

There was only one thing to say to that. "I hoped so."

She snorted. "Hope'll kill you slow, Chris. Truth is, I don't know you. The man I loved, the man I married, it's not you."

"I quit the CIA," he said. "I gave it up. I wanted to-"

"You don't look quit to me."

There was nothing to say to that either. She was right.

"I don't think you're going to try and abduct me, or kidnap our kids. So I'm telling you to leave. You may be a killer out there," she waved a hand vaguely, "but right here you've not got a leg to stand on. Ask any court in the land. They're going to find in my favor."

He said nothing. There were ways to surveil his family without being seen. Keep them safe from a distance. It wasn't ideal, but…

Something struck him. Something he'd never really thought about.

"You called me 'Saint Justice'. How did you know about that?"

She set the knife down on the counter. "True to form. That's what you want to talk about, how your cover was breached?"

Suddenly, that was the only thing that mattered. For the past half a year he'd just assumed she'd had enough. But knowing his CIA nickname? It sent him operational: sizing up the windows, the house, even the guy. James.

"Yes," he said. "Nobody knows that. Tell me, Loralei."

She gave him *that* look, like she was humoring him, then

brought up her phone. She spent a few moments scrolling, then held it out. "You want to know, have at it."

He took the phone, looked at the screen, which showed an email message. Every word came like a shot in the head.

Your husband, Christopher Wren, is a CIA agent known as 'Saint Justice'. He has been involved in the following operations:

A long list followed, complete with dates coinciding with his every 'business trip' away. There were photographs too, of him in far-flung locations, overseeing cartel arms deals in Mexico, meeting with princes in Saudi Arabia, exchanging briefcases in dank Swiss parking lots.

The email scrolled on and on. It was pretty close to his full CIA record, all of it beyond Top Secret designation. There was no way she should have this.

He looked up, already planning what he'd say.

"Don't try to explain," Loralei said. "I didn't just believe some random email. I checked everything. I went back through some of your contacts. Your trips. The hotels you stayed at. You always brought so many mementos, Chris." Her voice cracked. "Stationery from every place you 'stayed'. Gifts for the kids. I spent days calling hotels. Not one remembered you." A tear ran down her cheek, and she wiped it angrily away. "Not one record anywhere. You were lying constantly. You're a liar."

He felt gut-shot, spiraling now, eyes roving for unseen threats.

"You said you were in Thailand for the last trip?" Loralei went on. "Chris, I flew out there."

His heart drummed hard.

"You'd talked about the hotel, all the beautiful nature, the people you were meeting? I guess they gave you an information packet, details to repeat, because I found hardly any of it. Not the people. Not the places, at least not the way you said. Not you."

The world spun. "I'm sorry."

"Too late, Chris. The decision's been made. This is it, and we are over. You'll get divorce papers as soon as there's a place to send them. Now you need to leave before the kids come back.

He didn't know where to look. The threat from the Blue Fairy felt very nearby. He looked at the phone again, scrolling through the list of his ops like there might be an answer there.

Then he found it.

The sign-off was the last name he'd expected. A man twenty-five years dead, America's most famous serial killer and cult leader, and Wren's own father.

The Apex.

3

FAKE TOWN

Wren left the Delaware duplex without another word, mind buzzing and heart racing. The Blue Fairy was out there dancing on the darknet and some copycat jackass was pretending to be his dead father.

The Apex.

Leader of the Pyramid death cult that Wren had grown up inside. Maybe the first man to use the Blue Fairy symbol. His death had been uncertain at the time; had he died along with the thousand who died in his suicide cult?

Nobody knew. He had to be dead, though, had to have been dead for twenty-five years. Now some copycat was trying to tear Wren's life apart in the Apex's name.

He called Sally Rogers.

"Agent Rogers," she answered.

"It's Wren. I'm sending you a file; there's been a massive data breach of my agency record. Someone claiming to be my father sent it to Loralei. That's why she cut me off."

A few seconds passed. "Your whole record?"

"Check the file. It's unprecedented. We need to look into who would have that kind of access."

Seconds passed. Wren figured she was looking through

the file. A quiet curse came down the line. "Boss, I don't have the clearance to even look at this."

"So put it onto Director Humphreys. In the meantime, I'm going to need everything you've collated on Apex copycats and residual cults."

He'd given her the assignment as soon as they'd started working together. For decades he'd been doing that job alone; collecting any sign of his father or his father's followers. None of it had led anywhere.

Now he needed a target.

"I'll send you what we've got," Rogers said. "It's pretty thin, though."

"Not many targets?"

"Really just one. Some kind of non-profit. They've set up in the ruins of the Pyramid cult compound in Arizona."

Wren's blood ran cold. "What?"

"I'll send it to you. I can't figure out what they're doing there, something about body reclamation? You think that's a good lead?"

Wren didn't need to think. His father's Arizona compound, housed in a fake town originally built as a set for a cowboy western movie that was never made, had long been a mecca for Apex and Pyramid freaks. Wren had run creeps like them off the land multiple times before.

"Watch my family," he said, feeling the anger surging. "I don't care if they're rejecting witness protection; do it from a distance if you have to. I'm getting on a plane. Send me everything you've got on this non-profit."

"Done and done. I'll also relay the file to the Director. And Boss?"

Wren was already climbing into his Jeep, bringing up the website to order a short-notice flight. "What?"

"Be safe, OK."

He hung up and hit the gas.

A flight and three-hour drive later, Wren arrived. Standing in the desert emptiness of Arizona, some wild time after midnight, he looked out over the fake town.

Heat radiated up from the cracked, sand-covered blacktop, carrying wafts of tarry creosote sap, though the sun had dropped six hours earlier. The sky was so black it seemed blue, overhung by a wicked sickle moon.

Wren ran his eyes ran along the fake town's silhouette, like a thumb along a blunted knife. Moonlight dappled the last few buildings in place. The saloon stood to his right, but only just; the front façade was badly bowed by two decades of rain, its boards bleached gray by the sun. Next to it lay a bare cement base; that had been the hardware store, before an arson fire claimed it. Beyond that it was just bare cement bases stretching away into the desert like toppled tombstones, keeping their secrets in the shifting sands.

The fake town had taken on a second life when the Pyramid had bought it and sealed off all access, until the day they all died. They'd burned themselves alive at the Apex's command right here, an act that Wren had witnessed as a twelve-year-old child. Official records stated he was the sole survivor, though of course they'd never found his father's body…

Now there were fresh tire tracks in the sand. Wren toed them with his boot. Wide wheelbase, cutting deep. Carrying something heavy.

Copycats.

He could sense them watching him now. There were CCTV cameras perched on the corners of the few structures still standing. He knew the outline of those decrepit buildings by heart, and something had changed.

Now several stood bolt upright. Last time he'd been here, the townhouse off Main Street had been only a drooping front wall. The film hadn't required many interiors. Now the structure had been repainted and rebuilt. Wren had only vague memories of the atrocities that had taken place there, back when the 'rooms' had been caravans towed and staked into place, used as isolation cells for disobedient members.

A movement came from the end of Main Street.

Wren advanced toward the townhouse, SIG Sauer .45 shifting against his hip. From the darkness there came a muffled clank of metal. The greased slide on a rifle, filling the breach.

Wren stopped ten yards from the townhouse, and a security flood-lamp switched on behind him, casting his shadow large across the newly-painted boards. He didn't move. Let them get a good look at him just standing. I know you're there, those seconds said. I'm waiting.

He turned.

They stood at the Main Street crossroad, cutting off his route back. Five dark figures, rifles held at the ready.

"Who in heck fire are you?" one of the five called. "What are you doing here?" Wren caught the faint twang of a Boston accent. Long-distance transplants weren't unusual out here. The Pyramid had gotten under the nation's skin twenty years ago, and there were always sick people looking to come pay homage. They didn't often rebuild buildings, though.

"I used to live here," Wren called. "I drop by sometimes."

"You don't live here now," Boston said. "You have to go."

Wren let that hang. He thought about picking these five off where they stood, but didn't like his odds, long-range with a handgun against hunting rifles. He could ping a few, but not before they'd fired back.

He imagined a route back to his Jeep, where he had a Mossberg tactical shotgun and an M27 infantry automatic rifle in the trunk. A tight sprint down the side of the townhouse, then he'd be in the dark desert. His eyes would adjust before theirs, and they'd have to come at him through the security light. A few might branch right immediately, try to cut him off on an angle, but they wouldn't know where to intersect.

Wren would pivot sharply and hit them by the saloon. He could take two of them that way, lead two around the loop and take them on the other side.

It would be a bloodbath. That was no problem for Wren, if they deserved it. But he had to be sure.

"I'm looking for the Apex," he called. "You know anything about that?"

Boston frowned. His face wasn't clear at this distance, more a shadowy emoji. "You're looking for a dead man?"

"Or a copycat. This is where he had his last stand, and now you're here. I need to know why."

Boston stared. "Why we're here's none of your business, friend. Fact is, you're trespassing. I got five armed men here telling you to get. You go on and get."

"Bullshit," Wren countered. "This is Federal land, designated persona non grata in perpetuity. If it belongs to anyone, it belongs to me. So actually, you're trespassing on my land."

It was a stretch. Wren was just looking to see what shook out.

Boston said something into his radio about a whack job in the street. A crackle came back, then he gave instructions to his team. Three advanced, one coming head-on while the others spread out in a pincer to left and right. The one on the right had his rifle up now, the stock butted hard into his shoulder.

"We're asking nicely," Boston said. "We'll start shooting soon."

Wren switched his attention to the lead man in the pincer. "What's your name, hoss?"

The guy spat in the sand. "Don't you mind. You been told to go."

Wren counted the yards between them. It would be six big strides which he'd follow with an elbow to the trachea. The guy slacked off on his aim when he spoke, and that opened a window. Wren could ask another question then charge while he was distracted, bat the muzzle aside, hold him like a shield and absorb fire from the other two while leveling his Sig. Seven seconds, maybe, before the two in back got their weapons up. Doable, but foolhardy. High casualty count before he could end it, and a good chance he'd get hit.

Not ideal. They were closing in now. Wren switched back to Boston. "Last chance. Clear your people out. Walk away from this town and never come back. I'll even give you a running start before I come looking."

The pincer movement finished. Now there were men to his back left and right with one in front.

"You're leaving now," called Boston. "This can go easy or hard, so start marching."

"I've never gone easy in my life, and that's because-"

Wren moved, back and to the left. The man there had his rifle barrel pointing down. Four strides was three seconds for Wren, the move slotted in and executed while the guy's brain was still jammed up with that 'because'.

Reasons always followed a 'because'. You set yourself waiting for the sentence to close, when all that happened was Wren hit him with a clothesline in the throat. It lifted the man up and spun him horizontal, slamming hard to the sand.

Wren ducked behind him, lifted him like a hostage and pulled his Sig. Shoot now and they'd tear their own man up.

The others stared down their barrels. It had happened too fast. Boston's mouth was wide. His radio crackled.

"Now put down your weapons," Wren said, not showing any exertion. "Begin your exodus from the promised land."

4

MAGGIE

Nobody moved. Seconds ticked by with weapons aimed.

"I'm not putting my rifle down," Boston said at last. "None of us are. If it comes to shooting, so be it. We'll not be driven off. We've children here."

Wren squeezed the trigger, instantly seeing red. Children? Boston would go first. "How many?"

"I'm not telling you that."

"In cages?"

"What, cages? Man, who do you think we are?"

"Where do you think you are?" Wren countered, letting his anger show. Last time he'd busted a Pyramid clone, they'd been experimenting with parboiling apostates. Big iron cauldron atop a raw fire. Wren had dropped three explosive charges around the perimeter then walked in firing. "To my left the Pyramid had their main torture cells. All day the screaming went on. Did you really think I'd let it happen again?"

"Wait, again? Are you saying you were in the Pyramid?"

Wren trained the Sig on Boston's face. "I already said I was in the Pyramid. Now put your weapon down."

Boston's rifle was already slack. Shock was getting the better of him. He let it slip to the ground.

"You need to understand," Boston said, "that's why we're here. The crimes of the Pyramid-"

"Stay in the past," Wren interrupted. "Everyone puts their weapons down, steps away, and you get your boss out here now. Are we clear?"

Boston's radio crackled. "Yeah," he said. "Clear. Weapons down. It'll be OK."

The weapons dropped. Wren stood up. A few moments later the door of the townhouse opened and he turned. In the doorway was a woman dressed like a Shaker school teacher, in a plain tan smock, white blouse and dress, with tawny ringlet hair tied back loosely.

"Christopher Wren," she said, with a hint of a question. Her voice was powerful, like she was used to projecting to the back of an auditorium. She was around his age, a handsome and sturdy woman, looking frontier-rugged.

She knew his name. Of course she did. "You're trespassing on hallowed ground," he said. "Explain."

She strode out of the townhouse. Wren caught a glimpse of the hallway beyond; candlelit, with no sign of cages. Two children stood either side of the door, peering out wide-eyed in their long cotton pajamas.

"Can I check the man you struck?" she asked.

Wren backed away a few strides and she advanced, kneeled by the man, said his name and touched his throat lightly.

"He's fine," Wren said. "I barely touched him."

She ignored Wren and helped the man up, sending him back toward the others, then she stood and looked at him. She didn't have a weapon, but she didn't seem intimidated by him in the slightest. He imagined her facing down a charge of Sioux warriors with that steady gaze.

"It is Christopher Wren, isn't it?" she asked. "Sole survivor of the Pyramid?"

Wren steeled himself. This could still go bad. Any Pyramid clone that could get their hands on Christopher Wren, last son of the Apex left alive, would have a field day putting him in a cage.

"That's me. And you are?"

"Margaret. Maggie. None of this is what you think it is, Christopher. I apologize for you finding us this way. I tried to contact you, to seek your blessing, but never found a way. The Order of the Saints raised your profile, and I thought…" she trailed off. "You're here now. Good. May we talk?"

"We're talking."

She allowed for that with a slight incline of her head, like a teacher brushing off the smart Alec at the back of class. "Walk with me. My men will stay here. They won't pick up their weapons, I promise."

Wren scanned the five of them. They looked sullen.

"We have children here," she went on. "Vulnerable people. If you don't like what I've got to say, then I'm a better hostage than they are."

"Maggie," said Wren, tasting the syllables. Weighing what he'd seen. "You're the leader of this cult."

"We're a non-profit charity, not a cult. But yes, I'm the leader. Now shall we?"

She gestured toward the darkness.

5

PYRAMID CLONE

Into the desert they walked, and Wren thought about what she'd said.

Female cult leaders were rare. The vast majority were male, and usually followed the same old drives, seeking greater fulfillment of their own whims. With women it could be different. They were more unpredictable. Some of them had harems, like the men. Some of them were serial killers. Others just liked the idea of a big, happy family.

It didn't seem like a profile for the Blue Fairy

Maggie walked alongside him. She seemed to know the rough terrain underfoot well. She didn't say anything, but it didn't feel combative, it felt generous, like she was giving him time to process.

"You're not a Pyramid clone," he said at last.

"We're not."

Their pace slowed. "So what are you?"

"The opposite, in fact. We're a refuge, really. Cult survivors come to this place. We focus on rehabilitation."

Wren gritted his teeth. "I'll need to see it. I'll need to look inside your buildings. I'll need to interview your people."

"Because you're the governing body on cults?"

He looked over at her. She wasn't angry. If anything, her confidence was infectious.

"When it comes to this place? I am. Whatever you're doing here, it's dangerous. This place, it's…" He trailed off, moderating what he wanted to say. "You shouldn't be here. No one should."

She didn't say anything for a long moment. They walked in silence until Maggie stopped.

"What we're doing here," she began, "I think you'll approve. Let me show you."

"So show me."

She took a flashlight out slowly, clicked it on and aimed the beam on the ground ahead of them. It took Wren a second to realize what he was looking at. A flat oblong of gray stone laid down in the sand. There was a name inscribed, some dates, a line of description.

A chill ran through him. "It's a grave."

"It's how I got started here," Maggie said, and ran the flashlight beam sideways, over more of the flat oblongs stretching away in a squarish plot. "We scour the desert for them. Victims of the Pyramid. Animals have dug many of them up and scattered the bones, so we do what we can. Metal detecting helps with fillings in jaws, with heart fittings and such. We have several contacts on staff at nearby universities for radiocarbon dating and DNA checks. We're not high on their priority list, but we push it through."

Wren's head spun. This was not what he'd expected. "You're digging up the Pyramid?"

"Less digging, more hunter-gathering," said Maggie. He looked at her. "You'll know these numbers better than any. Your father, the Apex, killed far more people than those that died in the final firestorm. Many hundreds more, by anyone's best guess. Many of them are buried in the desert around here. We've found approximately forty-three so far. We've been doing this for over a year."

Wren blinked. Over a year. "And you're burying them?"

"What we can find. We notify the families and arrange for re-consecration in line with their wishes. We set up headstones, so they come out here and pay their respects. It's why survivors come stay. They meet with the families, they come with their own children, and we all move closer to some kind of forgiveness."

Wren studied her. He didn't know how he felt about that. "Why?"

She shrugged lightly. "It's a good thing. I don't like to think of those bones scattered throughout the desert, alone. Unmourned."

He shook his head. "No. Why you? Why are you doing this?"

"Let's just say I'm a concerned citizen."

"Bullshit. No one's that concerned."

She eyed him, a measure of fierceness showing through. "Then how about this? I grew up watching the Pyramid on TV. The day it broke open was huge news in my little town. Your father took dozens of people from us. It's been a hole in me ever since. I never stopped thinking about the bodies in the streets, burned by napalm they'd brewed themselves. I imagined all the lost souls who'd tried to stop your father on his path to destruction, and they called me here."

"Not good enough."

She went cold. "It has to be."

Wren let a little of his own cold anger through. "It's not. It's bullshit empathy; people don't just do that. If I believed you, then all these graves would sicken me. You'd be an emotional parasite like the other Pyramid clones, living off the pain of the families. I'll burn the whole place down and break you six ways from Sunday, if that's true. So tell me why."

Now her eyes bored into him, catching the moonlight and swimming with anger.

"OK. Your father destroyed my family," she spat. "My mother joined his cult. My aunt followed, then two uncles. They all went willingly, and it ruined us. Emotionally. Financially. A year later my dad killed himself and I was put into foster care. I bounced around the system and I came out angry. Like you. And I never forgot." She took a breath. "When the Pyramid fell, they couldn't find my family. Not burned up, not anywhere. So I started hunting. I'd come out alone and walk in the wilds. I got my doctorate at the same time. I thought about starting a family, but this place was in my bones. Now we've got Federal approval, we're a listed NGO with rights to identify and consecrate any remains we find. Does that answer your question?"

She let out a breath.

Wren sagged a little. Bullshit empathy, he'd said.

"So do we have your permission?" she demanded.

Wren met her gaze. This flipped everything. "You've got it the wrong way around," he said. "This is your place now. I see that. You don't need my permission."

A tear broke down her cheek.

"I hope you find your family," he said. "I'm sorry I scared your people. I'll make a donation. You should get better security to keep out the Pyramid crazies."

She started to say something, but Wren was already walking away, back into the desert.

"Come back, Christopher," Maggie called out, but made no move to follow, and maybe that wasn't what she meant anyway. "Whenever you want. Whenever you're ready. This is your home, after all."

Wren strode on and the darkness swallowed him.

6

ROGERS

Wren's Jeep was waiting. He got in and drove away, along the old road headed for I-40. There'd been no answers from the desert. No Apex, no Blue Fairy, just another dead end.

At some point cell signal returned and his phone rang. It was Director Humphreys. Wren watched as seven text messages dropped in telling him to pick up, along with choice insults and reminders that despite his new 'AWOP' Agent WithOut Portfolio status, he still had to file constant progress reports.

He hadn't filed one since Minsk nearly two days back. The phone kept ringing and he answered.

"What is it, Humphreys?"

"What is it?" Humphreys snapped. "I've been calling since midnight. That's five hours, Wren! What have you been doing?"

Wren took a moment. "I was off-grid."

"Off-grid? There's no off-grid for you. You've got a team and right now they're on red alert, with the trail getting colder every second. I need you on the ball 24/7."

"What trail?"

"Do I sound like your PA? Call your team. And as of this moment, consider yourself seconded to the FBI, since this attack's inside the continental USA."

Humphreys ended the call.

Attack?

Wren called Sally Rogers.

"Boss," she answered. "We've been trying to reach you."

"I just heard from Humphreys. He said there's been an attack?"

She took a deep breath. "Yeah, I'm there right now. Six hours back, in the middle of the evening commute, the Blue Fairy took a huge leap. This is action taken in the real world: one murder and a double kidnapping in downtown Detroit."

Wren's blood ran cold. "What?"

"I know. It's unprecedented."

"Action in the real world? But the Blue Fairy's a darknet group. They've never acted openly before."

"This was definitely them. I've got dozens of witnesses here who watched four guys in creepy Pinocchio masks just baseball bat a man to death and drag a woman and a man into a panel van."

Wren gritted his teeth. "Pinocchio masks? Like they wear for their darknet videos?"

"Same thing, as far as I can tell."

Wren sat very still, heart pounding as the truck sped into the night. He checked the dashboard clock. Albuquerque Airport was four hours' drive, with Detroit a three-hour red-eye flight away. He could be there just after three in the afternoon.

"Boss?"

"I'm here. I'm thinking. Send me everything you've got. I'll be there in about ten hours."

"Will do."

"And get some sleep, Sally."

"Not much chance of that. Nothing's open right now but some vegan coffee booth selling soy milk coffee, but I'm slurping it down with the blue light crews anyway. Leads to chase up."

Wren smiled. The only trouble with hard-chargers was they burned themselves out. "This is going to be a marathon, Sally, not a sprint. Lay off the soy and get at least an hour's sleep before I land, OK? I need you sharp."

She chuckled. "OK, Boss, you too."

Wren hung up. Sleep. Despite his advice, he didn't think there'd be much chance of that for him either, not with the monsters crawling out into the light.

7

BLUE FAIRY

Wren reached Albuquerque airport with the dawn. It was a blocky mesa-like structure in clay-colored stucco, already bustling in the hot sun. Wren pulled into long stay parking, fed the meter one of his credit cards and shouldered his bag. It was light; one change of clothes, various documents and IDs, his netbook and a small clutch of phones. In the past five months he'd adapted well to his Agent WithOut Portfolio status.

At the walk-up counter he bought one-way to Detroit, got a piping hot Americano and sipped it at the gate. His CIA ID got him through and boarded early. He took the mid-wing seat for the legroom, logged into Wi-Fi and downloaded the intel Sally Rogers had sent him.

It looked thin.

The case summary stated there was no CCTV of the attack at all. It seemed these 'Pinocchios' had pulled off a cyber-coup and shut off all CCTV within two blocks of the Michigan Avenue People Mover elevated tram line station. It was in a high traffic area of central Detroit, flanked by four-lane roads and skyscraper office blocks, with dozens if not hundreds of camera watching the crowds, the turnstiles and the roads.

All were gone. That suggested significant cybercrime capability

Wren scrolled on. With no CCTV available, they were left reliant on witness statements, of which there were plenty. He skimmed them. All were highly emotional, but offered nothing on ID or even the panel van's license plate. They did have a time, approximately 8:10 p.m., and an outline of the attack.

Four men in Pinocchio masks had exited a white panel van, pushed through the crowd, then attacked two men standing in the middle of the People Mover's forecourt with baseball bats. One man went down, the other fled, and two more people were captured, a man and a woman, dragged back to the van and driven away.

Wren scrolled on.

Next up was a map outlining the route the van might have taken on escape, heading west. There was no shortage of blind corridors leading that way into Corkdale and Warrendale and from there into areas of heavy blight, where it would've been easy to disappear. Large portions of Detroit were basically ghost neighborhoods, steadily falling apart. A panel van out there would be as good as invisible.

Wren tapped out an email to his team as the plane taxied toward the runway.

'Get forensic data scientists on the CCTV blackout. For a hack this size, they must have left a trail. Also throw out an image search spider on social media. Somebody had to have been filming on their phone, video doorbell or dashcam at that moment somewhere along the route. Maybe we'll get lucky and pick up the van or the guy who got away.'

He scrolled further through the intel packet to the section on victims. Here things got interesting. It seemed the dead man and the two who'd been taken were members of an activist 'catfishing' group; volunteers who spent their evenings mocking up the social media identities of young children, then went online to lure pedophiles out of the dark.

Wren read deeper.

These three were members of a group called 'Marcy's Heroes', with seventy members nationwide, but based primarily in Detroit. They had their own message boards, it seemed, with good data encryption. Rogers had already requested further details, but they only had ID so far on the dead man.

Wren read his profile. Malton Bruce was a lawyer by day, catfisher by night. Coached Little League on weekends. A big guy, but he didn't stand a chance against a baseball bat to the head. The coroner's cause of death was included: blunt force trauma to the skull. It looked like he'd been struck five times and his skull shattered. He had no known enemies, at least so far.

The three of them had been targeting a male in his 40s, according to witnesses; maybe a perp? Some accounts claimed this 'perp' had been standing out in the open dressed in a designer suit with a clipboard, running a questionnaire on passing commuters. The catfishers had circled around him and Bruce had confronted him with a thick folder.

Wren had seen catfisher stings before. There was one lead, usually a large man to dissuade attempts at flight or violence, who approached the perp and showed him the evidence they'd collected online; sometimes months' worth of text messages, photos passed back and forth and so on. The others invariably filmed the confrontation and called the police.

Instead of the police, though, the panel van had pulled up and the Pinocchios had approached. Bruce had been struck in the back of the head and the two other catfishers had been dragged back into the van. Several of the witnesses said the perp had looked as stunned as they were, like he had no idea what was going on.

Nobody knew where he'd gone, though.

Wren fired another email as the plane lined up with the runway.

'We need IDs on the kidnap victims and the perp and everything Marcy's Heroes have on him.'

Next up was a section of witness statements dealing with the Pinocchio masks. They described a darker version of the Pinocchio image, closer to Carlo Collodi's original vision of the little wooden boy than the cheerful modern-day depiction.

Wren did a quick search before he lost the Internet, and saw dozens of Pinocchio mask models available commercially, widely shipped, some fitting the description of the witnesses. His team were already requesting data from the big online markets using Freedom of Information laws to try and track the purchases, but that seemed a long shot to Wren.

He skipped to the details on the attackers. There'd been four of them, all wearing masks, with check shirts and blue jeans. None stood out as particularly tall or short. There was nothing on race or even gender, though it was assumed they were men. 99.9% of all Pinocchios had been men so far.

It wasn't much to go on. He wrote a final email.

'Recall the witnesses. All of them. We're going to squeeze them.' He thought for a moment. 'Call them for evening, same time as the attack, outside the People Mover station on Michigan Avenue. I want to jog their memories together with a re-enactment.' He thought some more. 'Get a white van, masks and fake blood. Hire actors. We'll rehearse the hit just like it went down, like a rolling re-enactment. We'll spring it on the witnesses, so keep this quiet. Maybe something will shake loose on the perp.'

He sent the mail. A moment later the plane sped along the runway, rose into the air and the Internet died.

Wren put his phone down. There was nothing for it now but to get to Detroit and start knocking on doors.

He looked out the window, watching as first the city then the encircling desert receded below, spreading out to the horizon. He knew he should sleep but was too wired.

This was something new. Something big. The timing was too close to his raid on the Minsk data hub to feel like a coincidence. Something was beginning here, and he didn't like it.

8

PEOPLE MOVER

I t seemed Wren had barely blinked when the pilot's voice came over the PA, announcing they were on final approach. He looked out the window and saw Detroit passing like a broken circuit board below.

He traced its patterns through neighborhoods with components missing. There were green patches spotted throughout, where abandoned homes had become blight, and blight had been burned and wrecked by bored kids then demolished by the city. It made Wren think of a cancer metastasizing, dots here and there blasted by the chemotherapy but always reseeding itself and spreading wider.

The plane touched down. Wren was first off, through Departures in minutes and into a cab. Out the window, Detroit thickened like a broth on the boil, with broad streets and residential zones giving way to malls and parking lots. The roads narrowed, the green blips of blight melted away and the city's few skyscrapers grew larger in the distance. The abandoned Michigan Central Train Depot appeared on his right, its empty windows gazing across the bare grass of Roosevelt Park. It made him think of Maggie's graves in the desert. Here was a tombstone for the scattered bones of a city.

Michigan Avenue People Mover station was waiting for him. Around 3 p.m. on a Tuesday, he got out of the cab and surveyed the scene of Malton Bruce's murder.

The station was a slim two-floor block, really just walls around a flight of stairs. In front of it lay a broad forecourt that narrowed like the prow of a ship, pinched off by the intersection of Michigan and Cass Avenues. In the rough center stood a single tree in a brick planter.

A People Mover tram clattered in on the elevated line overhead. Cars bustled through midday traffic behind him. People hurried this way and that. Just ahead, only sixteen hours ago, Malton Bruce had been bludgeoned to death.

There was no blood left on the stone flags, no police tape or forensics tent. The air smelled of the city at the end of winter: diesel fumes, frost in the air, a hint of wafting coffee.

Wren called Agent Rogers.

"Boss," she said.

"I'm at the People Mover. Where are you, Sally?"

"We've got a temporary office ten blocks south. You need me there?"

"I'm walking the scene. I could use your eyes on, but there's something I want to check first."

"Fire away."

"The panel van, do we have any idea where it went?"

"We know it went west on Michigan. But without any read on the license plate, and no CCTV for two blocks, we've got nothing further. White panel vans are ten-a-penny."

Wren nodded along. He'd expected as much. "What about the perp?"

"The perp?"

"The guy Malton Bruce was catfishing. Do we know where he went yet?"

"Nothing on that, Boss. Nobody was watching him by then."

"But they did watch him earlier. In the witness statements, it said the perp was surprised by the attack."

"Uh, yeah." There was the sound of paper flicking in the background. "Yeah, that's right. Like he wasn't on the same page as the Pinocchios."

Wren grunted. "OK. So if that's true, he probably didn't know the CCTV was out, either. He would've been careful, approaching the station in a way he couldn't be seen."

Rogers pondered that. "Sure, I guess, if he had any tradecraft."

"Which rules out the People Mover itself. I'm thinking he drove. A guy like this, meeting a 'girl' for the first time, he wants to impress her."

"I don't know. Maybe?"

"We do know he was dressed in a designer suit. Probably he came in a flashy car. He'd have parked nearby, because no one's impressed by a long walk back, but he'd want a CCTV blindspot, nothing that could be traced. Ideally somewhere he could watch the crowd."

Rogers took a moment. "Sounds plausible."

"I'll take a look. Come on over, I'll be here."

"Heading now."

Wren stepped up to the narrow 'prow' of the forecourt and looked out over Michigan and Cass. He watched the traffic and the cameras overhead, calculating lines of sight. Doubtless the perp had done this too, in the days before his meet with the girl.

Cass Avenue was well-covered by CCTV. Anyone approaching the station from the north or south would be captured in footage, so Wren ruled that out. Michigan was a different story, though. To the west the People Mover had cameras on the sidewalk and road, cameras the perp would have thought were live, but not on Michigan heading east.

Wren started walking that way.

The air was brisk and fresh, the sky a painful wintry blue. Past the People Mover lay a narrow parking lot, and beyond that numerous shuttered buildings lined either side of Michigan: a closed law office on the right, graffiti on large boarded panels to the left. It was a broad street, four lanes wide, with beautiful old wrought-iron lamps.

No CCTV, though. Largely unobserved, with parking at the curb.

Wren picked the nearest parking spot and looked back at the People Mover. The sightline was good. Parked on the south side of the street, the perp would have had a clean run east.

He must have come this way.

Wren kept walking.

It was two blocks east on Michigan Avenue until he found the first business still in operation, a nice-looking artisan coffee spot at an intersection. On the left turn there was no obvious CCTV, but in all other directions there was.

The shop was called the Orange Pip, and promised a pure Columbian blend. Wren entered and ordered one Americano, one latte and one soy milk latte from the woman behind the counter.

She was in her early thirties, with a sarcastic look in her eye, a pin pierced through her cheek and an odd bowl-cut hairstyle. On her chest she wore the A-in-a-circle symbol for anarchists.

"Were you on duty last night, around 8 p.m.?" he asked, while she frothed up his lattes.

"Yes," she said, almost biting off the word. "Why?"

"I'm investigating the attack at the People Mover last night. You heard about that?" He held out his CIA badge; she gave it a good long look, like she would know if it was fake or not. "A suspect fled the scene and likely made a left turn here." Wren pointed through the glass. "It would've been around 8:20 p.m., and he would've been driving a nice car, something expensive. Did you see anything like that?"

The woman frowned. "CIA," she said, slowly drawing out the letters. "You're not supposed to operate in the USA, right?"

He smiled. "I'm on loan with the FBI, just waiting on the badge and jacket. We're all pals. Now about the car, did you see anything?"

"You said it was nice?"

"Something expensive, like a Tesla, a new-model BMW, even a Porsche or a Ferrari."

She regarded him flatly. "I don't know anything about cars."

"OK," said Wren patiently. "One more question. Was anyone else on duty then?"

Her frown deepened. "Monday night? I close at 8:30. It's dead in here by then. It's just me."

Wren nodded. He'd have to get a team crawling the left turn, asking the same question at any other businesses they could find. "Thank you, you've been very helpful."

He headed for the door. Her voice stopped him before he opened it. "Maybe there was something though."

He turned. "Yes?"

"I didn't notice it myself. A couple of customers did, just as I was cleaning up, so around the time you're looking for. A Firebird, I think they said. Is that a car?"

Wren took a step back. "A Pontiac Firebird?"

"I don't know. They just said 'Firebird'."

Wren thanked her and left, juggling the coffees with his phone as he dialed Rogers again.

"Almost there, Boss," she said.

"Maybe we've got a lead. Let's look into ownership or rental of a Pontiac Firebird in the Detroit area, could be the perp's." He paused a second. It was a rare car, so it should be easy to check. "Scratch that. Widen it out. Give me a two-state radius and an APB, all units we can get looking out. And send some officers to canvass the route north of the Orange Pip coffee shop on Michigan Avenue. Have them asking after the Firebird."

"On it.

He ended the call. That felt like progress.

9

MARCY'S HEROES

S pecial Agent Sally Rogers was waiting at the triangle forecourt for him, sitting on the central planter and looking at her phone.

She was 5' 9" and thick in the shoulders; a prize-winning weightlifter in her college days, and she'd clearly kept it up. She had a sweet, earnest face, leafy blond hair and the wicked mouth of a trooper.

"Boss," she said, looking up as he approached. "Good to see you. The Director said you'd gone dark."

Wren smiled. They hadn't touched base since Minsk, and he hadn't kept her informed of how his trip out to Arizona had played out. "Just something I had to follow up on. Here." He handed her one of the coffees. "Soy milk latte, just as you like it."

She made a face. "Soy? When did I ever say I liked soy?"

"You said it while I was on the plane."

"I said I hated it!"

Wren hid his grin and took a long, satisfying pull on his Americano. Rogers took a tentative sip.

"This is just as disgusting as the last one," she said flatly.

Wren sat on the planter and shrugged. "When life hands you lemons."

"This is not lemons, this is soy," she protested, then pried off the sippy-cup top and eyed the foamy drink beneath. "You know soy's a bean, right? It's not even close to milk."

Wren chuckled. She took another sip and sat down beside him.

"Oh, man. This is not fit for human consumption. This is the kind of thing they feed to cows to make milk. You'd need five stomachs to properly process it."

Wren laughed, then held out the second latte he'd bought. She stared at it, then at him.

"More soy?"

"I promise, that's real coffee."

She looked at the cup in her hand then back at him. "So you spent the bucks on this one just to have a chuckle, is that it?"

Wren smiled. "Worth it."

She sighed and took the latte, made a show of tipping out the soy coffee into the soil, then sat beside him and took a hesitant sip.

"Better."

"Pure Colombian," Wren said.

"I never pegged you as a practical joker."

"Sometimes you have to laugh."

A calm moment passed. Wren figured it might be the last one for some time, so he savored it. But not for long.

"Have you cracked the catfishers' database yet?" he asked. "We need to see those chat logs, start building out IDs on the perp and the kidnap victims."

Rogers nodded. "The team's working on it, but Marcy's Heroes, that's the catfishing group? They're stonewalling. Claiming right to privacy."

"Privacy of what?"

She punctuated the air with her coffee cup. "My guess is, they're worried they crossed boundaries, maybe verged into entrapment with some of these perps? They're demanding we go through the courts. MacAuley's trying to get us a warrant but the judge is slow-walking me."

Wren sucked air through his teeth. Robin MacAuley was heading up their team back in Washington, a hotshot pattern analyst he'd head-hunted for his team right after Rogers, seconded from the FBI. She was slim and short, but had a devilishly fast mind, winning bronze in the national math Olympiad when she was only fourteen.

"During which time they could clean their records," Wren said.

"Or erase them."

That was frustrating.

"This is what happens when you play vigilante," Wren said. "You're always breaking laws and covering your own tracks."

"Speaking from experience there, Boss?"

She was smiling. Everyone knew Wren had taken on the Saints largely solo, acting as a vigilante himself. His AWOP status just made that official.

"It takes one to know one," he countered. "Give me the number for the head of Marcy's Heroes. I'll see if it can get the ball rolling."

"Sure." She brought out her phone and sent him a text. A second later the number for Marcy's Heroes pinged through on Wren's phone, along with a contact for its president, Reince Jeffries.

Wren stood up and dialed.

Seven rings in, the line was answered. "Hello?"

"Reince Jeffries?"

"Yes." He sounded to be an older gentleman, well-spoken, likely a professional with a lot to lose. "Who is this?"

"You've been speaking with my colleague, agent Sally Rogers with the FBI. My name is Christopher Wren, I'm leading the investigation of the death of one of your volunteers and the abduction of two others in central Detroit last night."

He let that hang.

"Yes," said Jeffries cautiously.

"She tells me you're blocking our request for your files. I'm calling to ask you to reconsider. This is an issue of national security, and your cooperation would be appreciated, noted and passed along."

An uncomfortable few seconds passed, filled with the older man's light, wheezy breathing. "I'm afraid that won't be possible, Mr. Wren. Our records are of a highly sensitive nature."

Wren gave Rogers a look. She just raised her eyebrows in a kind of shrug.

"Mr. Jeffries, I'm enabled to offer rewards if this information pans out," Wren went on. "I can also assure you that this is not a fishing expedition for flaws in your record-keeping. You've seen the news. I'm after a hardcore group of child-killers. Not your organization. As far as I'm concerned, you're the good guys here."

Jeffries paused a little longer this time. Maybe he was considering it. "As I said to your colleague, I'm afraid that won't be possible at this time."

Wren cursed under his breath. There had to be something rotten in the records of Marcy's Heroes, something Jeffries felt he had to protect. That left only one way to get it.

"Mr. Jeffries, I've asked politely. The fact is, I have a team outside your office this moment, another team outside your home, and I'm ready to pull the trigger on an immediate raid. You just fell into the jurisdictional Twilight Zone, sir, left after the Patriot Act lapsed. Due process does not apply today. I do not need a court order or a warrant to deal with this terrorist threat. Send your full, unredacted files immediately, to this number, or things will become very unpleasant for your organization, your employees and for you personally."

A long silence followed. Roger's eyes widened. Wren had Jeffries pegged as a lawyer or a professor maybe, an intelligent not easily cowed, who was likely trying to figure out if this was a bluff or not.

"You can't threaten me like that," he settled on.

"I can and I am. This is a marathon investigation, Mr. Jeffries, one I intend to win, and you're standing in my way. Imagine how unhappy I'll be if you bog me down in the opening yards."

A long pause followed. Maybe Jeffries was moving to the window and looking out for signs of a strike team. "I think you should contact my lawyer."

"Unless your lawyer is standing at your front door with an AR-15, it's not going to make a difference. Ninety seconds now. Quit wasting my time or I'll nail Malton Bruce's death to your forehead and offer you up to the press. Is that what you want?"

"I…"

"Sixty seconds, Mr. Jeffries. You're already bending. Bend further. A little yoga will do you good."

Silence but for raspy breathing.

"Thirty seconds. That's it, we're coming through the door."

"Wait!" came the older man's panicky cry. "I'll send what you want. My family is here with me. I'll send the files."

"Good man. You're on the clock. Don't tamper with a thing."

"Yes," said Jeffries. "Thank you."

Wren rang off.

Rogers was staring at Wren. "That was intense."

"He said 'thank you'," Wren said. "That was nice."

"And probably not legal."

Wren tilted his head slightly sideways. "Maybe. It's just a phone call, though. I don't actually have a team ready to raid his house."

Rogers surveyed him like she couldn't be sure if he was telling the truth or not. "Maybe not?"

He smiled. "It's OK. It was just a bluff, Sally. The man's hiding something, but the files should come through soon."

She nodded along. "Off book. That's what everyone says about you."

"A dark horse," Wren said, deepening his voice and looking off into the distance. "Still waters, running deep."

Now Rogers laughed. Wren grinned and sat. "Enjoy your real coffee."

For a few moments they sat, sipping and watching people flow through the People Mover. The trains came and went. Traffic bustled by on Michigan and Cass. It was hard to imagine a man had been murdered only yards away, just hours earlier.

"On the plus side, all that soy should help with your Spanish," Wren said.

Rogers frowned at him. "What?"

"Soy milk? Yo soy milk?"

She stared, got it then groaned. "Dad jokes? Are you kidding me?"

He grinned. He hadn't busted out a 'Dad joke' since Loralei took the kids. Thinking about that flattened the good humor somewhat.

His phone pinged. He brought it up.

The records from Reince Jeffries.

10

CHAT LOG

Wren airdropped the records to Rogers's phone. In a zip file titled 'Sophie - Ravenous6' there was an untitled pdf and a document titled 'Notes'.

"His handle's Ravenous," Rogers pointed out. "Like he can't stop himself."

It wasn't lost on Wren. "And the girl's Sophie," he said. "You take the pdf, I've got the notes."

They both tapped at their phones.

"We do have an office we can use for this," Rogers said helpfully.

"Drink your soy."

"Bigger screens," she went on, "access to printers. What the normal people do."

"I'm a vigilante, we like the fresh air. Now what are you seeing?"

Rogers took a few moments, scrolling down. "Looks like the full chat log. There's hundreds of pages, the transcript of every communication. Photos too. Yours?"

"Highlights from the log," Wren said. The 'Notes' file was a neat document with four columns: the date, the recording catfisher's name, the page reference to the full log and a comment for follow-up. Malton Bruce's first name appeared frequently, interspersed with others. A Tom. A Clara. "Have we got full names for the two they took?"

Rogers answered without looking up. "Tom Solent. Clara Baxter. Photos too."

She scrolled then held up her phone. Tom Solent was in his late twenties, a thin-faced, dour-looking man with dark, sad-looking eyes. Clara Baxter was in her early twenties and attractive, with curly red hair curtaining her features, accentuating deep green eyes.

"They've both been in Marcy's Heroes for around a year," Rogers said, bringing her phone back around. "They're responsible for two and three perps being arrested respectively; Solent lives in the metro area, but it seems Baxter flew in special."

"Flew in? So she's not local?"

"Seems not."

"Where's she from?"

"It doesn't say."

Wren flagged that and scrolled on. The comment column held key quotes lifted from the full log: promises, boasts, sexual descriptions. Wren whipped the document down; it extended for fifty-three pages. More photos loaded the further he went. The catfishers had invented an identity to hook Ravenous6, a girl named Sophie who was fifteen years old, a cheerleader by the looks of the photos they'd shared.

Ravenous6 requested pictures from her in specific poses, or holding a newspaper displaying that day's date and headline, then getting impatient when 'she' didn't reply quickly enough.

"He's got basic tradecraft." Wren said.

Rogers looked up. "How's that?"

"These photo requests. He knows digital 'deepfake' photos

take time to crunch through even an advanced supercomputer. He asks her for a pose, then gets pissy if it takes her too long, to rule out catfishing."

"He's suspicious. Feeling her out."

"Tradecraft. Most likely he studied up online, another self-radicalized abuser."

Rogers considered. "Yeah. But do the catfishers even have deepfake capacity? That takes high-level tech skills and serious computing capacity to pull off well. Faking a convincing photo is hard."

Wren scanned some of the photos 'Sophie' had sent. "These are convincing. Either they deepfaked them, or this 'Sophie' is a volunteer too."

"We can look into that."

Wren scrolled on, reading through sets of links Ravenous6 had sent that passed as online games, but actually implanted spyware, designed to further test if 'Sophie' was real. She, or Marcy's Heroes, seemed to pass all his tests, at least as far as Wren could see. He recognized some of the spyware games but not others. The field was rapidly evolving. As the perps cooked up new means of verifying their targets, the catfishers came up with new workarounds. The CIA, FBI, NSA and other agencies occasionally dipped their massive feet in the waters and shut down a whole strain of code, but the waters always returned to a churning balance after.

"Do you know all of these testing links?" Wren asked.

Rogers looked up. "Not all. Some are new."

"Our database is out of date."

"It's always out of date," Rogers said. "It's a digital arms race, Boss."

Wren grunted. She was the expert, and this was why he'd picked her. "What about digital forensics? Can we lock into the coding style of these tests and narrow it to known hackers?"

Rogers made a face. "Difficult. The field changes fast and the tests are easy to design. Anyone with basic coding can dash one off." She pointed at the screen. "Many of the ones listed here are already outdated. Look, I know this one, two months ago?" She tapped the link for a ball-bouncing game. "It got nerfed." Wren frowned. "That's gamer speak, it means defanged, made useless, by a simple workaround. All the catfishers know about it so the perps don't use it anymore."

Wren considered. With deepfake images, poisoned links and testing 'games', the Blue Fairy and the catfishers went back and forth, using higher-grade tech every time, executing better attacks, causing greater collateral damage.

"This real-world attack is the logical next step," he said.

Rogers set her phone on her lap and looked at Wren. "In the arms race? You think this strike is an expansion of the battlefield?"

"We know they've been organizing," Wren said. "The Blue Fairy knows we can't crack them and they're getting confident. We don't even know how many Pinocchios they have. It could be thousands or even tens of thousands worldwide. We could be talking accomplished figures, with wealth, ability, power. Now it seems they figured out a way to catfish the catfishers. My guess is it's in these test links." He tapped his phone. "They hid malignant code and smoked out Marcy's Heroes. But they didn't warn the perp. Ravenous6. They let him walk right into it. Why is that?"

Rogers' eyes lit up. "They needed a patsy. A guy as bait for the catfishers?"

Wren nodded along. These thoughts had been forming on the plane and on the drive here; that this Pinocchio strike was just the beginning.

"We call it an arms race, but what if this was actually a declaration of war?"

Rogers' eyes widened. "You think there'll be more?"

Wren churned through the last twelve hours of data, projecting forward. "I don't know. Maybe." He stood up. "Let's get those witnesses in. The rolling re-enactment I asked for? We're doing it. I want to see what this strike really looked like."

"The re-enactment, sure. When?"

"As soon as it gets dark. Police escort to get them here on time, whatever. Maybe we'll smoke out a few more witnesses. Let's have big signs up in front of the People Mover where they can see it from the train."

"Understood," said Rogers.

Wren strode to the tip of the triangular forecourt. It felt like standing at the prow of a ship, looking out into an ocean of traffic. Down Michigan, police teams were going from business to business already, knocking on doors, but he didn't expect much. Half the places had been closed for years.

One dead, he thought. Two adults taken, and potentially more to come. The ship was sinking already.

He opened his phone and ordered a total lockdown of the support group he maintained of ex-cons, called the Foundation. It was an organization he'd built over years, absorbing an eclectic batch of ex-cons, intelligence officers, cult survivors and addicts with a diverse set of skills. The Foundation worked on a coin system, like AA, with regular meetings and tight-knit discussion groups, to keep all his members from falling into bad ways.

Now he set a block on all new member admissions, as well as requiring password changes for every user. He double-locked his inner files in the cloud on the dark Internet, where he stored names, addresses and coin status, then sent a warning message out to all his members to be on the lookout.

58

When he finished, Rogers' hand came on his shoulder and he turned. He could read the excitement in her eyes.

"Your social media search spider came back," she said. "We have a sighting on the van."

"I thought you said van's were ten-a-penny?"

Rogers grinned and held up her phone. "Not like this one."

The screen showed a black-and-white still-frame capture that showed the front windshield of a white panel van, and the three figures seated across the front.

All wore Pinocchio masks.

11

DEARBORN

"Where was it taken?" Wren asked, instantly on the ball.

"Dearborn. That's fifteen minutes west of here, mostly zoned for residential. The sighting came from some punk kids shooting up a STOP sign, posting footage for their dumb little buddies. We have the van turning right off Michigan Avenue onto Williamson Avenue."

Wren's heart leaped. This could be it. "OK. Are uniforms in attendance?"

Rogers shook her head. "Nobody knows about this yet. So far, it's just us."

"Call them in. Where's your vehicle?"

Rogers grinned. "This way."

She set off across the triangle at a fast stride, placing a call to Robin MacAuley to bring in local police. Wren followed. In less than a minute they reached a canary yellow Chevrolet Camaro in the People Mover's parking lot.

"You're kidding," Wren said as Rogers went to the driver's side.

"Same car since college," she answered with a grin, ducking in.

"I won't even fit."

Rogers laughed. "I've had bigger men than you in here."

"I don't want to think about that," Wren muttered and followed. It was a tight squeeze into the passenger side, forcing him to hunch over. He went for his seatbelt but Rogers didn't wait, punching the muscle car into reverse and revving straight out onto Michigan Avenue.

Wren clipped in as she skidded across the median, then braced both his hands on the dash. Rogers laughed and cranked the Camaro into drive, hit her sirens and peeled off west.

"Let's make it in one piece," Wren advised.

"They might still be there," she said, accelerating around traffic and across intersections. "Are you armed?"

"No. Too much paperwork to bring my weapon on the flight."

"There's a Sig Sauer in the trunk gun safe," Rogers said. "It's sighted in, a good piece, we'll get you kitted up."

"We cruise by first," Wren said. "Maybe we'll spot the van."

"Sounds good. What do you think the chances are?"

Wren was already bringing up Google maps on his phone, zooming into Williamson Avenue then swapping to the satellite view. It was plainly residential; nice looking houses with decent-sized yards, but with the familiar gap-tooth appearance left by blight. Numerous houses had been leveled along the length of the street, leaving empty green blocks of lawn in their place.

"Good," he said. "Williamson's heavily blighted. Those kids were shooting in a real quiet spot. Not a lot of community left, no curtain-twitchers watching out. Easy enough to pull a panel van in, park up and get off the grid. Pick the right house and you've got no neighbors for a hundred yards in any direction."

Rogers whistled low then whipped through another intersection, barely avoiding getting sideswiped by a big Audi SUV. "You think one of those houses is their destination?"

Wren scrolled the map. Williamson led nowhere special. If the Pinocchios had wanted to go north to Ford road, they could've just turned off Michigan Avenue earlier. "I think so."

Rogers smacked the wheel. "Bingo."

"Don't celebrate yet. They killed Bruce in seconds. There's no telling what they've done to Solent and Baxter."

Rogers turned to him. "You think they're dead already?"

"Only one way to find out."

The ride passed swiftly, a straight shot on Michigan all the way to the turnoff to Williamson.

"Siren off," Wren said, and Rogers hit the button. The car fell silent and she made the turn onto a street that was more than gap-toothed with blight; it was virtually barren.

Rogers cursed.

"I didn't think it'd be this bad," Wren allowed. "It's gotten worse since the map was shot."

The street was wild; scarcely any buildings remained after the blight clearance campaign, and those few that did looked like they weren't far off the grave. Every scrap of space bar the road itself was wildly overgrown, with grass tufting thick and tall, Japanese knotweed spreading like an infection and strangling up the bare branches of dead elms and sycamore, and great overflowing tangles of brambles surging in places like strange, lumbering beasts.

"I would not want to be here at night," Rogers said.

Wren couldn't argue with that. They passed one of the dead homes. Its once-white picket fence and weatherboard fronting had all chipped, peeled and blanched, leaving it a corpse-colored gray. The windows were all hollowed out, the door hung open and kids toys poked their sun-bleached plastic tips through the thick ocean of knotweed in the yard.

"It's like that house in Edward Scissorhands," Rogers murmured. "Before Johnny Depp turns all the bushes into sculptures."

They drove on. Wren scanned the driveways and garages of the few remaining houses. It only took a few minutes, but there was nothing to see.

"Damn it," Rogers grunted as they closed on Ford Road.

"Go back," Wren said.

"There's nothing to see, Boss. Where would they hide a white panel van? You can't just drive it straight into one of the houses."

"I'm not looking for that. Take another pass."

She spun and passed back. This time Wren didn't scan the houses, he scanned the wilderness between them. A third of the way down he saw what he was looking for, and his heart began to pump harder.

"Stop here," he said.

Rogers stopped. "What do you see?"

Wren was already getting out. Stretching to his full height felt good. He strode to the trunk and popped it. Rogers was right behind him and keyed in the code for the gun safe.

"Seriously, what did you see?"

"I'll show you," Wren said, and retrieved the Sig Sauer P226; a classic and solid choice for an agent. It felt good in his palm, always accurate, reliable and durable. He checked the slide and chamber then racked a shell into line.

Rogers was doing the same.

Wren held one finger to his lips then jogged toward the wild undergrowth, pointing dead ahead, gun held low in both hands to his side. "Right there," he said quietly. "See the crushed stems and slow spring-back? Twin lines, just what you'd expect from a van taken off-road."

Rogers stared for a moment, then cursed. The lines made

by tires were faint but present. "How on earth did you see that from a moving car?"

"I'm good with pattern analysis," Wren said. "I'm thinking they took one more turn here, just to confuse us a little bit longer. Come on."

Wren strode into the overgrowth, following the partly crumpled track lines left by the Pinocchio vehicle. The grass was damp and clogs of knotweed slowed their progress, reaching up to Wren's waist in places. The tracks snaked left and it soon became plain where they were headed.

Wren pointed at a house that fronted up to the next street over. It was even more dilapidated than the rest, literally falling down before their eyes. Where the upper floor windows should have been were round, gouged-out holes scarred by black soot. The ground floor seemed to be standing on stilts, with large sections of wall stripped away.

"Maybe they did drive right into the house," Rogers whispered.

Wren vaulted the rickety picket fence and advanced low, scanning the cracked blacktop drive and peering into the darkness of the house. Everything was black inside, burned down to a shell. The van tracks led right in and he followed.

The van was there.

Tucked into the shadows of what might have been a living room once, invisible from outside. A plain, unremarkable panel van.

Wren's heart-rate shot up and he raised the Sig, nodding smoothly for Rogers to take the left. He circled right.

The van's rear doors hung open, nothing inside. He reached the passenger side and pivoted around the open window. Empty.

Then he paused.

There was a smell in the air. Unmistakable. Wren had come across it many times in the past. Half a day had passed since the abduction, not so long, but in the blazing heat of a Chicago summer, half a day was enough to really bring on the rot.

There was also the low drone of flies.

"Oh no," Rogers whispered, meeting him by the van's hood.

"Come on," Wren said softly, and advanced deeper. Shafts of sunlight cut through the ceiling and walls at stray angles, illuminating patches where the patterned wallpaper had burned directly into the wood. It was an odd reminder of the lives once lived here.

A corridor, a door, then they arrived.

Wren stood and stared. Sally Rogers stood at his side, looked dead ahead then looked away and cursed again.

"That's Solent," she said. "Tom Solent."

Wren surveyed the naked figure seated in the chair, in the center of a dark, shabby, stinking room. It was a terrible, lonely place to die. The figure was a male, late twenties, dark hair, skin paled out by blood loss. Undeniably Tom Solent. The chair had been bolted to the floorboards, with Solent's upper arms and thighs zip-tied into position. His face was untouched, and if it weren't for the clouds of flies and the rest of the damage, he could almost be sleeping.

But there was plenty of damage. Wren strode closer, watching his footing. Pieces of Tom Solent were everywhere. His fingers lay amidst the low weeds, along with his toes. The floor was still wet with blood, unable to sink into the already-sodden carpet, and Wren's every step sank in a little, sending clouds of flies and bluebottles buzzing away.

There, resting on the glossy floor between Solent's mutilated feet, was his genitalia. Wren leaned in to study the cuts to Solent's knuckles. The wounds were clean, likely cut with some kind of shears, and had started to scab. He noticed individual zip-ties fastened tightly, like tourniquets, at the base of each finger. That meant only one thing.

"No," said Rogers. "Come on, Boss."

"They didn't let him die," Wren said, speaking in a flat monotone. He'd seen worse before, but not by much, and every time it was sickening. "At least not right away. They took all his fingers, his toes. The wounds started to scab. I'd guess they were at it for a few hours. At the end, pièce de résistance, they castrated him. No zip tie there, so that was when he bled out."

"Sick freaks," Rogers spat.

"We already knew that," Wren said, and turned. "We shouldn't stay. We'll only contaminate the scene for forensics."

At that moment the sound of sirens grew louder.

"I'll go out and wave them in," Rogers said. She'd turned pale. Wren didn't blame her. Kill rooms had that effect.

She left. Wren stood in the corridor outside the site of Tom Solent's painful death, thinking hard. The Pinocchios had come here and done this for a reason. They'd wanted something from him.

What?

It took moments for him to clear the rest of the ground floor. The stairs leading to the second floor were gone, ripped away in the fire. There was no sign of Clara Baxter.

He stepped out of the building as the first police unit was pulling in over the grass. Men in black strike armor with rifles spilled out.

"Clear!" he called. "No perps, one dead. We need a coroner and CSI."

They brought up their radios. Wren found Sally Rogers in the back yard, gazing out at the grass.

"Are you OK, Sally?"

She turned back to him. There were tear trails down her cheeks.

"I was just thinking about the girl," she said. "Clara Baxter."

Wren gritted his teeth. He'd been trying not to think of that.

"They still have her. Why? What are they going to do?"

Wren looked at the sky, as if he was afraid the sudden surge of anger he felt would slosh out of his eyes and be lost. You had to keep it all in, every drop.

"We'll find them before that's a factor, Sally. I promise you. Now come on. We need to get that re-enactment started."

Rogers looked around. "The re-enactment? What about here?"

"Forensics, but I don't think they'll find anything. Those four guys only needed to take off their masks and swap to another vehicle, and they're clean away. Nobody would've seen the vehicle, not here. The trail's gone cold."

Rogers' jaw clenched. Wren could see she was about to burst out in a rush of curse words, and put his hand on her shoulder to stem the flow.

"Hold it in," he said. "Use it."

Steadily, her jaw unclenched. Wren could almost feel her swallowing the outrage. It wasn't easy, but it fed the fire, and his long experience said that the fire needed to be tended constantly. You couldn't ever let it go out.

She nodded once, then started away through the thick greenery, back toward the Camaro. Wren joined her.

12

CATFISHERS

They were largely silent on the ride back to the People Mover. The weight of what they'd just seen was heavy, and it pushed the rest of the world further away.

Wren was lost in thought, trying to figure out the purpose of torturing Tom Solent. His mind drifted back over the conversation with Rogers earlier, about the digital arms race between the catfishers and the abusers they hunted.

It shook something loose.

"These catfishers," he said, breaking the silence and causing Rogers to jerk in her seat.

"Heck, Boss, give a girl some warning."

"Sorry," he said, and smiled. "It's a lot to take in, right?"

"It sure is. Like a Saw movie. I wouldn't want to go out like that."

Wren shuddered at the thought. The pain of having all your fingers and toes cut off would be more than matched by the horror of watching it happen. "Me either. Now, about the catfishers. What do you think the chances are they talk to each other?"

Rogers frowned and glanced at him. "You mean, like, be friends outside their ops?"

"I mean across groups. Marcy's Heroes is one group. There's gotta be others they coordinate with. You said Baxter flew in from out of state; why's that? I'm thinking, maybe she's hooked on the thrill. Maybe she's got a group where she lives, but she wants more, so she commutes just to do it? I can see that the face-off moment, when the perp sees his life falling apart around him, would be a real adrenaline blast."

Rogers nodded along. "OK, I can see that too. So, you're saying there's communication across a wider network. Members in multiple groups. Makes sense." Her eyes narrowed, then it hit. "Oh."

"Yeah," Wren said, already bringing up his phone and dialing Gerald Humphreys.

"You think that's why they tortured him?" Rogers asked.

Wren nodded, then the voice of Gerald Humphreys spoke in his ear. "What is it, Christopher?"

"We found one of the abduction victims," he answered swiftly, "in a blighted house in Dearborn, fifteen minutes away from the abduction site. Tom Solent. He was mutilated heavily, looks like torture, and we're thinking the Pinocchios extracted intel on him about other catfisher groups. This thing we're seeing, it could be about to spread wider."

A few seconds passed. "Is this supposition or do you have any evidence?"

"Well, Solent's dead, so he's not talking," Wren said flatly. Rogers smirked. "But it's a solid inference. We need to start spinning up switchboards and get the message out to every catfisher we can reach. They need to lay low until we can start providing protective details."

"Protective details based on an inference?" Humphreys asked. He sounded skeptical. "And how many people is that, do you have any idea? What's the geographical range? It has to be in the hundreds, perhaps thousands."

"I'll put my team onto Reince Jeffries and try to narrow it down to close affiliations and nearby states, but the warning stands, Gerald. The attack here was brazen, and it looks like there's a plan behind it. This is going to get bigger."

Humphreys sighed. "Just because the Saints' terror attack was national doesn't mean this is also, Wren. Focus on the local until we have more to go on. Find the missing girl."

Wren's jaw clenched. It wasn't an unreasonable piece of advice from a man in Humphreys' position to give, but it felt shortsighted. Unfortunately, gut feelings didn't count for much in the bureaucracy of Intelligence.

"I will, but at least spin up those switchboards. Put the warning out, or it'll be your body parts rolling when the next attack comes."

He could imagine Humphreys' grimace. "OK. Find me some likely targets and I'll spare some agents to make calls. That's proportionate. Any other leads?"

"We'll have forensics on the kill room soon, maybe we'll get some IDs, but that place was a bacteriological swamp, and it looks like the Pinocchios ran a clean ship, so I'm not optimistic. We're also setting up a live re-enactment at the People Mover, try to squeeze our witnesses for some identifying details on the perp or the Pinocchios."

"Get us something, Christopher. Heaven forbid, if this does go bigger, I do not want to be caught flat-footed like last time."

Wren hung up. There was no benefit in pointing out that the flat-footedness last time had entirely stemmed from Humphreys' unwillingness to believe Wren. He looked at Rogers; she was bringing her own phone down from her ear.

"The team's onto Jeffries," she said. "We'll get the affiliations for Marcy's Heroes and relay to Humphreys."

"Good," Wren said. That was something. He looked ahead. It was coming on for late afternoon, with the sun halfway down toward the horizon. Somehow they'd spent over an hour in Dearborn, though it had only felt like minutes. "Set someone to watch him, too. If they tortured Solent for intel, Jeffries is a natural next stop."

"Agreed," Rogers said, and brought her phone back up.

Wren gazed out the window. Back in the kill room, the shadows would be deepening. CSI would now be arriving, putting on their white suits and booties, erecting a clean tent around Tom Solent fitted with clinical white lights. They'd track footsteps, take samples of the mushy blood and ash mix in the carpet, dust for prints, even capture several flies to help nail down time of death.

Such was the procedure of death.

"The re-enactment," he said, interrupted Rogers' call. She looked over. "Let's bring it forward, Sally. We need to do this now."

13

LIVE RE-ENACTMENT

I t grew dark, and the live re-enactment came together under Wren and Rogers' careful oversight.

"The actors are an improvisation group," Rogers explained, standing at Wren's side as a rented white van parked at the curb. The People Mover triangle wasn't taped off. The street wasn't blockaded. The whole re-enactment was guerrilla, unauthorized by the city but with the knowledge of local police, just the way Wren wanted it. "The best I could get on short notice."

Wren said nothing. Three of the actors were sitting in the panel van now, waiting for their first take. They had on the Pinocchio masks Rogers had bought, over hoodies and jeans, and just looking at them made Wren want to stride over and start breaking jaws. They were actors only, he told himself. He'd dressed them that way. They weren't the real Pinocchios.

Traffic rolled on behind him. The People Mover came in overhead, emptied and re-filled, and a fresh flow of people came out of the ticket gates.

Their three witnesses stood at the side, with the best view. A woman and two men, all apologetic that they couldn't remember more, still stressed from what they'd seen the previous night. Wren hadn't pressed them.

The actor playing the perp, Ravenous6, was in position, matching the description as best they could gather from witness statements; a middle-aged, medium-height, white male wearing a suit, ball cap and carrying a clipboard. The three catfish actors were in waiting; a big guy with a binder as Malton Bruce, a blond woman with a camera as Clara Baxter, a slimmer guy with another camera as Tom Solent. At the edge there were signs up requesting information. Police and agents stood on the periphery, ready to harvest testimony.

8 p.m. on a Tuesday, heading into twilight and the witching hour.

"Go," Wren said into the radio.

The catfishers heard the order and sprang into action, following the script. The guy playing the perp took up position in the midst of the outflow of genuine commuters, plying them with his clipboard. Moments later, the big actor playing Malton Bruce approached him. Tom Solent came closer with his camera raised, while Clara Baxter occupied a middle distance, tracking the scene.

Moments passed as Bruce confronted the perp. Angry improvisation led to raised voices and a real tension. The perp did a good job of looking terrified. The commuters passing by opened up a gap around them organically, like a big rock splitting a stream.

Wren looked to the van.

The Pinocchios took that as their cue. The van doors opened and they emerged, holding baseball bats, wearing masks. They walked swiftly up the triangle, and in seconds one of them was behind Bruce. He brought the bat around, faked the hit to the back of the big man's head well, and Bruce went down on cue. Four more mock hits followed.

Commuters nearby screamed and scattered. They didn't

73

realize this was a mock-up, and Wren was aware he was potentially traumatizing a fresh load of citizens, but he couldn't think about that now. The intensity their cries brought was essential to get his witnesses back into the right emotional state to optimize recall.

He pulled his gaze from the action, as the other Pinocchios corralled Solent and Baxter, and instead watched his three witnesses intently, looking for signs of recognition or confusion.

Their faces were fraught with emotion, but Wren wasn't sure what that meant. Maybe something didn't feel right; about the re-enactment, about the reactions, and Wren tried to pin it down as the Pinocchios ran back to their van, dragging Solent and Baxter with them. The perp was standing there shocked, commuters were running and shouting and making emergency calls, everyone was in the right positions, just as they should be.

So what was wrong?

"Run, you idiot," the lead Pinocchio shouted through the window at the perp, a guess at what he'd actually said, then mimed hauling ass back into traffic, though the van didn't move. A big reverse U-turn, Wren figured. Sweep east, stay out of surveillance, then beeline back west along Michigan. They already knew where that ended up.

The perp would follow in his Firebird from its perch around the corner. Witnessed, maybe, from the Orange Pip, but there was no social media confirmation on that yet.

The scene ended.

The cries of terrified Detroiters stilled as the dead catfisher, Malton Bruce, stood up sheepishly, rubbing the back of his head. People ebbed out then back in, like a wave, curious then angry. Were they filming a movie? What the heck was this? Wren let his team handle the explanations and studied the witnesses.

Two were young men, high-powered financiers working downtown, dressed in smart chinos and expensive designer jackets. They looked nauseated, and that made sense. Seeing it all over again would bring it back.

But the woman? She was in her mid-thirties, an office worker in the Guardian building a few blocks over. For a time in the middle there'd been something like confusion on her face. Now she just looked blank. Not nauseated. Wren had read her profile, and there was no sign she had psychopathic tendencies or anything to explain a lack of empathy. She should be nauseated like the men, thrown back into the trauma, but she wasn't.

Something about the performance hadn't rung true to her.

Wren strode over. She was a tall woman, with dark hair, brown eyes and summer freckles across her cheeks.

"Mrs. Reveille," he said, reading her name from his clipboard. "Janet, if I may?"

She nodded. "Sure, go ahead."

"I'm Christopher Wren, investigating officer. I was watching you during the re-enactment. You saw something after the victim was struck with the baseball bat, something that didn't seem right to you. What was it?"

Her lips pursed. That told Wren she wasn't sure. Maybe it wasn't something she really remembered, lost in the stress of the moment. "I don't think so. I think..." she paused. Questioning herself, now. That was exactly the sort of thing Wren had rigged this whole thing to avoid. He wanted their automatic responses and emotional memories, with the filter of their thinking minds out of the way. He wasn't getting that here, and she seemed to know it too. "It was horrible," she said, offering a measure of certainty. "It seemed right."

"No," Wren shook his head, sticking with the feeling. "In the middle, I saw your reaction. You weren't even looking at the bat. You were watching the other one. The Pinocchio with the female victim. What happened there?"

"Oh. Well, I don't… I mean…" she paused, trying to get a grip on it. "Maybe it was louder?" Her dark eyes now shone. Tears suggested she was heading back into the memory. "The clown, the Pinocchio, I don't know. I was nearer to him. Over there." She pointed. "There was so much shouting, I could hear it but I couldn't really *hear* it, you know? They were right beside me. I was worried it would be me next, but I just froze. I wanted to run but I couldn't move."

Wren cursed inwardly. Of course. He'd set the witnesses aside like they were neutral observers, like they were watching a movie, but that wasn't right. When it had happened, they'd been in the thick of the attack. The Pinocchios had waged a disciplined attack designed to maximize shock and awe, and the fear in the midst of that would have been intense.

"If you try, can you remember what they were shouting?"

"I really can't. I'm sorry."

"Let's try something. Would you close your eyes?"

She stared at him, then closed her eyes. Wren went on, starting slowly but building in pace. "OK, you were in the midst. The men in masks were shouting. You feared for your life, so you were hyper-aware. You heard everything, even if you couldn't process it at the time. I want you to focus on what they were shouting. Any scrap of dialog, a name, anything will be useful."

Seconds passed. Janet rocked her head side to side, then opened her eyes. "I'm sorry. Maybe there was a name? But I can't remember. I really can't."

Wren kept the disappointment off his face.

This was his fault. No wonder the re-enactment had rung false to her. He needed to replicate the original conditions as closely as possible. Sensory details were key to recall, right alongside emotional state, and he'd muted both by setting the witnesses aside.

"We'll re-run it," he said.

"That's not necessary-" she began, but Wren held up a hand.

"Help me here, Janet. Please. These men have already killed twice. They took a young woman and we need a break in the case to help find them. I need you to be brave. We re-run it one more time, with you standing where you stood last night, and we try to grab hold of that name. Can you do that for me?"

Now her pupils dilated. The fear was coming back more intensely. It was obvious now that the first re-run had been too safe. Even she'd seen that. Too quiet, too distant, and that was the problem.

She gave a tiny nod, mustering herself as much as she could. "OK."

Wren squeezed her shoulder. "Thank you."

Rogers followed after him as he strode away, moved into his path. Her eyes were wide and bright.

"What are we doing here, boss? That woman has been traumatized enough already. Doesn't matter if she gives consent, it was bordering harassment to put her through it once, but again? Not to mention that her testimony will be muddied. You're going to insert yourself into any sense memories she comes up with."

There wasn't much Wren could say to that. "She knows something, Rogers. I can see it. We need to get it out. I'll apologize when it's over."

"Apologize?" She gestured around at the re-enactment. "Everything we're trained to do in witness testimony is about minimizing the trauma to the victim. They're victims, not toys. You can't use terror as a tool for recall."

Wren looked over Roger's shoulder to the witness. She

was already walking back to the position she'd been in for the strike. Already turning pale.

But was something else still missing? Something she'd said about the real strike being louder?

Rogers was talking. Wren looked at her but barely heard a thing, like he'd dialed the volume way down to the silent fuzz of CCTV. He fast-forwarded through the strike in his head again: the van, the attack, the escape. He'd had the actors improvise angry dialog, but that wouldn't have been the only sound. There was one more, maybe the most traumatizing of them all.

It could be the key.

"What does it sound like when a baseball bat hits a human head?" he asked.

Rogers blinked. "What?"

Wren tried to guess. He didn't have long. He'd pushed the witness into the right mental state. She'd hold that for maybe ten minutes, but afterward she'd be too exhausted to do it again. He'd set the fuse burning; now he was on the clock and had to get it right. "Not a ham," he mused. "And it's not good enough just to hit the ground. Or a tree."

Rogers stared at him, beginning to glimpse the logic. "You're talking about hitting a skull. Malton Bruce's skull?"

"A thin bone globe with soft meat inside. A thunk, kind of hollow. What sounds like that?"

Rogers frowned, her anger fading already in the thrust of this new angle. "It depends on the bat, I suppose. One of those metal bats, it's going to ping. A wooden bat, more of a thunk and a crunch."

Wren thought back to the witness statements. None of them had mentioned the type of bats used. He looked back at the two male witnesses. An agent stood by them filling out forms. Wren strode back over. They were young, desk

78

warriors who'd never experienced anything like this before, each in their own state of heightened emotion.

"What did the bat sound like?" he asked. "Hitting the guy's head? Was it metallic or wooden?"

They stared at him. They looked at each other. "Sound like?"

"Metallic or wooden?" Wren repeated. 'Like a ping or like a crack?"

"Uh, wooden," said one. The other nodded. "It was loud. Like wood."

Wren sucked through his teeth. Of course.

"The actors are using a wiffle bat," Rogers said, getting into the spirit of it. "They're not even hitting anything. The blows are pulled."

"That's it," Wren said. Aside from the Pinocchio and the perp arguing, there'd been hardly any noise through the whole re-enactment. It was almost like a silent movie. No impact of the bat on Malton Bruce's skull, no groans as he died.

Nine minutes. He brought up his phone and clicked into the maps app.

"Does it matter that much?" Rogers asked.

"It might," Wren said, scrolling the map as he talked. "Research says memory is highly linked to context and emotional state."

"Context and emotional state?"

Wren looked up; he needed her on-side for this. "The textbook example is taking a math test. Imagine you're given an hour to prep for the test, and they put you in a blue room with Mozart playing in the background. When the test comes, you either stay in that blue room with Mozart, or you go to another room and it's Bach. Which condition will you perform better on the math test in?"

Rogers frowned. "What color is this room?"

"It doesn't matter. Not blue."

"Sounds like bullshit to me."

"I haven't even told you the result. It's the blue room with Mozart, you'll definitely do better. Recall is tied to emotional state and context, could be auditory input, color; anything could be a keystone memory that'll trigger greater recall." He looked back at the map.

Rogers stared. "Sounds like I need to read this research."

"I'll send you a link. Either way, I can't do it alone. We've got less than nine minutes to pull this off. Are you in?"

Rogers gritted her teeth, jaw clenched. Some anger, maybe, but putting that aside. "I'm in. What do you need?"

Wren held up the map on his phone and pointed east along Michigan. "There's an athletics store on Woodward. Sprint over and get a wooden baseball bat."

"What about you?"

"I'm going to source a skull."

14

SKULL

Wren ran, hit the ticket gates for the People Mover in seconds and vaulted over them. People dodged either way and he sprinted up the stairs, onto the long narrow platform and dropped down onto the track.

Somebody shouted, then he was away and sprinting north. The track was shallow, with two rails for the People Mover, the electrified third rail in the middle and low cement walls to either side, like a human aqueduct flowing through the city, cutting corners and shooting over the tops of buildings.

He'd worked the angles already. If he took Cass north on foot and ran east, he'd reach the nearest grocery store in ten minutes, probably even slower if he took the van, thanks to traffic. Call it a minute to select what he needed, ten to come back the same way, and the witness would be long out of the emotional state they needed.

The People Mover track was his only shot. A train ahead was pulling into the next station: Times Square Grand River Avenue, less than a mile away. Wren pumped his elbows hard, banking on three minutes sprinting there, three back, two to get a 'skull', that gave him a rough one minute to play with.

The train ahead pushed through the station, clearing his route in, and now faces were leaning down from the platform looking back at him. A minute later he was amongst them, hauling himself off the track and bustling through the crowds. He sped down the stairs and hurdled the ticket gates out onto Grand River Avenue, two blocks north of Michigan.

Before him stood Adam's Market.

Organic produce, it looked like, farmer's market-style with minimum food miles, all very ethically responsible. He dashed in and scanned the aisles: Fruit, Household, Seafood, Meat.

Seafood was in back, an artistic display of fish, crabs and shrimp on a bed of ice chips and kale. Wren vaulted over the glass display counter, snatched the prize King Crab from its place in the center then rolled back across.

"Sorry," he called over his shoulder, tucking the crab under his arm.

In the Meat section a big man was coming up the aisle already, store security. Short hair, thick tight beard, hand going to his waist for a taser.

"Sir, I'm going to have to ask you to-"

"Sorry," Wren called and charged the guy like a tight end. The man wasn't expecting it and took Wren's shoulder below his center mass, sending him crashing into a pyramid of cans.

Wren reached the pork products in the refrigerator bay and scooped the largest ham joint they had, packaged in plastic with a thick fatty rind. On the way out the security guy was getting up.

Wren jumped over him. By the registers he grabbed a roll of duct tape and sped outside. People were staring now: a huge man running at full speed, carrying a giant crab under one arm and a huge ham under the other. Late for the dinner party of a lifetime, perhaps.

A transit worker stood in front of the People Mover, looking this way and that, and Wren breezed by him, jumped the gates and ascended again to the platform.

"It was him," somebody shouted as he dropped back down to the track. "Now he's got a crab!"

He ran, already at five minutes and counting. A train came directly toward him, the driver opening his mouth. Wren leaped onto the track's thin outer wall, grabbing a support column with his free hand, and the train whipped by inches to his left. People inside pointed and started. A child shouted, "Crab!" like they'd sighted a rare bird.

The train passed and Wren dropped into its wake, hitting the Michigan Avenue platform two minute later. Eight minutes gone already. Down the stairs he went and out onto the triangle, where his witness had drying tears on her cheeks and Rogers was already standing by the tree, panting, with a baseball bat in her hands.

"You went for groceries?" she asked.

"What they had," he said, dropping to his knees. He stripped the plastic packaging off the pork and slapped it on the ground. "Get them all ready. Tell the guy with the bat to hit this with everything he's got. Hard. Five times."

Rogers stared. "Yes, boss."

"And tell them all to make some noise."

Wren dug his fingers under the flap of fat covering the pork joint. It was slippery but he dug his nails in and yanked. Fat skinned away with a ropey tearing sound. Next he smashed the crab on the concrete so the shell cracked, allowing him to tear the creature apart. He pressed the top shell on top of the pork joint then swung the flap of fat over the top.

It was the best approximation for a human skull he could come up with on short notice.

He swiftly duct taped it into a tight, compact package, then rapped the top twice with his knuckles. It gave a solid, boney thunk. He looked up; the actors and witnesses were all in position, swallowed in a fresh flow of evening commuters. Rogers was staring at him, a look that said he was either a genius or a madman. That would depend entirely on what happened next.

He got to his feet and strode over to the actor playing Malton Bruce. The guy actually looked scared. Wren set the bundle down on the floor.

"As soon as this gets hit, you shout and you go down," he said softly. "Each hit, you shout. Then you die. Sell it, OK?"

The guy's eyes widened and he nodded jerkily. Probably he'd never taken a director's note so fully to heart before.

Wren checked on the witness, Janet. She was in position, standing near where the Clara Baxter actress was lurking, glancing around like she didn't know quite what was happening, like she wasn't sure this was really a re-enactment anymore. Wren raced on to the van and leaned through the open window. Three Pinocchios leered back at him, their noses obscenely long.

"You hit that piece of meat with everything you've got," he told the lead. "Don't screw around. Pull a muscle in your back if you have to. Five times. Hit it like you hate it." He looked to the others. "The rest of you go in hard. Shout. Improvise. Throw some punches. You hate these people. This is your big break."

He stepped back. Out of the fray, to the roadside where he could watch his witness. There was silence across the triangle now, all eyes on him, even the pedestrians coming out of the station were muted, as if they knew something important was about to happen. Waiting.

"Action," Wren shouted.

15

RECALL

The re-enactment began again. The catfishers swooped and things got heated fast, more heated than the first time, louder and more desperate. Emotions were running high after Wren's frantic disappearance onto the People Mover and his rushed reappearance with the meat. The air felt charged and everybody breathed it in.

Commuters stopped in their tracks to watch as Malton Bruce and the perp yelled. It hadn't happened that way at the start; Wren knew from witness testimony that they hadn't raised their voices, but he didn't care. He wanted high emotions, and Janet Reveille was clearly feeling them. She looked terrified, like she truly dreaded what was to come.

The door of the white van opened and the Pinocchios flooded out, coming up the triangle like a tide, bats swinging, pushing commuters out of their way. This was better. The atmosphere was thick with fear.

The Malton Bruce actor played it beautifully. He was caught in his moment of righteousness, making this pitiful perp squeal, but all the time listening for his cue. The bat went up then came down hard.

The thunk on the crab and pork package was gruesome, sounding out across the triangle. It didn't matter that the Pinocchio was only hitting a piece of meat on the ground. The sound of it went right through Wren, married to the sudden violence of the strike. It sounded like a person dying.

Bruce dropped to his knees with a blood-curdling shout. The Pinocchio struck again swiftly, hitting just meat and a crab shell bundled on the floor, but nearby commuters froze where they stood, staring in horror, too stunned now to scream. Violence was violence, and with each blow Bruce cried out and jerked like he'd been hit.

Had he been hit? Even Wren wasn't sure. It felt real.

Three more hits and Bruce lay on the floor convulsing. The other three Pinocchios were rampaging through the crowd now, snatching Solent and Baxter, and the screaming of commuters began.

Wren's eyes swept the chaotic scene. The Pinocchios were rough this time, as per his instructions and it looked like Baxter and Solent were actually resisting, probably doing their best to not actually get hurt. There were barely-pulled punches to the stomach, slaps around the head and shouting. Wren had orchestrated it and still he couldn't take it all in.

Commuters cried out and ran. The Pinocchios dragged their two victims toward the van. Through the midst of the madness, Wren strode toward Janet Reveille. She had turned ash-white, hurled right back into the moment. He stepped in front of her like he was popping into her personal nightmare, and it took her a moment to register him, too caught up in her private terror.

"Janet," he said, firmly now, because softly wouldn't cut it. "Tell me what you saw?"

"I-" she began, but couldn't get it out. He saw something moving behind her eyes, like a shark swimming in the depths.

Wren leaned closer and pointed without looking. "That

man broke another man's head open. The others were beaten and kidnapped, and you've never seen anything like that before. God forbid you ever see it again. Now help me make that true. What did you see?"

Her eyes flickered then settled on an empty space in the air.

"There," she said, pointing.

Wren looked. Nobody was there now, but Wren rewound the action. It was where one of the Pinocchios had grabbed the female catfisher, Clara Baxter. Reveille's finger trembled.

"Tell me."

Reveille's body shook. Wren thought she might vomit. "Shouting. The man in the mask was shouting. She was screaming. He elbowed her in the face and there was blood."

"Go on."

"He said something."

"What did he say?"

"I couldn't hear clearly. The mask." Janet's face was locked now, seeing it happen again. Feeling it. "He was so angry. I've never... I've never seen anything like that." Her eyes flickered to Wren and away again, like she couldn't hold focus. "I couldn't see his face, but the way he moved, the way he held her? He hated her. He wanted to rub her out."

That was all new, and Wren felt his calculus shifting. Until now, Clara Baxter had been just another victim, taken as collateral. But maybe there was more to it than that.

"He hated her generally, as a catfisher?" he asked. "Or he hated her personally?"

Janet's eyes ran cold. "Personally. Definitely."

"What did he say?"

She twitched. "A name. I think."

Wren's heart skipped a beat. "What name?"

"I can't- I don't know. I don't know."

Now Wren dropped his tone to soothing. She couldn't

take much more before the stress overloaded her nervous system. "Give me a letter. Just one letter."

She strained at the air, her vision wavering like she was trying to pin down a mosquito with her eyes. "L? I think, L."

"Keep going."

"Maybe Lance?"

"Lance," affirmed Wren, "good, Janet. Now give me the rest. Give me a last name."

She stared. She weaved. Then she went still. Wren had seen this before. She was about to pass out. It happened when people drove their bodies to the extremes, in faith healer churches, in exorcisms, at rock concerts. Their emotions went up to the edge of what their minds could take, and found there was nothing to hold them back, no safety railing before overload. Without someone to pull them back, they tipped over into unconsciousness.

He put both hands on her shoulders to steady her, looking into her eyes.

"I'm here. You're safe, Janet. We're just spectating here, it isn't real. Tell me the name."

She nodded faintly, taking the tiniest step back from the edge. "Hepbert," she said, staring right through him. "Hebbert. Heppert, something like that."

Wren nodded. That was it.

Reveille's gaze went stone cold, like she was speaking from the fall on the other side. "This is for Lance Hebbert", she said weakly. "That's what he said. Like a vendetta."

Wren took hold of her hands; they were ice cold. He had to get the reframing of this experience in before she collapsed. The nightmare had to end better than this for her, or she would suffer for it. Wren knew all about PTSD, panic attacks and night terrors.

"Thank you for what you've done here today, Janet," he said, speaking clearly and making sure her wide eyes registered his lips moving. "This shouldn't have happened to you, and I'm sorry for my part in it, but you've been incredibly brave. You have definitely saved lives tonight. We will use what you've given us to catch these men and bring them to justice. Thank you. You're a hero in my book. You should be very proud."

She nodded vaguely. Wren felt he could see right into her heart. Then her eyes rolled back in her head, her body went limp, and Wren caught her. He guided her gently to the ground as a medical team came rushing in.

The world rushed back in with them. There was a sense of people gravitating toward them at the center. In the seconds after the wave of attention crested, Rogers appeared by his side, staring at him in disbelief. What she'd just seen probably looked like magic.

Wren felt about the same. A witness who'd known little suddenly gave hard testimony. The first time Wren had seen his father fundamentally manipulate people from the inside out, rewriting the way they thought about the world, it had been the same.

"What did you get?" she asked.

"A name," Wren said, straightening up. "Lance Hebbert. This wasn't just a random hit. They were after these catfishers in particular. Maybe Clara Baxter above all, for something she did to Hebbert."

Rogers' eyes lit up, spooling through the possibilities. "Clara Baxter? She's the only one still alive. So Malton Bruce was just collateral?"

"Maybe. Tom Solent they tortured, because why not? They had him. But they wanted Baxter."

"So she did something to this 'Hebbert'? This was a revenge hit?"

"This was revenge," Wren confirmed. "And I think they're just getting started. We need to scour every record there is for the name Lance Hebbert or Hepbert or other derivations of that name. We need everything we can get about Clara Baxter. Who is she, where did she come from and why would they hate her so much?"

Rogers nodded and brought up her phone. "On it, Boss."

16

WORKING THE CASE

W ren looked across the triangular forecourt as federal agents and cops ran clean-up in the middle, debriefing witnesses and corralling commuters. The evening was dark and the air was still fraught with the sense of threat.

Rogers was working her phone, liaising with their team of analysts back in Washington, but her usual cocksure manner had faded somewhat, replaced by uncertainty. This was footing she didn't understand, and he didn't blame her. The death of Tom Solent was bad enough, and it left Wren feeling like he was standing at the edge of a very high precipice. They needed something solid.

Wren started to pace around the forecourt, working the case in his head. The organized chaos of passing traffic on Michigan and Cass bombarded him; horns, lights, shouts, engines and exhausts. Detroit after sundown had always felt dangerous.

Worse yet, they knew his name. They knew about his kids.

After half a circuit of the forecourt, he brought up his phone and hit redial for Reince Jeffries, head of Marcy's

Heroes. He was the only person they knew who might have met Clara Baxter. As the line rang, he caught Rogers eyes through the crowd.

She shook her head. Nothing yet.

After six rings, Jeffries answered.

"I'm recording this call," the older man said angrily. "I have spoken with my lawyer, Mr. Wren, and-"

"Mr. Jeffries," Wren interrupted, "that's all fine, record as you like, just please answer one more question. Have you ever catfished a man named Lance Hebbert?"

There was a moment of silence. Wren pictured Jeffries stewing, wondering if there was a team outside his house this time, wondering if he should expose himself to more legal jeopardy. Wren expected prevarications and delay in reply, requiring another push to crack through Jeffries' resistance, but what he got was unequivocal.

"I have never heard that name, Mr. Wren. Be assured I know the details of every evil man my organization has incarcerated. I cannot help you. Do not call this number again."

He hung up.

Wren completed his circuit of the forecourt, ending by the ticket gates. The machines chimed manically as dozens of people swiped their phones and tickets. Another People Mover carriage pulled in overhead, rattling and clanking the metal bolts in the ceiling beams, then rattled off again.

Jeffries said he didn't know Hebbert, and Wren believed him. That meant Marcy's Heroes hadn't captured him, which meant, what?

He worked the facts he had. Interlinking lines stretched out from Clara Baxter, reaching out to the Pinocchios and the Blue Fairy, to Marcy's Heroes and Reince Jeffries, and to Wren and his children. A cloud. Connections.

Who was Clara Baxter?

He brought up his phone and scrolled to the full chat log, looking again at her picture. She was young and beautiful, with that red hair and green eyes, but there was something off about her, something he couldn't quite place.

Rogers had said she'd flown in specially for this hit, but what kind of catfisher did that? He imagined a woman with resources, possibly hiding her true wealth; not a usual position for a young person to be in. That could make her far more than a hobbyist predator of predators. Had she somehow taken her mission pro?

How else would she have earned such hate? Bringing Pinocchios down could be her vocation. Maybe this Lance Hebbert was one such Pinocchio.

Rogers intercepted him at the tip of the forecourt's triangle.

"Boss, it's not looking good," she said.

"No records?"

She shook her head. "There's nothing on 'Lance Hebbert' or any variation of that name, at least not a single relevant criminal conviction, arraignment, or arrest that we can find. The team's already checked every national intelligence service directory there is, along with Interpol, international police databases, prison records, army files, airport customs logs, and anything else they could think of. They've tried cross-referencing just Hebbert, just Lance, then those against Baxter, but still nothing. According to the census there are plenty of Lance Hepperts or Hebberts out there, tens of thousands even, but not one we have a single relevant lead on." She sucked air through her teeth. "The man is a ghost."

Wren's fists tightened. It was possible their witness had completely misheard, but he didn't think so. Janet Reveille's revelation felt genuine.

"What about Baxter?"

"Almost nothing to tell," Rogers said. "Facial recognition

scans bring up a social security that places her as a grade school teacher in Webster City, Iowa. She went to Iowa state and studied Fine Art, now she teaches kids how to paint still life. She's got a minor social media presence; she plays basketball in an amateur league, supports her school's football team and goes to the movies a lot."

Wren frowned. "That's it?"

"I get the same feeling," Rogers said. "Classic fake ID, right, just enough life to make it look legit? Kind of like the fake Sophie account."

"She's running a sock puppet of herself? A fake?"

"Could be. The team's running checks on everything they can; voting record, address, arrests, bank accounts, family. It's late, but we're reaching out to her school colleagues, see if we can get confirmation on anything."

"Good. Keep at it." A thought struck him. "Have we had anything on the perp?"

Rogers frowned. "Yeah actually. There was something. One second." She swiped sideways rapidly on her phone, scanned something then looked up. "We got another hit on the social media image spider, looking out for a Pontiac Firebird heading away from the scene."

Wren focused in. "What do we have?"

Rogers held up her phone. There was an image of what looked to be the hood scoop of a cherry-red Pontiac Firebird. "It's fleeting, barely visible apparently, with no shot of the driver, captured in the background by a social media influencer riding on the People Mover."

"Do we know which direction it was heading?"

"Looks like north on Cass."

"License plate?"

"Nothing on that, Boss."

Wren's mind spun. "The color's going to narrow it down some."

"Looks that way." Rogers swiped through emails. "We have five teams out right now canvassing owners: according to DMV records, there are seven red Firebird owners near Detroit, with a few possibles further out, and one we like out of state."

"Out of state?"

"His Internet traffic is through the roof. He's got VPN, IP masking, looks like serious cryptography on his data. Could just be peer-to-peer piracy of TV shows, or..." she trailed off.

"Videos of kids," Wren finished. "OK. Prep the teams to move in on them all, including the guy out of state. We should have enough to run warrants and start taking vehicles and searching them for contraband. We can also set up our witnesses here with photo ID parades of the Firebird owners. One of them's gonna recognize him."

"Will do."

Wren nodded. "OK. Baxter's the center of this thing, but the perp's a solid lead. Work them both. I'm going to try Jeffries again and squeeze something on Baxter."

Rogers nodded and brought up her phone, heading back over to the agents working with Janet Reveille and the two finance bros. They wouldn't be going home just yet.

Wren dialed Jeffries, but this time he didn't answer. After eight rings it went to voicemail. Wren tried again, but still nothing.

He sighed. The old man had clammed up. Wren called his team.

"Yes, Boss," came the sprightly sound of Robin Macauley.

"Who've we got watching Reince Jeffries?"

"On Jeffries? That's Mather."

Robert Mather was a stalwart FBI agent from cybercrime, with twenty years clocked in cyber-defense, often involving in-person stakeouts to scoop encrypted signals out of the air.

He'd busted countless cybercriminals on their data use, which technically didn't need a warrant once it had left their computers and entered an open, even spoofed, wireless Internet network.

"Put me through."

"Sure thing, Boss," MacAuley said. The line clicked. Wren waited as Mather's cell phone rang.

And rang.

After twenty seconds Wren hung up and called MaCauley back, at the same time as pushing back through the crowds toward Rogers.

"Boss?"

"He's not answering. Ping his car radio."

"Calling." Wren heard the beep as MacAuley keyed the transmission. "2-Gamma, this is 1-Alpha, acknowledge."

No answer. Wren's heart rate accelerated, and he waved to get Rogers' attention as he drew near.

"2-Gamma, this is 1-Alpha, please acknowledge," MacAuley repeated.

Still nothing.

Wren cursed then reached Rogers, who pulled the phone slightly from her ear.

"What is it, Boss?"

"Mather's not answering his radio or cell. I think Pinocchios have just taken Jeffries. Come on."

He started running toward the parking lot, whipping by the ticket gates in moments.

"Pinocchios have taken Jeffries?" Rogers called, following along behind.

"If I'm right, they're at his house right now," Wren called back, then reached Rogers' yellow Camaro. "Give me your keys."

She handed them over. "We'll need backup."

Wren unlocked the door and slid in. "Agreed. We need a

squad sent to his home right now, along with drone recon overwatch equipped with heat-tracking, plus helicopter overwatch."

"Helos?" Rogers asked, sliding into the passenger side as Wren fired up the engine. "But what about Mather, you think-"

"There's a good chance he's already dead," Wren said, then hit the gas and reversed the Camaro out into traffic faster than Rogers had, pulling the handbrake and skidding hard to face west. "But maybe there's still time. Now, direct me to Jeffries' house."

Rogers absorbed that for a second, then nodded. "West on Michigan," she said, then lifted her phone to her ear and started barking commands. Wren cranked the car into drive and shot forward.

17

REDFORD

W ren took the Camaro up to seventy in seconds, sirens wailing, sweeping out into oncoming lanes to bypass traffic heading west. A large Ford Super Duty came barreling toward them and Wren shifted across the median at the last possible moment, let it whip by then flung the Camaro back to the left.

"Boss, are you serious?" Rogers asked, staring at him wide-eyed.

"I should've said 'hang on'," Wren allowed, letting the tunneling effect of adrenaline and the riotous thump of his pulse push him to the limit.

"Noted." Rogers took firm hold of the ceiling grip. "We have a rapid response squad inbound from Redford PD; they'll beat us by a few minutes. A tactical helicopter should join soon after. Turn left here!"

Wren ran a red light and skidded hard onto Rosa Parks Boulevard, rising to ninety alongside the freeway. Five seconds passed in acceleration, then he pulled a hard right going the wrong way onto the exit ramp. Rogers braced her other hand against the dash as exiting traffic sped toward them. Wren pushed the pedal down and swung over to the shoulder.

"Unh," Rogers grunted as the stream of oncoming vehicles honked and peeled to the side, missing them by inches. Three seconds later they merged into oncoming traffic; Wren spun a hard handbrake turn into the middle of the three-lane expressway, stopping two lanes of traffic and nearly getting reamed by a speeding semi. He cranked the gear stick, the tires squealed and burning rubber backwashed into the car, then they were accelerating like a cannonball along with the rest, back up to ninety in ten seconds and wailing west.

Rogers took a breath. "Hot damn, Boss. And you acted like I was driving too fast."

"The occasion demands it," Wren said, willing the road ahead to empty out so he could go over a hundred. "Only Jeffries so far knows anything about Clara Baxter. Maybe that's why the Pinocchios went for him. We should've put on more units."

"Shoulda coulda woulda," Rogers answered with a heavy exhale. "We'll get there."

"Let's hope he has all his fingers and toes."

She winced.

"What's our ETA?"

"Redford's near enough," Rogers answered, then held her phone to her ear. "MacAuley says a normal journey takes twenty minutes, should be less given we're speeding."

"That's what the blue lights are for." Wren crested a hundred, overtaking a long Lincoln Navigator limousine, already out of central Detroit and arcing northwest. "Still nothing from Mather?"

"Nothing."

Wren cursed.

"You think they're going to torture Jeffries?" Rogers asked.

"That or just kill him. If he knows something about Baxter, something which could lead us to Hebbert, that could lead us to them. If I was them, I'd just cut the old man's throat and be done."

Rogers shook her head. "Some day you'll have to tell me all about your CIA days."

Wren snorted and flashed her a glance. "You don't want to know, Sally."

"Because you broke laws?"

"Laws? I'm barely even house-trained. I can't believe Humphreys gave me AWOP."

Rogers laughed. "Maybe I'm glad he did."

"Maybe?"

"Let's see how this turns out."

"Fair point," Wren said. "This exit?"

"This'll work."

Wren zagged over the lanes and dragged the Camaro off the freeway and into Redford Township at seventy, barely letting up as the off-ramp veered right. Gyroscopic force pushed Rogers against Wren and made the vehicle's grip on the road seem a tenuous thing, then they slammed into a straight and tore through one, two intersections, cutting up traffic with sirens wailing.

"Turn right," Rogers barked.

Wren cranked the handbrake and pulled hard onto Inkster Drive, leaving burned rubber trails behind as he accelerated into nighttime traffic, past the Tim Horton's and the Dollar General and into an all-American suburb of wide streets, spreading lawns and porch swings.

"Who's with him?" Wren asked. "Jeffries."

Rogers had the information ready. "He lives with his

daughter, her husband, and their two kids. We don't have their confirmed locations right now."

Wren looked ahead. The skies were empty. "Where's my overwatch?"

Rogers pressed her phone harder to her ear. "Choppers are twenty minutes out, but I'm wired into a Redford PD drone already up on heat seek."

Wren was impressed; that really was a rapid response. "If we've got one the Pinocchios could too. What are we seeing?"

Rogers tapped through to the live footage and held it up so Wren could see. "It's that one," she pointed at a hot orange building at the end of a row. "Vehicle in the driveway with a cold engine, looks like the saloon belonging to Jeffries. I count nine people in the house, which could just be his wider family or maybe the immediate family plus another gang of four Pinocchios. Nobody running, nobody hiding, no movement at all."

Wren cursed under his breath, glancing at the phone's dark heat-map then swiftly back at the road before he could sideswipe an old GMC Sierra changing lanes without a signal. "How are they clustered?"

Rogers studied the heat-map. "Two figures positioned closely together near the front bay window, looks like they're sitting around a coffee table, one figure at the head. Five in the back parlor, one by the front door, one at the rear."

Wren worked that through. "Sounds like they've got the exits covered," he reasoned. "Unless two of his family went out for a smoke at the same time but in opposite directions."

"Agreed."

"Then the four in the parlor are the family, with one Pinocchio standing guard. In the front window'll be Jeffries and his torturer." Rogers winced. "Heat signature shows they're all alive?"

"Right now, yes."

Wren chewed his lip and blew through another intersection, thinking about the Blue Fairy catfishing the catfishers with a patsy, about Internet games that doubled as traps, about an MO he'd already seen play out once in the real world and now...

"Jeffries' house, is it steel frame or brick?"

Rogers frowned, but fed the question to MacAuley and got a reply. "Brick, why?"

Wren's mind raced on: Pinocchios on both front and back sentry duty came close to ruling out a stealth assault. Besides, it would take seconds only to kill Jeffries. If they had the slightest warning, he was done.

Wren pushed the pedal down harder, blowing past Bell County Park at sixty. "How many officers inbound?"

Rogers listened to the answer. "Seems like the whole station's on its way, but we've outpaced them. We'll hit first."

Wren absorbed that, then hit the button to kill the siren. It spun down at once.

"What are you doing?"

"Any warning and they'll kill him."

Rogers frowned. "OK. So what do we do, try to slip in the back?"

"Too much risk we'll tip them off, and we can't risk it. Right now, Jeffries is our only lead. We need shock and awe chased by total takedown. Get your weapon out and buckle up."

Rogers turned to look at him, lips framing to ask a question, then the light came on in her eyes. "Wait. No. Don't tell me you're going to-"

"We are," Wren interrupted, flying through the final intersection. "Buckle tight, Sally, and hold up that heat-map."

Rogers cursed then cinched her seatbelt and held up the phone. Wren tugged his belt tight with one hand then locked his gaze on the small screen.

The Camaro shot into frame like a heat-seeking missile. Jeffries' house was on the left, Victorian style with large bay windows up a sloped front yard set to grass. Wren judged the moment then yanked left, whipping the car hard to mount the curb with a chassis-cracking jolt.

"Daaamn!" Rogers shouted as they tore up the grass at forty miles an hour, then grabbed the back of her neck and braced.

They hit.

The fender struck brick just beneath the bay windows and crumpled instantly, followed by the grill which squashed flat, then the safety roll cage which sheared back on itself but didn't buckle, stripping a bolt in the undercarriage. Beneath it the building's outer layer of brick powdered with a terrific bang, sending fracture lines shooting out too fast for the structure to settle onto, opening a cavitated hole that the roll cage blew through in an explosion of bricks. The headlights ruptured as they hit the crumbling wall, then the indicator lights, sending glass sprinkling with brick dust and mortar as the car punched into the wall. The bodywork scraped and tore as the roll cage pile-drived into an inner layer of cinder blocks like a hammer splitting a coconut husk. A run of electrical cabling tangled on the front axle, then the flat front fender barked through the interior wall.

Pillows and throws flew through the air from the bay window seats, along with an airborne avalanche of masonry, timber and glass. The three-paned window above shattered under the warping stress, blowing back across the Camaro's roof. The front wheels tore off like pencil erasers on jagged brick ends, the wing mirrors clipped neatly away and the windshield smashed inward as the A-pillars hit the base of the wooden window frame and plowed through in a burst of heat, sound and motion.

As the car decelerated from forty to zero with an almighty

bang, Wren and Rogers flew on; the seat belts caught their bodies and the brace positions helped prevent hyper-extension of their necks, until the airbags deployed with a double blast of air that was masked in the overall crash. Hard canvas balloons punched them both in the face, bruising their eyes, noses, lips, but halting the whiplash and pushing them back into the soft recesses of their seats.

The patrol car buried its momentum halfway into the Jeffries' dining room then rocked to a stop in a cloud of dust and tumbling debris, less than a second all told. Wren blinked and craned his neck over the airbag as it deflated. The car hummed and the structure above them teetered, the engine still growled but the front end was buried too deeply in masonry to push any further.

Wren saw them then through the dust-filled air, two people laid out in the rubble, one of them Jeffries. He was lying in his chair still, clearly zip-tied down and unable to move, a bead of blood running down his temple. The other wore a Pinocchio mask and was already trying to get up.

Wren kicked his door open just as the first Pinocchio emerged from the rear and fired.

18

DEAD MAN

Bullets spat through the Camaro's shattered windshield and thumped into the upholstery. Wren rolled smoothly around the open door and returned fire with Rogers' Sig P226, pinging the nearest Pinocchio in the chest and face.

He tumbled down and Wren advanced, mirrored by Rogers to his right.

The Pinocchio at the rear of the house took cover behind a couch in the den, grabbing one of Jeffries' grandchildren as a hostage. Wren had no time for that, and fired through the cushions. The hollow-point bullet shredded through the soft furnishings and into the Pinocchio, who dropped his weapon, released his hostage and fell.

A gunshot rang out near Wren's side, and he spun to see Sally Rogers dispatch a Pinocchio in the front hall. Another rose up in the den and Wren shot him in the abdomen. The torturer lay still by his feet and Wren stepped over him, kicking his mask away to reveal the face of a ruddy teenager.

"-om!" came a shout. Wren scanned the space and settled on Jeffries.

"Secure these," Wren told Rogers, then kneeled by the old man's side and pulled a knife from his belt, setting to work releasing his zip-ties.

Three fingers were already missing from Jeffries' right hand, each wound with a zip-tie tourniquet. His eyes were wild but his mouth was trying to frame words.

"You're OK now," Wren said. "Everything's going to be-"

"... bomb!" Jeffries managed to get out.

Wren spun.

"Dead man's switch, Boss," came Rogers's cry, kneeling by the man toward the rear of the building. "This freak's holding a button."

The world tunneled. "Down!" Wren shouted, then threw himself across Jeffries as all hell broke loose.

A tsunami wave of heat, blast wind and noise hammered into Wren and flattened him across the old man, scraping shrapnel across his back. Jeffries' chair broke beneath the force and the old man cried out.

Then it was over, and Wren reared up.

The world around him was black and dizzy. The Jeffries' dining room, only moments ago wrecked but recognizable, was now a dark cave filled with smoke and fire. Wren turned to seek out Rogers, but the air was too black and noxious to see. He glimpsed the ashy outlines of bodies, maybe Pinocchios or Jeffries' family, then a figure rose up ahead.

He seized up a brick, ready to hurl it, then recognized Rogers.

She was on her knees and weaving, lit by the sickly light of flames spreading across the carpet. Her eyes roamed then fixed on him, blasted red with pinkish tears running down her cheeks, face pale and mouth open like she couldn't get a breath in.

"Holy crap, Boss," she croaked.

"You OK?"

"I'm alive," she answered. "I think. You?"

"I think so. Took some shrapnel. But what about..."

Wren looked down at Jeffries, his mind working fast to make up for his deadened limbs. The ceiling lights had blown out and the floor was scoured clear of furniture and cratered by the rear doors. The walls were peppered with fracture lines and shrapnel holes and fires were catching everywhere, lending more smoke and flickering light to the chaos.

"This was a booby trap," Wren growled, dropping to one knee to check Jeffries' pulse in his neck. "Like their online attacks, moved into the real world."

"That was a substantial explosive," Rogers added, shambling closer. "Had to be several pounds of Semtex."

Wren found Jeffries' pulse, rapid and thready. "Jeffries is alive. Find his family."

"Already on it."

He scooped the old man carefully out of the broken sticks of the chair frame and started forward, stumbling over crushed brick and scorched carpet.

"Somebody here!" came Rogers' voice.

Wren moved toward her. She was lifting up a child. In the chaos it looked like Wren's own son, seven-year-old Jake, but of course it couldn't be. This was Jeffries' grandson. By his side lay the granddaughter, wrapped in the protective embrace of her mother.

Wren rolled Jeffries over his shoulder then dropped to one knee and hiked the boy under his arm. Silver lights flashed behind his eyes as he stood, then staggered on through smoke, while Rogers alongside him carried the girl.

The crater by the rear French doors was torn two feet deep through the parquet oak flooring, and he edged around its scorched rim. The doors were encased within a frame of flame as the curtains caught fire, but Wren ducked through and into the chill evening air.

A generous garden spread before him, laid largely to grass. He staggered twenty yards until he was clear of the smoke and shrapnel cast by the blast, then laid the bodies down gently and turned around.

Jeffries' home was an inferno already. Rogers' restraining hand came on his arm.

"It's done, Boss."

"Two people left," he said, and ran back into the house, leaping through the halo of flame to find the son-in-law coughing on his knees in the black. "That way, go!" Wren pointed, gave him a shove, then turned to Jeffries' daughter.

She lay still, her face pale and shrouded with shrapnel. Judging from the wounds in her back and side, it looked like she'd taken the brunt of the blast to protect her kids.

Wren lifted her quickly and carefully, her body lolling like a baby cradled across his chest. He pushed up and ran back past the crater, but saw the son-in-law had collapsed inside, unconscious. Wren dropped to one knee, balanced the daughter with one arm and pulled the son-in-law out.

He staggered through the rubble and blazing French doors to burst out onto the cold, damp grass. Rogers appeared by his side and took the son-in-law's arms. Wren sucked in air and looked to the sky. Now he heard the rotor beats of a helicopter coming in. A little too late, he wondered, and chuckled.

"What's ... funny?" came Rogers' voice nearby.

"This is the kind of thing," Wren wheezed, "we did ... in the CIA."

She laughed too, which lapsed into a coughing fit, which prompted her to roll to her knees and check the vital signs of the children. Wren watched until she gave him a thumbs up. That was a blessed relief.

He checked Jeffries' pulse again. It was there, but only just.

"Stay with us, Reince," Wren said, then stood and started waving both arms at the helicopter as it circled in.

19

BENNETT

There was no room for the helicopter in the rear yard, so Wren headed to the front as it descended. The house was fully ablaze now. A paved alley ran between the red brick wall and a tall fence, but it was utterly engulfed in smoke, with flames shooting out through two gaping windows.

Wren vaulted the fence into the neighboring garden then padded down through the shadowy copse of Douglas firs as the rotor blades swept overhead, fanning the flames.

The helicopter's floodlights lit a scene of carnage on the street, littered with burning blast debris from the bomb. Rogers' Camaro looked like it had been through an industrial shredder. Ahead, six figures rappelled down fast ropes, rifles raised and beading on Wren.

"Identify yourself," the lead SWAT officer shouted, a rugged-looking man in his early thirties with a strong jaw and commanding features.

Wren slowly raised both hands, stopping in the midst of a bank of lavender. "Special agent Christopher Wren. There were four perps here, but they're all in the house. One ignited a suicide vest." He nodded sideways at the conflagration.

"My partner's in the back with a family of four. We all survived a bomb blast and need medical attention. Have you got a medic?"

The lead officer talked into his helmet mic in a low voice, getting confirmation, then nodded, turned and starting giving swift commands. Two of his team broke left and two broke right.

"My name's Jack Anderson," said the officer. "We'll clear the surrounding properties and secure the family. Here," he turned, to where a fifth SWAT officer came forward carrying a large black satchel, "Caleb Bennett, our medic. Lead the way."

Wren nodded and turned.

The medic exclaimed loudly.

"What is it?" Wren asked, spinning back.

"Your back," Bennett said. "It's shredded. You've got to be losing a lot blood."

Wren grimaced. He did feel light-headed. "Patch me up later. I've got kids in back plus a witness with vital information, elderly male, in poor condition."

He didn't wait for further comment and ran back through the fir trees to the fence, where one of the advance SWAT officers was already standing guard. She nodded at Wren and he vaulted back over the fence.

The children in the yard were crying now, which seemed a good sign to Wren; better than lying still and silent. Jeffries' daughter and son-in-law were holding and soothing them, which was even better. Only Reince Jeffries was motionless, with Rogers kneeling over him now, administering CPR.

"He started coughing then he crashed," Rogers said.

"Right here, Bennett," Wren said.

"Don't stop," the SWAT medic said to Rogers, then dropped his backpack, kneeled opposite her and began an expert, swift inspection, probing Jeffries' ribs, listening to the wheeze of breath as Rogers pumped his chest and inspecting his eyes.

He looked up. "You said you were hit by a bomb?"

"I had him covered," Wren said. "I don't think any shrapnel hit him."

"Doesn't matter," said Bennett. "It's the shockwave. He's frail. I think he's got an intrapulmonary hemorrhage and maybe TBI."

"In English?" Rogers asked.

"Damage to his lungs causing hypoxia; not enough oxygen in his blood. TBI is Traumatic Brain Injury; he's got one pupil bigger than the other. Options are limited, but they get better the faster we put him on the helicopter and get him into an OR. He might make it." His gaze drilled into Wren. "But you said he has vital information?"

Wren gritted his teeth. Exigent circumstances gave special agents in the field a lot of latitude in how they treated injured witnesses in time-critical cases.

Bennett gazed flatly, waiting for Wren to make the call. Rogers kept pumping.

"Can you bring him around now?"

"Probably. An adrenaline shot from an epipen should bring him back, but it might also drive him deeper into cardiac arrest."

"Can you pull him back, if it does?"

"Possibly. It's less likely than an immediate air evac to hospital, though I'll be honest, I'm not hopeful in either case. Odds are he doesn't survive these injuries. "

It was a hard choice. Wren looked up at Jeffries' burning home. Nothing was going to survive that conflagration. No evidence, no records, nothing to lead him back to Clara Baxter, and from her to the Blue Fairy.

Only Reince Jeffries knew who Clara Baxter was. Only Jeffries could help save her.

"Wake him up."

Bennett pulled a slim box from a slot on his belt and popped the clasp. It was foam-packed inside, cushioning a narrow tube filled with yellow liquid. He slid it out and pulled the plastic lid off, exposing the thick silver syringe.

"Boss," Rogers cautioned, "you sure this is right?"

"My call to make, on my head Sally," he said, and nodded at Bennett.

Bennett opened Jeffries' shirt, positioned two fingers either side of the sternum, then raised the epipen back. "This is intra-osseus infusion," he said calmly, "into the bone, the best route to reach the venous system," then he brought the syringe down.

The tip stabbed into Jeffries' sternum with a crack and a crunch, then Bennett depressed the plunger.

The old man bolted upright at once, gasping hard. His eyes flashed wide and his neck quivered like it was under tension from some hidden inner spring. He shook once, then looked jerkily at his burning house, at Wren and Rogers, and it was clear panic was only seconds away.

Wren put one hand on his shoulder, another on his chest beside the syringe and spoke in a soft, soothing tone.

"Mr. Jeffries, everything's all right, your family are fine, there's nothing to worry about. I'm sorry to ask this right now, but I need to know everything you know about Clara Baxter."

20

CLARA BAXTER

The old man's eyes fixed on Wren. Dark processes turned behind his pupils, trying to come to grips with the things that had happened, that were still happening.

"My house is on fire," he said. His voice sounded strange, too high. Now his eyes were roaming. He'd see his grandchildren on the grass any moment and get distracted.

"Mr. Jeffries," Wren said, and clicked his fingers in front of Jeffries' eyes. "Your family are all healthy and well. What I need to know about is Clara Baxter."

Jeffries' eyes steadily focused on Wren. His breathing was high and whistling, but some of the deep, commanding timbre returned to his voice. "You."

"Me. Whatever it is you're not telling me about Baxter, I need to know it right now."

More deep processes turned, like cogs in an ancient machine. Reaching a calculation. "That's not her real name." He paused to wheeze. "Clara."

"OK. Is this what you didn't want to tell us at the start?"

Jeffries stared for a moment, then nodded.

"So what is her real name? Why did the Pinocchios take her, but kill the others?"

Jeffries drew a shuddery breath. "She came … five years ago. Before I started … the Heroes. Encouraged me."

Wren frowned. "You mean she got you started?"

Jeffries nodded. He was paling further. Wren worried he'd lapse back unconscious before he got the information out. "She emailed. Many times. Different addresses, different names. Eventually she came out to see me. She knew I had money." Long pause. "She wanted me to work with her."

"So she ran your group?"

Jeffries coughed. Wren glimpsed Bennett from the corner of his eye, readying to step in and push him away, but he held out a stalling hand.

"Ran it. Designed it. Coded it. Enlisted the people. I just…" He coughed.

"You bankrolled it?"

Nodding.

"So who is she?"

"Emily," said Jeffries. "Mona. Gloria. Lots of names, half-mentioned, half-forgotten. She'd done … this before. Made groups. To catfish them."

Wren felt like he was back teetering at the edge of a high precipice, with answers on the other side. "How many groups? Which ones?"

Jeffries gave a weak shrug. "Dozens, I think. Across the country."

Dozens. Wren reeled. "Give me something more. Where's she from?"

"Idaho," Jeffries asked. His eyes rolled up in his head, only rolling back when Wren gave him a light shake. "Maybe Idaho, from the accent. A farm. She gave hints about growing up with pigs. I think … she was lonely."

"Why would she be lonely?"

"This was her whole life. Hunting them."

"Why would she do that? What happened to her? What's her connection to Lance Hebbert?"

"To who?"

"Lance Hebbert."

"I don't know that name."

Wren cursed. He looked at the fire, then back down at Jeffries, who was now unconsciously clutching his wounded hand. Three fingers missing. Maybe Wren could use that. Humphreys had told him to narrow the target list of catfishers; maybe this was his chance.

"The Pinocchios asked you about other catfishers. What names did you give them?"

Jeffries just stared.

"Any name could help, Reince," Wren said. "I can protect them. What did you say?"

"They didn't," Jeffries began, then gulped hard, "not about catfishers."

Wren frowned. "What do you mean, not about catfishers? What did you tell them?"

Jeffries sucked at the air once, twice, perhaps straining to answer, then his eyes rolled up in his head and didn't come back down.

Bennett jumped in and took Jeffries' pulse. "He's flagging. Help me get him to the helicopter."

Bennett took his shoulders and Wren took his legs. Together they ran back to the fence, which had been hammered flat by the SWAT team. They ran through darkness pulsed by the blue lights of half a dozen police cars, right up to where an air ambulance had put down next to the SWAT helicopter.

Wren fed Jeffries in, then Bennett took over, beginning emergency intubation, and the helicopter took off. The downdraft blasted Wren like a wave of relief.

He brought up his phone and tapped in a number.

"Yes, Boss," came the voice of Robin MacAuley on the line, somewhat less sprightly than usual.

"We just got hit by a suicide blast, four Pinocchios down, but we're OK and Reince Jeffries offered some intel. Feed new data points into our search for Clara Baxter and Hebbert. She might've grown up or spent time on a farm in Idaho, maybe a pig farm. Potential aliases include," he thought back, "Emily, Mona and Gloria."

"Running that now," she replied. "And when you get a moment-"

"Agent Wren," came a firm voice from his right. Wren turned to see SWAT team leader Jack Anderson striding over.

"With you in a second, Robin," Wren said.

"You need that medical attention right now," Anderson said. "An ambulance just came in, this way."

He started walking.

"Come on," Wren said to Rogers.

She shook her head. "What we got on Baxter, it's hardly anything to go on. I don't know if it was worth-"

"Jeffries is on me, Sally," he said gently. "Now come on. Your back's a mess too."

21

EVERYWHERE

T he lead EMT at the ambulance, Mia Sullivan by the name on her badge, was stunned when she saw both Wren and Rogers' backs.

"How are you two even walking around?"

"Coffee," Wren said.

"What? We need to get you into an ER and operate."

"Can you stitch us up here?" Wren asked.

Sullivan blanked for a moment, then turned to a colleague who shrugged, then turned back. "It's possible, I guess. Are you sure you want to do that?"

Wren looked at Rogers, and she nodded. "Please do. We need to be here co-ordinating the response."

Sullivan paled slightly but nodded. "OK then. We'll, uh. We'll lay out some gurneys and start stitching, I guess."

"Sounds good." Wren smiled and turned to Rogers. She looked like he felt; pale, red-eyed from the blast, soot-stained and weaving slightly on her feet.

"Suicide blast," he said. "They were ready."

"Booby-trapped, like you said. Maybe every strike they go in hot, in case something goes wrong."

"Nobody gets taken alive," Wren murmured.

"But suicide vests? It's crazy. It's normally jihadis who do that, because they'll get all those virgin brides in heaven." she stoped to suck in a breath. "What's in it for a Pinocchio?"

"You've seen the videos catfishers put up on WeStream?" Wren asked.

"Some, yeah."

"Then you know. Getting caught is worse than death for these guys. Jail means a lifetime of humiliation and violence for child abusers. They lose everything."

"So they'd rather die?"

"Extremists, Sally," Wren said. "The Blue Fairy's been radicalizing them; darker content driving them deeper into their sickness."

She nodded, absorbing that. "OK. So you're thinking there's been more of these."

"Let's find out," Wren said, and called MacAuley back on speakerphone. "What have you got for us, Robin?"

"Bad news, I'm afraid."

Rogers winced.

"Don't sugarcoat it."

"It looks like you were right about the Pinocchios having national targets," MacAuley said. "The first attack hit four hours back, but we're just putting the pieces together now. It was a sister network to Marcy's, one that never responded to our calls since midnight, when we started the phone banks. I'm seeing," she scrolled, "two more anti-abuse volunteers dead, and their two children were taken. Mutilations that match Tom Solent." She paused. "In their home. No evidence yet, no trace."

Wren stared ahead, feeling the scale of the Blue Fairy swell around them. Bigger than Detroit. Faster than he'd expected, and now taking children. "Any sign of suicide vests? Unexpected explosions in civilian areas?"

"I, uh, don't think so."

"All teams going out to protect the catfishers need to be warned. The Pinocchios are willing to kamikaze themselves to take us out."

"Yes, Boss, I'll-"

Just then Mia Sullivan appeared, wheeling a gurney which she braked by his side. "If you could get on," she said.

"One second, Robin," Wren said, then laid down facedown. His whole back cried out in pain. Rogers did the same beside him, grunting throughout. It gave them a front-row seat to the burning of Reince Jeffries grand home. Fire trucks had rolled up now, and firefighters were aiming jets of water into the blaze, but at this point it was too far gone. The best they could hope was to stop the flames from spreading through the neighborhood.

"Don't move your left arm," Sullivan said, then fed a needle into a vein in the back of Wren's wrist. He tracked it back past a cannula and plastic tube up to a blood bag hanging from a pole. "I'm going to cut away your jacket and shirt. This is going to hurt."

"Thanks, Mia," Wren said, then alongside him Rogers cursed as the first strip of clothing was peeled from her back. Wren grunted as Sullivan began on him, but refocused on the phone.

"Where was this attack, Robin?"

"Sacramento," she said, then paused for a moment and continued. "Also Seattle and Orlando."

Wren looked over at Rogers. "Three cities?"

"Three cities," MacAuley confirmed, her bright voice flattening out under the barrage of bad news. "Three different corners of the country. Four dead in total." She took a heavy breath. "Sacramento was the family, Seattle and Orlando were single victims, with all bodies tortured and left at the scene."

"Four dead," Wren repeated. "And two children taken. All in the last few hours."

"You think they were connections from Tom Solent?" Rogers asked.

"Could easily be." Wren worked the numbers. "The Pinocchios here were done with Solent at least twelve hours back. It's possible, but impressive that they could put together three attacks across the country in that time."

Rogers looked like she wanted to spit. "They're like cockroaches; they're everywhere."

Sullivan put the first needle into Wren's back. He stiffened but didn't cry out. "Little warning?" he said.

"Forgive me," Sullivan replied, "I don't normally stitch people together out in the open at a bomb site." She closed the stitch and pulled it tight, forcing Wren to suck in a sharp breath. "I'm a little out of my element."

Rogers winked. "I think she likes you, Boss."

Sullivan sucked air through her teeth and Wren ignored them both. "Send everything you've got to my phone, Robin. And Rogers, get Humphreys on the line with the warning about suicide vests. Tell him this thing is going to snowball. They're targeting catfishers and anyone who comes to help them. We need to do more."

"More like what?"

"Mass protection details. Safe zones in police stations or even army bases. Whatever it takes."

"On it."

She brought up her phone and made the call, just as Wren's phone chimed with the email from MacAuley.

"That's everything, Boss," she said.

"Thanks. Anything on Baxter yet?"

"I'll let you know as soon as there is."

"What about the red Firebird?"

"Ah, yes. I was going to say." A few seconds passed as keys clacked in the background. "OK, we already had teams stop by five of the seven possibles near Detroit. One guy was infirm, could barely walk, and one was actually dead but nobody updated the DMV." More keys clicked. "One had his Pontiac up on blocks, rusted to bits, while two were out of state with solid alibis. We'll be with the other two within thirty minutes, and the out-of-state guy in an hour."

"OK, keep me apprised."

He brought up her email as the stab of needles into his back continued.

The intelligence reports were shaky and brief, a loosely organized collection of crime-scene photographs and scraps of after-the-fact CCTV footage. Wren burned through screen after screen, drinking from the fire hose. Judging by the coroners' time of death certificates, each hit had been perpetrated in the afternoon, in broad daylight, but there were no witnesses. It looked like proficient work, with no fingerprints, no 911 calls made and very little on CCTV but for the Sacramento hit, which was caught on a neighbor's hidden security cam.

It was another team of four men in Pinocchio masks, dressed in jeans and black hoodies and armed with baseball bats. Wren watched them break in fast and easy. The security video showed they were inside for an hour, long enough to extract more information before the kills were made. He imagined their snowball of intel rolling downhill, gathering mass and speed until it became an avalanche.

He looked at the pictures of the victims. Blood was everywhere, despite the zip ties on every finger and toe. Like Solent, the men had been castrated at the end. Blood loss was the cause of death in all cases.

Each was a fresh beachhead in the Blue Fairy's war.

Wren rubbed his temples. Rogers held out her phone across the gap between their gurneys. "Humphreys."

Wren took it. "Gerald."

"You were right," Humphreys said immediately, which

was a rarity. He never admitted mistakes. "This is a major nationwide terror organization. We're looking to correct that oversight now, with a flood of agents and police sent to protect catfishers, taking into account the Pinocchios' zealotry. But there are still too many to cover them all, Christopher. You're in the field, you know the Blue Fairy best. I need you to get me specific targets."

Wren winced as a needle ran deep.

"Sorry," Sullivan muttered.

"We will," Wren said. "Jeffries almost gave us more. We've got a lead on Baxter that may lead to this Hebbert, plus there are a few possible IDs on the perp's vehicle from the People Mover. We've got teams en route to brace them."

"Get me something I can use, Christopher. The President's talking about a statement to the nation with the dawn; we'd better have some good news for her to relay."

The line went dead. Wren handed back the phone.

"Next steps?" Rogers asked.

Wren thought. The needle rose in and out of his back. The blood bag drained into his wrist. He cast his mind back over his rapid-fire interview with Reince Jeffries, looking for anything he could use, anything that felt like a missing link.

Then he found one.

"Jeffries had three fingers missing," Wren said. "So they'd already tortured him."

"Agreed."

"But when I asked him about that, he said he didn't give up any catfishers."

Rogers was silent for a moment. "Did he say that? I don't.... I'm not so sure that's what he said."

Wren re-wound the conversation in his head. He'd asked about catfishers, and Jeffries had said something, but maybe it had been...

He stiffened on the gurney, accidentally driving a needle in too deep.

"Obviously don't do that," said Sullivan calmly.

"Sorry." He turned. "Sally, you're right. I framed the question about catfishers. He said they didn't ask that. So what did they ask?"

Rogers's eyes narrowed. "What else could they want from a man like Jeffries? They've already got Baxter, so it wasn't about her."

Wren thought, mind turning in circles until finally it hit him. He felt the blood drain from his face. "Perps."

"What? You think they were asking about other Pinocchios?"

"Maybe Pinocchios, maybe wannabes. It's the only other thing Jeffries would know; a full target list."

"OK. But why would they want that?"

Wren could only think of one reason. "Recruitment."

22

RECRUITMENT

Both Rogers and Wren lay in silence, reflecting, as Mia Sullivan and her colleague finished stitching up their backs.

The house fire was finally tamping down. Some of the police vehicles were leaving.

"All done," Sullivan said at last. She came around to face Wren. She was pretty, with tan skin and broad cheekbones that accentuated her eyes. "First time for everything."

"Thank you," Wren said, and Rogers echoed him.

"Right around now, your ER doctor would order up enough anesthetic and sedative to keep you out for at least twelve hours. Those stitches need to bed in and start to heal."

Wren smiled and pushed himself up to a sitting position. Sullivan wrapped a silver mylar blanket around his bare shoulders, keeping out the worst of the cold. The stitches pulled tight but held. He felt like he'd been worked over by a Pinocchio gang wielding baseball bats, but it wasn't incapacitating. The worst thing was the dizziness. Maybe traumatic brain injury, after all...

"I'll sleep en route," he said.

She cocked her head to one side. "En route to where?"

"I don't know yet. Nowhere good, I'm thinking." He stood.

Sullivan just looked at him, seemingly thinking about something, then rustled in her pocket and came up with a scrap of paper and a pen. She scribbled something down and held the paper out. "My number. In case there's complications. I put the stitches in, so I'm best to advise if something goes wrong. I've spritzed you with disinfectant and bandaged you tight, but sepsis could set in easily if you open them again. Call any time."

Wren took the paper and smiled. It just said MIA with her number. "I'll call if I need you."

"Do that. And eat something, plus make sure you drink lots of fluids. You lost a lot of blood." She hovered for a moment. "Good night."

She pushed the gurney into the back of the ambulance, then climbed into the driver's seat. It pulled away. After perhaps twenty seconds, Wren turned to Rogers. She wore a faint smirk.

"Still got it, Boss," she said.

He tucked the paper in his pocket. "I'm a married man."

Rogers snorted. "Really? It's been six months, way I heard it, and the whole team knows she's got a new guy."

Wren grunted. "None of your business, Agent Rogers."

"The new man, he's some kind of Nerd Squad cable guy, right? He sets up home stereos and surround sound and such."

Wren sighed. That was a little too personal for his taste. "Recruitment," he said, changing the subject.

"Hit me," Rogers said.

"One second." Wren pointed at Captain Anderson, striding by with his squad. "Captain. Can you spare tactical shirts for us both?"

Anderson strode over, taking a cursory look at the patch-up job on their backs. "No problem. I've also got strong coffee brewing for the family, and MREs. You'll need it, I'll set you up."

"Thanks."

He strode off.

"Maybe you'll get his number too," Rogers murmured.

Wren fixed her with a glare.

"Sorry. Giddy from blood loss. Maybe the blast."

"Back to recruitment. If we're right, then the Fairy are using these attacks on catfishers for two reasons simultaneously."

"Sure. Plant the fear of hellfire into other catfishers, which is one heck of a show of force. They leverage that show into bringing more people in."

Wren nodded. "Exactly. It could be a way in."

"We just need a perp."

"And maybe we've got one. Ravenous6, could drive a Firebird."

"The Firebird, right. You want to go for him?"

"Until something shakes out on Baxter, Mona, Gloria, whatever, he's what we've got." Wren thought for a moment, and just then Anderson came back with MREs and coffee on a tray. Both Wren and Rogers thanked him, then tucked in. The coffee was strong and the MRE was a cold tuna melt that tasted delicious. "You like the guy out of state, right," Wren went on, "big Internet traffic and a lot of encryption?"

Rogers nodded, munching on her spaghetti bolognese. "Sure, down in Ohio. All we've got on him is a car and a color, though."

"Right, but the team's already ruled out five of the seven locals. The other two we'll get answers on any time now." He chewed and thought. "Didn't we get images of these guys to the witnesses to ID?"

"We did, yeah, but not a single definitive ID. Nobody got a good look at him, apparently."

Wren turned that over. "I think Ohio's our best shot. He's out of state, which would appeal to a guy with some tradecraft like Ravenous6. Crossing a state line makes him harder to track back." He considered. "What's the guy's name?"

"Name? One second." Rogers put her coffee and meal tray down and brought up her phone, scanning through contacts until she paused. Her eyes widened. "Oh, man.

"What is it?"

"His name's Charles DeVore."

"DeVore?" Wren leaned in. "Like devour? Like he's ravenous?"

"Yeah. I just noticed that."

"That's strong circumstantial evidence, in my view."

"Agreed."

"Any reports to social services? Any record of abuse?"

"Nothing like that. But he has got two kids. Just bought the Firebird recently."

"How recently?"

Rogers scrolled and scanned. "Ah."

Wren read that easily. "Let me guess, three months ago? Around the same time Ravenous6 started talking to the catfishers posing as 'Sophie'?"

"Got it in one."

"He's our guy," Wren said.

"OK. So you want us to go now? It's still all circumstantial, and that's a three-hour drive. It's a lot of time on a hunch, Boss."

Wren looked over at Captain Anderson's SWAT helicopter, resting in the middle of the street. "Who said anything about driving?"

23

WHATEVER IT TAKES

W ren and Rogers flew southeast at two hundred miles an hour in Anderson's Bell UH-1 Iroquois helicopter, a 'Huey', swiftly leaving the fire in Redford behind. Detroit's city lights shone briefly like a setting sun then sank below the horizon, until soon they were hammering blindly over dark, empty wilderness.

Every part of Wren hurt. The seat did nothing to cushion the explosive drumbeat of the chopper's blades, sending daggers down his neck and spine. There was no escaping the whiplash of the crash or the damage of the blast. The fresh stitches in his back sparked like firecrackers under the skin.

Heading for Canton, Ohio, home of Charles DeVore.

Just twenty minutes earlier they'd had the call from Specialist Bennet. "I'm sorry," he'd said. "Reince Jeffries didn't make it."

Wren had thanked him and ended the call. Neither of them had spoken since, until Rogers broke the silence.

"Jeffries," she said.

Wren turned to her. There was little to say. "We have to make this count. Two kids taken, Sally, plus Baxter."

She said nothing.

Wren thought about his own children. He didn't want to imagine the pain and fear those kids would be feeling right now. It went the same for Clara Baxter and anyone else the Pinocchios snatched tonight. He hoped they were all alive still. He hoped they could save them. Jeffries was a hard cost, but he'd already made the play. there was no taking it back now.

"What if this guy is Ravenous6?" Rogers asked.

"Then we flip him, ensure he's recruited and insert him deeper if we can. Use him as a lever to crack the whole Blue Fairy open."

She looked away. He could see the death of Reince Jeffries was weighing heavily on her.

"You've got to delay it, Sally."

She didn't respond.

"Jeffries. This kind of thing, it's going to hit. We all feel it. Right now you use it and make time to feel it later."

"I know. It's OK."

He reached across the Huey's aisle and placed one hand on her shoulder. "Maybe it's not OK. You could have saved him but I chose not to. It's a gamble we'll save more lives this way, but that's my gamble. the decision's on me, not you."

"Yeah."

"Yeah," Wren echoed, and leaned back. Words didn't mean much at a time like this. "So, what have we got on DeVore?"

Rogers blinked several times, like she was mustering herself, then brought up her phone and scanned through pages of notes.

"He's married with two kids, both girls, aged seven and nine. Lives in the south side of Canton, affluent, off Cleveland Avenue. He's an accountant; the Firebird looks to be a recent hobby. Medium height, forty-five years old."

"Eyes on his house?"

Rogers scrolled further. "A squad car rolled by ten minutes ago, but sirens off, like you requested. We have a heat-tracking drone up, too. Signals are fuzzy, but looks like one figure in the den, three laid out in bed."

Wren checked the time. Just past 10 p.m.

"I bet that's him in the den. Wife and kids asleep. He's having a long dark night of the soul."

"Or maybe he's just watching TV," Rogers countered. "Not everyone's a psycho just because of their name."

Wren said nothing.

"Sorry, Boss," Rogers said quickly. "It's just..." She trailed off.

"It's OK. Go on."

She shook her head. "Forget it."

"Not gonna happen, Agent Rogers. If you've got a problem with me, say it."

She raised her eyes to his. "OK. First the witness at the live re-enactment? You manipulated her, digging around in her head. It may have worked, but it's pretty far from protocol, and you just kept pushing her buttons until she was close to popping. You could have given her a heart attack."

Wren said nothing.

"Then Jeffries? He did have a heart attack. He died, Chris!"

Wren nodded. She was right. "All true."

Rogers sighed. "Well, I don't know what to do with that. One minute, we're making jokes about soy lattes and hooking up with EMTs. Then there's a guy with his balls cut off, and you just flip a switch, and anyone in your way becomes expendable; just a bunch of human programming you get to rewire or execute at will."

Wren didn't like the sound of that. He didn't like that it was true. "So you're angry. Maybe angrier because you didn't stop me."

Rogers snorted. "Is that what I'm feeling?"

"I'm not trying to diagnose you. It's how I would feel."

"You'd feel guilty?"

He shook his head. "Sally, I do feel angry. Right now, I feel angry, guilty, all kinds of things. What I did with Janet Reveille, it's from a bag of tricks plucked from my childhood. You know I grew up in the worst death cult in US history, right?" She said nothing. "My dad was a narcissistic manipulator who talked all his followers into burning themselves alive. That's not pretty. I survived, though. I honed those tricks overseas against the worst terrorists in the world, where US laws don't apply. Now, should I apply them here, in the homeland?" He took a breath. "Maybe you're right. Maybe I shouldn't. They might even land me in a CIA black site one day, locked away from the world. Maybe they're morally wrong, no matter how many lives are at stake. But right now we're here, in a helicopter heading for Ravenous6, and I'll choose to call that a result."

Rogers just shook her head. "Maybe it's not the kind of result I want."

Wren thought about that. It was a good thing to know about yourself, he figured. He'd always been an all or nothing guy in the service of justice. It had earned him the nickname 'Saint Justice' in the Company for the most terror groups shattered, but it had cost him his wife and kids. Now, maybe, it was going to cost him Rogers as a team member.

"I don't blame you," he said quietly. "It's not for everyone. Maybe it shouldn't be for anyone."

She gave no answer, just looked out of the window at the passing darkness. The rotor blades hammered overhead.

"I'll go in solo for this guy," Wren went on. "If it is our perp, and I think it is, I don't want you complicit."

Rogers turned back. "What are you going to do?"

Wren met her gaze unflinchingly. "Whatever it takes."

24

CANTON

Wren had the chopper land in a dark, barren field near the Speedway on the Lincoln Highway, east of Canton and several miles distant from Charles DeVore.

He loped away from Rogers in back as the thumping rotor blades turned, stamping through old stalks of hay sticking up in the stubbly field. The highway ahead was four lanes wide and desolate. The Speedway had a handful of cars parked in front of its halogen white windows. Products inside cheered their brands on, competitors in a different kind of race.

The Huey took off in back, headed for a holding pattern with some measure of overwatch. Wren picked the waiting car out with ease; an unmarked Toyota sedan on the verge. Dark green. The driver gave him a nod as he dropped into the passenger side; a detective on loan from Canton PD.

"Any movement at the house?" Wren asked.

"Nothing since the last drive by," the guy said. "Your kit's in the glove box."

Wren clicked the button and opened the glove box. It held the gear he'd asked for, a Beretta M9 with a spare magazine plus a handful of small GPS tracker 'dots' in a small plastic baggy.

"These are Micro Hornets?" Wren asked.

"Model number 1511," the detective said. "We use them sometimes to track cars, mostly dealers. Technically, you need a warrant."

Wren snorted, opened the baggy and shook one out. It was one quarter the size of a postage stamp and looked just like a computer chip. "What's the range?"

"Like any wireless device," the guy said. "Obstructions will block the signal. If you're putting it on a car, don't bury it under the spare tire in the trunk. But soft furnishings, like stowing it in the back seat crevice, that'll be fine."

Wren nodded and pocketed the devices. The CIA had smaller ones, but these would do in a pinch.

"Thanks. Let's go."

The guy nodded and pulled into traffic.

Soon they were skirting the town center, but Canton was asleep already. Wednesday night, 11 p.m., and mostly residential plots lined the route. A small ballpark. A few patches of industry. A long strip with junk-food eateries. Wren's heart began to beat harder as they pulled into DeVore's road, 33rd Street off Cleveland Avenue.

He'd already picked his ingress point; rear entry through the home's sliding glass doors. There were no fences here but plenty of trees to cover his approach. The detective cruised slowly along like he was making a considerate run home. If there were Pinocchios here watching DeVore, Wren couldn't put a foot wrong.

His house was number 79. They rolled a hundred yards past it then pulled into an empty drive. The detective killed the engine and the lights died. Wren holstered the Beretta in his waistband and opened the door.

The night was quiet and cold and his breath plumed with

frost. Across the street somebody was watching TV; fuzzy light played through their thin lace curtains. Maybe it would snow; winter was still in the air. He mimed clicking the car fob then strolled up the drive and around the side of the house.

Once out of sight, Wren slipped into the shadow of an oak tree, all senses buzzing. There was nothing unusual though, just the drone of a plane passing by overhead. Screened by bushes and ducking low, he headed east toward DeVore's place.

In moments he was standing on the back porch of number 79. There was a BBQ and a swing in the yard, strewn about with a pair of pink scooters. Wren peered in through the rear sliding doors, but there were no lights on inside. He brought up his phone and hit dial.

"Rogers," came the response.

"I'm outside," Wren whispered. "Does the heat tracker still show him in the den?"

A moment passed. "He's there. Or someone is. No movement in the last hour."

That was suspicious; without the TV or a radio on, just sitting in the dark.

"Thanks," he said. "I'll dot his car then enter. Standby."

He stalked down the side of the house, hoping for another view on the interior, but there was none. The Pontiac sat on the drive, a dull crimson in the faint streetlight, its hood scoops each a small, gaping mouth.

Wren popped two Micro Hornets from the baggy and slid one inside a scoop, its magnetic surface clamping hold, then attached the other in the right rear wheel well.

"You read those signals, Sally?"

"Got them."

He hung up, padded back down the side of the house, drew the Beretta then tried the slide door. It opened silently.

Wren entered and moved deeper into shadow, away from the window and alongside a heavy oak dining room table, surveying the darkness ahead. To the right lay a breakfast nook still laid with cups, bowls and cereal packets, despite the late hour. Ahead lay a sunken den, with a long L-shaped sofa and a reclining armchair at one end; the man of the house's seat.

It was occupied.

Wren saw a flash of reflected light in wide and staring eyes. Charles DeVore was staring right back at him.

25

DEVORE

Seconds of eye contact passed in the darkness, and Wren realized two things at once.

First, there could be no doubt that Charles DeVore was Ravenous6.

He was sitting alone in his den with the lights off at night, not alarmed when a stranger broke in. Not shouting, not standing to fight, not calling the police. Just sitting and staring.

This was their perp.

Second, he was holding a gun pointed at Wren's face.

The moment stretched out.

"Charles," Wren began, breaking the silence gently, but DeVore cut him off.

"I know who you are."

His voice was high and fraught, like his lungs were too full of air and he could only manage clipped sentences. On the edge. Wren's eyes adjusted to the gloom. The gun trembled in DeVore's delicate, desk worker's fingers. A Remington 380, a hell of a piece of punctuation.

Wren took a sliding step forward. "So, who am I?"

"You're with the Blue Fairy. This is my test." DeVore's

tone was high and emotionless, but Wren felt the tension humming underneath. The moment heightened. Wren imagined his trigger finger squeezing.

"I'm not from the Fairy," Wren said calmly, trying to sidestep whatever fear DeVore was working over in the dark. He had no idea what the 'test' was, but intended to find out. "I'm here to help."

DeVore stared. "Help?"

"Help," Wren confirmed, sliding subtly to the end of the dining table. "I've been looking for you, Charles. I was there at the People Mover. I know what happened to you, what you witnessed. I know that you weren't involved." He paused, weighing the moment. "I've seen your chat logs. I know Sophie was barely underage."

DeVore twitched. He extended the hand holding the gun, riding a hint of anger now. "Sophie wasn't real."

"I know that. They entrapped you. They broke their own rules, Charles. A case against you would never stand up in court. You could sue for damages and they'd have to pay."

DeVore leaned forward, and the tension rang through in his voice, trembling somewhere between hope and fear. "You're a lawyer?"

"Better than that," Wren lied. "I can exonerate you completely. This isn't fair; it's obvious that the catfishers got you first, and now the Blue Fairy wants dessert."

DeVore stared. "You don't know that."

Wren slid to the steps leading down into the den. "They set a test, didn't they? Did you pass already, Charles?"

DeVore shuddered. "I tried. I'm trying."

As Wren advanced, the den revealed itself in stages, etched in silvery moonlight like an old-style photograph, taking on texture and depth. The sofa, the TV, the coffee table, the recliner. He'd half-expected to see DeVore's wife laid out on the floor, bound and gagged alongside their daughters, despite what the drone heat tracker had shown.

"What was the test?"

"Stop moving," DeVore said, as Wren slid the first step down into the den.

"What's the test, Charles?" Wren pressed, taking another step. If I'm going to help you, you have to be honest with me."

DeVore snorted. "How can you help?"

"Easy. Sometimes I'm a federal agent, sometimes I'm on my own. Today could be one of those days."

"Why would you?"

"Let's just say I hate to see an innocent victim. What was the test?"

DeVore shook his head fiercely. "I can't tell you. They'll kill me."

Wren slid another step down. "Without me, you're already dead. I know that you've been sitting in that chair for hours. Maybe since breakfast this morning? I've seen men like you before." Wren made the leap. "Men who've committed atrocities, or are considering them. Men deciding whether to eat their own gun." He advanced. "What's the test, Charles?"

"She was almost sixteen," DeVore whimpered, his voice sounding flat, like it was a sentence he'd been repeating for hours; so many times that any sense of meaning had long evaporated away.

"Last time. The test, Charles."

DeVore raised the gun to his head. "She said she was sixteen."

Wren ran and caught the barrel as it discharged, disrupting the shot so it only raked the back of DeVore's head. He wrenched and pulled the weapon away, leaving him howling.

Wren put a knee in his chest to keep him immobile and checked the wound in his head; shallow.

"The test, Charles," he demanded, seizing him by the throat and lifting him slightly.

"Please!" DeVore whined. "Please, I didn't mean to-"

Wren slapped him. The sniveling ceased immediately.

"None of that," he said, and leaned closer, so they were eye to eye. "You can still get through this, but you need to level with me. What is the Fairy's test?"

It took DeVore a long moment to find his voice. He gulped and stared at Wren, then he spoke in a bare whisper.

"My family."

"What about your family?"

"They wanted me to do things. Send photos."

Wren gritted his teeth. Photos were the currency of the Blue Fairy.

"Why? Why you?"

"I don't know. They said I'd played an important role."

"What role? You were their patsy."

"I know!"

Wren wanted to slap him again, but restrained the urge. "Did they say why it was an important role?"

"Something about a woman. That was all, I swear."

"Clara Baxter?"

"They didn't say."

It had to be her. "And what did they offer you?"

"What do you mean?"

"It's simple, Charles. They wanted you to do things to your family. In exchange for what?"

DeVore writhed but didn't speak other than to grumble and whine, trying pathetically to get free.

Wren shook him. "Stop. How did they communicate with you?"

"An app. On my phone."

"Show me."

DeVore stopped wriggling and rooted in his pocket, pulling out a Google Pixel. He tapped in his PIN then held up the screen for Wren to see. It showed a blue chat box with a long train of unanswered texts, each a word long, repeated every thirty minutes and stretching back through the whole day.

PICS?

GIFS?

VIDEO?

Wren scrolled further back and found the instructions. They were specific. Detailed. Exactly where the camera should be placed, the scenes of abuse they wanted to see DeVore carrying out against his own wife and children, ending in their bloody death. It was all spelled out; DeVore's test for admission, and it began with a simple message.

DO YOU WANT TO GO TO PLEASURE ISLAND? CLOCK IS TICKING.

Underneath it there was a timer:

18:05:36

The second counter ticked by. Eighteen hours. That placed it squarely at 5 p.m. tomorrow.

Wren stared. He'd never heard of any of this. "What's Pleasure Island? What does this timer mean?"

"What? I don't know."

"You don't know?"

"No! It's a myth. It's the dream."

"What do you mean, the dream?"

DeVore shrank under Wren's gaze. "Like in Pinocchio, the fairy tale? Pleasure Island's where you go to drink, smoke, gamble, have anything you want."

Wren's gaze sharpened. "Kids."

"It's not my dream! She said she was sixteen!"

Wren ignored that. "Is it a real place? Or just another hidden site on the darknet?"

"I don't know."

"But they're inviting you?"

"If I send them what they want, I think so."

"And this counter, what's that?"

"I don't know! I don't know anything! It's all there."

Wren scrolled back through the messages. It did seem like a physical location, geared around a specific event occurring at noon tomorrow, but there were no details. DeVore hadn't sent them anything yet, either. No PICS, GIFS, or VIDEO, but it was clear what was required.

"Did you complete the test, Charles?"

DeVore looked away.

"Where are your family?" Wren demanded.

"In the basement." The words slithered out of his mouth wet with shame.

Wren leaned back and listened, but heard nothing. No muffled screaming. No muted cries for help rising through the floorboards. He'd seen three more heat signatures from the drone, but that could mean anything.

"Are they alive?"

DeVore blinked up at him with eyes as wet as oyster shells, sobbing in self-pity. Wren wanted to punch into his chest and rip out his heart. You were to supposed to hold them close, he wanted to say. You were supposed to protect them.

"Are they alive?" he repeated.

DeVore answered in a nasal whine. "I don't know."

26

PIC

Wren copied the countdown timer over to his own phone and hit start.

18:03:21

The clock was ticking.

He passed back through the kitchen. Half-eaten bowls of cereal rested on the table, and the air smelled of curdled milk. The basement door stood beside the tall fridge-freezer.

He opened it on darkness, and another smell enveloped him like a warm cloud; the ammonia tang of urine and the rich stink of human waste.

He flicked a switch and white lights buzzed to life, illuminating walls hung with family portraits. Happy as a foursome at a beach. Charles DeVore smiling like a real person. At the bottom lay a bare cement floor and a wall filled with mildewed boxes on shelves.

Wren went down swiftly and smoothly, and found what he'd expected. The camera stood between him and DeVore's family; on a tripod, with the tiny fat tails of a Wi-Fi transmitter attached. Ready to stream video. Beyond that lay three pink deflated air mattresses with three people huddled upon them; the mother in the middle, the girls curled to either side.

They were motionless but alive, eyes wide in the sudden light.

"It's OK," Wren said softly, holding his hands out. "My name's Christopher Wren. I'm not going to hurt you. I'm here to help."

Dirty, wet gags in their mouths prevented them from answering. DeVore's wife tried to position her body in front of her daughters. Wren circled away from the stairs slowly, making no sudden movements. The smell was worse here. Waste stained their sparse bedding and pajamas. Their arms were zip-tied at the wrist to metal wall pipes, their wrists red and bruised. They'd been here all day.

Wren felt the choice rising before him. If Rogers was here, there'd be no question about it. She'd release them at once.

It wasn't as simple as that, though.

"I'm going to release you," Wren said, padding toward the camera. "I promise."

He hit the camera's power button to wake the screen, and the mother began screaming into her gag. The sound was horrible; like a wounded animal trying to escape a trap. She understood what the camera meant and what the blinking red light stood for, and yanked at her zip ties, thrashing her body like against the floor and trying to get free. Her girls screamed too.

There was nothing Wren could do except go faster.

"Almost done," he said, swiftly scrolling through the memory card on the camera's LCD screen, afraid of what he might find. There were still shots of the basement wall, of the set-up, a few practice runs of footage with DeVore's fingers fumbling over the lens, his family unconscious on the mattresses, and then…

Nothing.

No more stills, no video, no PICS. Wren let out a breath.

Good, but bad.

Good because DeVore hadn't done it. He'd brought them down here and left them, but ultimately been unable to go through with it. They'd spent all day gagged and bound in the basement, filled with terror of what might come, but nothing worse yet.

Bad because the scene wasn't there. The PIC. And Wren needed the PIC. The Pinocchios wanted it and Charles DeVore had to supply it, or there'd be no admission for him, no way into the Blue Fairy, no invite to 'Pleasure Island'.

Wren cursed. If he had time and access to a substantial supercomputer, plus high-resolution images of DeVore's wife and daughters to work with, he could order up a deepfake image within perhaps an hour, one that should pass muster and help insert Charles DeVore into the Blue Fairy's bloodstream.

But he didn't have that time.

Right now DeVore was a bomb ready to implode. Wren needed to fire him off right now or lose him, and that meant he'd have to get the PIC the old-fashioned way.

He'd have to do it himself.

He ignored the family's screams and ran back up the stairs. In the tall fridge he found a large bottle of tomato ketchup and another of BBQ sauce. Back in the basement, he popped the caps on both condiments and sprayed them out over the captives. It took only seconds. DeVore's family kicked and thrashed, smearing the stains and building the scene he needed.

He stepped behind the camera and sighted through the lens. The scene looked like a slaughterhouse, like a madman had been let loose with a hatchet.

It was the PIC.

"I'm sorry," he said, softening his voice and making eye contact with the mother. "I know this is hard to understand, but everything's going to be all right in about ten seconds time. I just need you to close your eyes and lie very still first. Can you do that?"

She stared back at him. There was no trust, but what choice did she have? She fell silent and the girls followed. One by one, they lay back and closed their eyes.

Wren took the PIC.

27

RED PILL

Back in the kitchen, Wren called Rogers.

"Yes?"

"I need a blue lights brigade here immediately," Wren said. "Ambulances plus a coroner's cart. DeVore locked his family up in the basement all day; they're alive, but terrified and dehydrated. I've released them and calmed them down, but we need them taken out of the house quietly. We need this reported as a triple homicide."

Rogers said nothing for a moment. "Do I even want to know why we're lying?"

"That's your decision. Can you set it up, Sally?"

Another beat passed. "I can do it."

"Good. Send them now."

Wren reached into his pocket and brought up DeVore's phone. The pic from the camera was already there and waiting, transmitted via Bluetooth airdrop and looking as gruesome as ever.

He tapped out a message, attached the PIC and sent it.

WHERE DO I GO?

There was nothing for a moment, then three dancing dots that signified someone was typing.

VERY GOOD.

Wren tapped a swift reply.

THAT WAS MY FAMILY. I'VE EARNED MY PLACE ON PLEASURE ISLAND.

More dots. Wren barely breathed.

PERHAPS.

More dots.

WE ASKED FOR VIDEO. WE ASKED FOR A LOT MORE THAN THIS.

Wren gritted his teeth.

THIS WAS FOR ME. THIS WAS PERSONAL. WHATEVER'S NEXT, I'LL SHARE.

More dots. Wren waited.

GET IN YOUR FIREBIRD. DRIVE NORTH.

I'M COMING, Wren responded.

DeVore was waiting in the den, staring into the darkness filled with terror as Wren approached. Wren held out his phone.

"Congratulations," he said. "Your family are dead and you have a place on Pleasure Island."

DeVore's eyes widened so far Wren thought they might bug out. "What? I didn't..."

Wren showed him the pic. "This photo says you did. You passed the test, Charles. You're good to go."

"What? I... What?"

Wren leaned closer. "You were right the first time. I'm from the Blue Fairy. You passed." He clapped one hand on DeVore's shoulder. "We're waiting for you, brother."

DeVore stared at the pic. His jaw dropped. "I didn't... I..."

"It's always hardest the first time," Wren said. "But the memories will come back. There's much more ahead. You won't need to pretend anymore, like you did with 'Sophie'. Fifteen?" He snorted. "It won't matter."

DeVore just stared.

Wren tapped the phone over to the chat box. "Read that."

DeVore read. He read it again and again.

"That's your new life," Wren said. "Go now. Don't look back. Oh, and swallow this."

He held up one of the GPS dots.

"What is it?"

"Red pill," Wren said, referencing the term conspiracy theorists used about the pathway down the rabbit hole. "It'll open your mind."

DeVore looked at the dot. He looked at Wren. A change seemed to come over him.

"I knew it was a test," he said.

"And you passed."

DeVore snorted. He took the pill and knocked it back in one.

"Attaboy." Wren handed DeVore the phone, who scrolled to the pic and stared at it.

"You should be proud," Wren said.

"I should've done this a long time ago," DeVore murmured. "This bitch kept me down."

"Now you're free."

DeVore looked up.

The change in him was setting in place now, as if a different person had slid into his skin. The tears had dried up. He stood straight and tall. This was the man he'd kept hidden inside for so long, living in shame, now coming out into the light.

A fresh recruit for the Blue Fairy.

"I only wish I remembered it. Maybe I'll go look..." DeVore started walking toward the basement.

Wren placed one broad hand on his chest, firmly barring the way. "Playtime's over for now, Ravenous. Or would you keep the Fairy waiting?"

Some of DeVore's new bluster vanished. "No. Of course not."

"Then drive north. Now. Go, or miss your chance."

DeVore stared into Wren's eyes, then nodded. He looked around the dark room a final time.

"You're a new man," Wren said. "Reborn today."

"Thank you," DeVore said, and walked away.

Wren remained, waiting until the Firebird engine fired up and the car pulled away. He felt sick at what he'd just played a role in, but that didn't matter.

He brought his phone to his ear, where Rogers hung on the end of an open line. "Do you have him?"

"Three tracker dots, all transmitting," Rogers confirmed. "Did you have to fire him up like that, though?"

"Yes," Wren said. "They'd never believe him otherwise."

"You just radicalized him."

"I think he'd done most of that for himself already, Sally."

Wren reached the door to the basement and opened it. Out poured Charles DeVore's family, dressed in beach towels. The girls went straight to the fridge and grabbed a carton of banana milkshake, while their mother glared daggers at him then went to the sink to wash up. He hadn't anticipated more than that.

"Where are my ambulances?" he asked.

"You should hear them coming now," Rogers answered, "along with the Huey."

Wren listened, and then there they were. Sirens drawing near, overlaid with the sound of helicopter blades.

"Oh, and one more thing," he said. "As of now, we're on the clock. The Blue Fairy sent DeVore an invite to something called Pleasure Island, along with a countdown timer. Less than eighteen hours remain, which is 1700 hours tomorrow. They're building up to something. Pass that on to Humphreys and the team, see if they can figure out what the significance is."

"On it. See you in a moment, Boss."

28

PROACTIVE

Wren and Rogers leaned against the hood of a squad car outside the DeVore residence, sipping takeout coffee brought by a second influx of blue lights vehicles.

People hummed everywhere. The 'Do Not Cross' tape had gone up three hundred yards distant, far enough to prevent any press from getting a peek at the DeVore family inside.

They were supposed to be dead, but Wren and Rogers had a ringside seat on them through the front window, as the girls and their mother were checked over by EMTs.

The girls were capering like mad things all around their den. It was rejuvenating to see. Maybe they were high off the banana milk, or the endorphins of release, or just the pent-up energy of being locked up all day long.

It seemed bizarrely poetic to Wren.

In that same space just moments earlier, Charles DeVore had been contemplating an end of one kind of another, murder or suicide, a doorway he could never walk back through. Now his family were facing the same doorway; the end of their old life and a new life going forward.

"Witness protection," Rogers said softly, sipping her coffee. "At least for some time. That photo you took is all over the darknet already, getting celebrated like some major victory."

Wren took a long draw on his coffee. "We'll get the bastards who did this."

Rogers shot him a look but said nothing. She had some idea now what he'd done to 'insert' DeVore, and almost certainly disapproved, but hadn't said anything yet.

Wren was happy to note that it didn't seem to have affected the girls unduly. They were singing on the couches, now. One of them was using a hairbrush as a microphone, reciting what looked like Taylor Swift's 'Shake It Off'. For the moment, their ordeal was over.

"So what did he say about 'Pleasure Island'?" Rogers asked.

"He'd never heard of it until today. He didn't know any more than the name. And the timer?" He shrugged.

"You think it's real? Pleasure Island, that it's a real place, not just a site on the darknet?"

Wren turned that over. He thought a lot of things. He suspected others. Now wasn't the time for his wilder speculations, though. "I think it might be. Location of some kind of endgame event in," he checked the synchronized timer on his phone, "seventeen and a half hours."

"And DeVore's invited."

"It seems that way. He played a role in the snatching of Clara Baxter, after all. Compared to any other recruits the Blue Fairy make tonight, that could make him important, whether he was a patsy or not." He paused a moment, thinking it through. "He also just 'killed' his family, on their command. How many other Pinocchios can claim that?"

Rogers' face fell. "It's like he's been vetted. Entrance to the inner circle."

"He's proven himself worthy. Where is he now?"

Rogers brought up her phone, where the GPS tracking app beeped with three red dots, just off I-77 by the Akron-Canton Airport. "Same place he's been for the past twenty minutes, at a rest stop fifteen miles north. We've got multiple agents tailing him."

"The Fairy will direct him onward soon."

Rogers seemed unconvinced. "Maybe. Or they might already know we're following and just run him around in circles for the next eighteen hours."

"Also possible. Have the team come up with anything significant about the date or time? Does it mark a particular event?"

"Couple of thoughts. One second." She brought up her phone and opened the Notes app. "OK, so Feb 18 is the date Detroit was founded. Back in 1701, some French explorer built 'Fort Pontchartrain du Détroit'." She looked up, saw Wren's flat expression and looked back down. "Yeah. Also, interestingly, it's the same date Michigan became a state, in 1837. Huh."

"Interesting, sure. But we're in Ohio right now. Attacks have come all across the country. I don't think it's localized to Michigan or Detroit."

"OK. It's also the date the Chicago Seven were found not guilty of inciting a riot at the Democratic National Convention in 1968."

"Unrelated."

"Probably not. One more? It's when Robert Hanssen, the worst double-agent for the FBI, was arrested on treason charges for spying for Russia."

Wren sighed. "So we've got nothing."

Rogers looked up. "I guess not."

"Have them keep looking. It means something. It might give us a clue on location."

"Will do."

They sipped their coffee and watched the girls goofing through the window. Wren thought back over the investigation so far, trying to tease out other leads. "What about Jeffries' intel, have we had anything back on the Idaho pig farm, linking it to Baxter?"

Rogers shook her head. "Not yet. Bad news there, actually. Apparently all digital municipal records for a large portion of Idaho were lost seven years back in a massive data breach. Births, deaths, marriage, land ownership, social security, business registration, tax, everything. We've had to send agents into city halls and records departments across the state, searching through hard copies by hand."

Wren whistled low. "Does that sound like a coincidence to you?"

"The wipeout?" Rogers shrugged. "I don't know. The Fairy did manage to hack all the CCTV around the People Mover, so they're clearly capable."

"They are. Did we get anything off that hack via data forensics?"

"No code signatures, no VPNs to track back. They got away clean."

Wren grunted. "No surprise. They're creatures of the darknet, after all. They know how to cast a shadow."

"Looks that way."

Wren drank his coffee. It was hot but a little weak for his taste. Through the window, the EMT was now trying to administer injections. Preventative antibiotics, Wren guessed, maybe some vitamin and mineral boosters. The girls were dancing a little too much, though, to make it easy. Folks inside were laughing.

"Meanwhile, more attacks are mounting," Rogers said.

That caught Wren's attention. "How many? Where?"

Rogers checked her phone. "Looks like a dozen so far, all across the country. News keeps coming in; kill scenes getting reported up the chain."

"How many dead?"

"Looks like twenty-five now."

Wren cursed. That was five times the number they'd lost already. "What about mutilations?"

"The same. They were all tortured like Tom Solent and bled out."

More bad news. "So they all gave up others in their network, or handed on the names of perps for recruitment."

Rogers' expression soured further. "Pretty much."

"Any suicide blasts?"

She scoured her phone. "Yes. One. Three FBI and one local police are in the ICU now, prospects not good. It was a stand-off and the Pinocchios blew themselves up rather than be taken."

"So none of these freaks have been captured."

"None."

"Twenty-five," Wren repeated. It wasn't a vast number, nothing like the three hundred and twenty-four ultimately lost to the Saints, but it was growing, along with the injury to emergency services personnel. Twenty-five families would be getting the worst news possible soon. "It'll have a chilling effect on other catfishers in the future," he said. "They thought they were safe behind their screens, and then..."

"Then the Pinocchios found them in real life and took them apart piece by piece," Rogers finished.

"It's revenge. And a warning."

"Right. No civilian's going to take on the Pinocchios again. Not after this."

"All targets dead except Clara Baxter."

"And she's personal," Rogers agreed.

Wren grunted. "Probably they're reserving an even worse death for her. Maybe that's what the countdown timer is for. A celebration of her death, with Pinocchios pulled in from everywhere to watch."

"Recruits like Charles DeVore. Ravenous6."

Wren rubbed his cheeks, speckled with stubble, soot and dried blood. He was getting tired of playing catch-up.

He took a swig of the coffee and stood up. "So let's be proactive."

"How so?"

"Go to Idaho."

"Idaho," Rogers repeated. "Wait, seriously?"

"Seriously."

"Looking for Clara Baxter or Lance Hebbert? Based on a fragment Jeffries maybe remembered?"

"It's all fragments," Wren said. "We stitch them into a quilt."

Rogers nodded, like she was trying to take that on board. "OK. Well, it's a big state. Where do we start?"

Wren checked the time on his phone. It was nearly midnight, with only a little over seventeen hours left on the timer now. "We'll figure that out in the air, redirect course if the right records come in. If they don't, we pick a spot, dig in and help sift through the paperwork. It's either that, or sit on our thumbs watching DeVore jack off to Pleasure Island in his Firebird, waiting for the Blue Fairy to play ball."

Rogers made a face. "Yeah, I don't want to see that either. But you do realize Idaho's on the other side of the country? We might be taking ourselves right out of the game, with only minutes left on the shot clock."

Wren took one more slug of his coffee then crumpled the cup. "This game's on the national stage, Sally. The Pinocchios are everywhere, and if Idaho holds answers, we need to be there to dig them up."

Rogers shrugged. "Can't argue with that. Do you think Humphreys will stretch to a private jet?"

Wren smiled. "Better to beg forgiveness than ask permission. That starts with the chopper. Come on, we can be at the airport in five minutes flat."

29

RECORDS

Within ten minutes Wren and Rogers were at the Akron-Canton Airport, sitting in the 330 Bar and Grille while a Cessna Citation M2 private jet was fueled up for imminent departure.

Rogers worked her phone and paced around the table, chewing a path through multiple layers of staff in Humphreys' retinue to pass along their intel about Pleasure Island. It seemed he was in the Situation Room briefing the President, though, so all she could do was wait.

Wren's mind strayed to thoughts of his family, and back to Minsk, and about the breach of his cover when someone calling themself the 'Apex' had sent his full CIA files to his wife.

He placed a call to Robin MacAuley.

"Yes, Boss," she said brightly, despite the ungodly hour.

"I wanted to check on the protective detail watching my family."

"Sure. One second." The second passed slowly. "All reports in. As of last check-in a few minutes ago, everything's OK. Sleeping soundly."

At least there was that. Wren breathed a little easier. "Thanks, Robin."

"Anytime."

Within ten minutes their burgers came: Rogers' was a buttermilk chicken double patty with blue cheese on rye; Wren had a double beef burger with 330 special sauce. Both got fries on the side.

They ate rapidly, and were called on the PA just as they gulped down the last of their fries. The Cessna was waiting on the apron outside, a light business jet with corporate stripes down the side, twin turbofan engines and a passenger capacity of seven.

They boarded and within minutes were in the air. Humphreys finally answered, and Rogers explained their progress and their goal in Idaho. Even to Wren's ears, it sounded thin. When she was done, she handed the phone to him.

"Christopher," Humphreys said.

"We need a team, Gerald."

"Of course you do. But you don't even have a target, do you? 'Idaho' doesn't count. It's eighty thousand square miles."

"A target will come in. This time we need to be ready. Every step we've taken so far, the Pinocchios were ahead of us. I don't want to be caught unprepared again."

"You think they'll be in Idaho ahead of you?" Humphreys sounded unimpressed. "Rogers just said the data you need's unhackable, spread in paper documentation across any number of archive facilities. You think the Blue Fairy could get into that?"

"I think that whoever erased all the digital records has the data already. Maybe it was the Blue Fairy."

Humphreys took a second. "The Blue Fairy did this?" Another few seconds passed. "That's a reasonable possibility.

I'll see what I can do. There aren't many operators in Idaho, and after the Saints fired up the country, all our best people are currently plugging holes in the dam. I already pulled dozens to seek and protect catfishers. I'll have to fly a team in." A moment passed as keys tapped away in the background. "Leave it with me. When you get a location, I'll have a team ready to land."

"Thank you."

The line died.

Rogers shot Wren a doubtful look. "That sounded unusually helpful of him."

"He's got kids," Wren said, as if that explained it all.

"Ah," Rogers said. "You do too."

"And you have nephews. This whole thing's personal, Sally."

She said nothing. Wren checked the timer on his phone. Sixteen and a half hours remained. "Now, how are we doing for records? I figure we can start sifting right here."

"Seconded," Rogers said, bringing up a pair of tablet computers. She handed one to Wren.

"Where'd you get this?" he asked.

She winked. "Poached them off Canton PD. Now, if you'll open to, yeah, OK, pretty much that."

Wren was already through the app screen and opening the Google Docs cloud server Rogers had downloaded. The file was live and undergoing constant updates, with what looked to be twenty two different editors currently active.

Wren scrolled and the file buffered, loading scanned documents from the cloud. Within seconds an onslaught of records appeared, some faded and yellowed with age, some arsenic-white and fresh out of the printer that had birthed them: marriages and divorces, births and deaths, land deeds and zoning records, business licenses and annulments and voter rolls and more.

Wren cursed beneath his breath.

"And they're just getting started," Rogers said.

"This is more than the catfishers' Notes app," Wren offered.

She laughed grimly. "By a fair way. I've seen photos of the warehouses holding all this stuff. They're like that scene in 'Raiders of the Lost Ark,' huge storage spaces crammed with dusty crates and filing cabinets."

Wren kept scrolling, pushing thoughts of Indiana Jones to the side. There looked to be three hundred pages already, and every second that number was growing. He scanned several documents: one was a municipal complaint about a pig farm waste overspill near Boise, owned by a 'Lance Hebbert'; the next was a birth record for a woman named Mona Brown, born in the early 2000s, the right age range to match Clara Baxter; the next was the marriage certificate for a Lance Gebbart in 1986 in Lewiston, with his occupation stated as pig farmer.

"The criteria are what we asked for," Rogers said. "Common areas subdivided by keyword. It's still jumbled right now but they're working on a system."

Wren kept scrolling, noting the keyword tags that distinguished various sections. "I see that. There's some organization by Baxter and her aliases, Gebbert and his, plus pig farms." As he scrolled the number of pages climbed, already past four hundred. The teams were working fast but the keyword structure wasn't flexible enough. "It's too hit-and-miss like this, Sally. Too rigidly divided. We need to allow for on-the-fly cross-referencing."

"OK. I'm all ears."

Wren thought for a moment. "These images need to be run through transcription. Set loose an AI, or a bank of data entry clerks in a bunker somewhere, to convert all this to searchable text. Then the whole thing can be manipulated. We can filter by the results we're looking for however we like, narrowing down or widening out. If there are documents with Gebhart, Mona and the pig farm all together, those could be our best bets. Or maybe not. Maybe we come up with some other search criteria. We'll never find anything like this."

Rogers nodded and brought up her phone. "Sounds good. I'll get MacAuley on machine transcription."

"Good." Wren drew in a slow breath. Every part of his body hurt, along with a throb in his head and leftover tinnitus from the blast at Jeffries' home. He needed to rest, and there wasn't much he could do now anyway, until the database was populated and transcribed. "Now, I haven't slept in a couple of days. I'm going to grab a few minutes, and I suggest you do too. Set your phone to wake us when the transcription's in."

"Will do, Boss."

Wren reclined his chair, switched off his seat lamp and closed his eyes. Something told him he was going to need every bit of strength he could muster in the hours to come.

30

FILTERS

It felt like only moments later that Wren woke with Rogers shaking his shoulder.

"Boss, we've got the transcription!"

Wren rubbed his eyes and sat upright. He felt groggy but better, with his head clearer and the tinnitus fading. "How long did I sleep?"

"About three hours. We're somewhere over Wyoming."

He looked at her through bleary eyes. "Three hours? To transcribe some documents?"

Rogers screwed up her face. "It's been a journey. We're into the tens of thousands of documents, now, and the AIs weren't effective. They kept missing obvious things. Any kind of damage to the document, or unusual fonts, or handwriting, they couldn't handle. So we enrolled a hundred proofreaders to check and correct their results. They're all working on the joint doc right now, and it's finally cleaning up."

"A hundred freelancers? From where?"

"They're all intelligence workers lifted across multiple agencies, all with L-level limited clearance. Humphreys pulled some strings."

Wren grunted, then fished for his tablet down the side of his seat. "All right. Have you run any filters?"

"Just the obvious ones, some combination of a Gebhart name, a Clara Baxter name and pigs. There's lots of results, still."

Wren brought up the joint doc and it buffered swiftly, showing full text transcriptions beneath every scanned document image. His mouth was dry and he plucked a bottle of water from the seat back and swiftly downed it.

"Nothing definitive?"

"Lots of leads. I figured we'd work through it together."

Wren scrolled the document. It numbered in the thousands of pages and the count was still climbing. He was an expert in pattern recognition, able to pick out meaningful threads from a muddled dataset, but that required intense critical thinking.

"We're going to need coffee."

"Already done," Rogers said, and offered him a steaming cup of black java.

"That's the spirit." Wren took a sip. Hot and strong. "OK. Let's dig in. I'll go Gebhart, Baxter and pigs. Why don't you take another combination, say Gebhart, Emily and pigs, and we'll see what shakes out."

"One variable at a time, I like it. I'll keep a record."

Wren took another sip then set the coffee cup on the tray table and began working on the joint doc. His filter returned hundreds of documents and he began to scan them. The first few seemed promising: a business license to raise and butcher pigs in Pocatello, co-signed by a Lance and a Baxter; voting records from Lemhi County that showed a Gebhart family with a brother and sister pair called Lance and Emily.

Then there was a third, and a fourth, and not just dozens more but hundreds, all with tenuous links. After twenty minutes of straining his eyes and draining his coffee, Wren looked up. Rogers was still bent to the task, but Wren wasn't sure what it was achieving anymore.

The patterns weren't there. The filters they had weren't tight enough and nothing stood out. All the critical thinking in the world wouldn't help when he was swamped by BS.

They needed another criteria, something more to constrain the search bracket.

He looked out of the window, watching the dark clouds drift below and casting his mind back over everything they'd discovered so far. Most of it came from Jeffries, though some came from the scant records on Baxter, and some from the recovered records from Marcy's Heroes, but that was it.

Nothing came from Charles DeVore. Nothing came from the Pinocchios, or Minsk, or...

Wren paused and swiped to the countdown timer. Something had come from DeVore: the countdown timer itself. They were down to less than fourteen hours remaining now. Something cataclysmic was coming, some personal climax for the Pinocchios, and he had to use that somehow.

The timer ticked and Wren's eyes defocused. Why that date? His team had come up with irrelevant markers so far, anniversaries scraped off the open Internet for the founding of Michigan or Detroit, but those meant nothing.

But maybe not completely nothing.

He felt his mind tighten, homing in on the idea of an anniversary. If this was an anniversary of something, it should be personal to Clara Baxter, maybe to Lance Hebbert too. Something important. A date that had to be marked because...

He brought up the document's filtering system. With a fresh rush of energy pulsing through him, he set the filters on names wide, then tapped in that day's date, fifteenth February, and clicked 'sort'.

The document shuffled and reduced.

Now there were just ten pages that matched all criteria,

maybe only five documents including the scans and transcriptions. Wren skimmed them swiftly, but halted cold at the fourth.

It was a death certificate. Bonneville county, east Idaho, where three members of a single family had died in a farmhouse fire on their pig farm: Lance Gebhart, Cindy Gebhart and their sixteen-year-old daughter, Mona Gebhart.

Wren's breath stopped in his chest. He checked the date, six years earlier. He read the brief coroner's report, and it hit like a slug in the face.

No bodies recovered.

He brought up the Internet and searched for news reports from that date using those names. An online newspaper called the Post Register popped up first in the listing, with an article headed:

MYSTERIOUS DEATH OF THE GEBHART FAMILY

Wren raced through the text, eating up the details. Their burned-down farmhouse was only discovered approximately three months after the fire raged, when a local slaughterhouse worker had driven by the Gebhart's farm once they'd skipped several deliveries and failed to answer the phone.

"It was all black and smoked out," the man was quoted as saying. "Like someone had taken a flamethrower to the building's south-east corner and just burned it off. But the pigs were the worst. They was all dead. Three hundred pigs, and I ain't ever seen the like. Dead in their pens, skinny to the bone. Starved. Was like looking at some kinda concentration camp."

The story picked up with local police investigating and forensics coming out from Idaho Falls, but finding no bodies to analyze. They'd assumed the fire had burned hot enough to incinerate bone, though that seemed unlikely, given the farmhouse's timber construction.

Wren lapped up the rest of the article, heart pumping

harder. No definitive answers were offered. The Gebharts were hermits. No one had even seen their daughter, Mona, since she'd been withdrawn from public school at age seven for home schooling. After the deaths, the farm had gone to probate, but paperwork was keeping the ownership issue stalled. That meant as of five years ago, the land remained untouched.

Wren whipped out of the search box and returned to the open work doc, plugging in Lance Gebhart, pig farm, probate and Bonneville County.

A welter of documents returned, land deeds and inheritance writs, testate and probate court records, all running up to the current year, all showing a trail of failure for the state to do anything with the land, locked up in some kind of legal wrangling.

Then there was a black and white photo.

It took Wren's breath away and sent his pulse shooting north of a hundred. It showed the Gebhart family standing on a red clay forecourt before their farmhouse, taken some fourteen years earlier. The farmhouse looked bleak and rundown, surrounded by ramshackle animal pens beneath a gun-iron gray sky.

Lance Gebhart was a thick, pig-like man with heavy forearms, deepset eyes and ham fists. His wife, Cindy, was willowy, pale and had the acne-ravaged face of a habitual meth-head. Between them stood their daughter, Mona Gebhart at six or seven years old, dressed in a simple white smock that could pass for a night gown, spattered with gray stains.

She had short dark hair and pale eyes that stared down the camera lens with chilling intensity. Looking into that child's eyes, any remnant of doubt Wren felt evaporated.

It was Clara Baxter.

Minus her contact lenses and wig, fourteen years younger

but unmistakably her. Somehow, she'd survived a nine-year disappearance and the fire that had taken her parents.

This was the date. This was the moment the Pinocchios wanted to commemorate, the day Lance Gebhart died.

Wren looked up at Rogers. She was scrolling hard, eyes drilling into her tablet. It felt like she was in another world, back through the looking glass. He reached out and touched her arm and she turned to him.

"I found her," he said, his voice dry and raspy. "Clara Baxter. Mona Gebhart. Lance Gebhart was her father."

31

FATHER

Rogers jerked like she'd touched a live wire. "Her father?"

Wren held up his tablet with the photograph full-screened. "That's their farmhouse, where Lance *Gebhart*, not Hebbert, raised her until she was seven years old, after which nobody saw her again. Nine years later, five years ago now, a fire ripped through the Gebhart farm, leaving no bodies, but the land's still tied up in probate." He took a breath, giving Rogers a chance to catch up it. "Five years to the day, as best as they could date it, after the burned-down structure sat there for three months before anyone reported it. The eighteenth of Feb."

Rogers' jaw dropped as she looked closer at the family. At little Mona in the middle, staring back. "You think this is her?"

"I'm certain. We can run aging software on her face and match it to Baxter, but I'm confident it'll confirm it."

Rogers trailed her fingers over the image. "There is a resemblance. Even in her mother, I see it." She looked up. "You said this farm burned down?"

"A portion of it, a witness said, with the rest blackened.

Who knows what happened? In any case, Baxter survived. Maybe it set her free from whatever Pinocchio bullshit they'd locked her down with."

Rogers looked up. "So Gebhart was a Pinocchio? He was abusing her?"

"It would check out. If so, they had her out of the public eye, withdrawn from public school, for nine years. God knows how many pics, gifs and videos he sprayed across the Blue Fairy network. Maybe Gebhart was a big fish. So when he died, and she set out to hunt Pinocchios across the country with all her catfishing groups, it painted a target on her back."

Rogers' eyes narrowed. "It's a big leap."

"It's the best lead we've got."

Rogers zoomed the image on little Mona's face. "Maybe. Maybe that's why she's so pivotal to them, why they're saving her death."

Wren grunted.

"How old was she here?" Rogers asked.

"I'd guess six or seven."

The same age as Wren's daughter, Quinn. The thought of her being taken by Lance Gebhart, of being kept by him for years, suddenly hit home with a blow that knocked him sick.

"Six or seven," Rogers repeated cautiously. "Boss, if you're right, and she is 6 or 7 years old here, followed by 9 years locked away and 5 after that, she'd only be 21 or 22 now."

That hung between them for long seconds. "It's young," Wren agreed.

"I'll say. And Jeffries said he first met her, what, a couple of years ago? She would've been barely 18, only a couple years after this fire and the death of her parents. But you still think she was flying around the country, setting up multiple catfishing groups and stinging perps?"

Wren gritted his teeth. "It's possible. Internet influencers these days make millions before they turn 16."

"And Mozart wrote his first concerto at the age of 11. It happens, sure, but it's incredibly rare; the behavior of a total outlier."

Wren thought back to his own youth. At 18 he'd run away from his adoptive father to join the Marines, after which he'd traveled the world killing terrorists to make up for the darkness of his days with the Pyramid. By 21 he'd racked up dozens of kills and joined Marine Force Recon in black ops.

"It's possible. Maybe Baxter is an outlier, Sally. A Pinocchio-hunter savant. Whatever these Pinocchios feel about her, it's deeply personal." He tapped Lance Gebhart's face. "They hold her responsible for his death, and now they're going to kill her on the anniversary of his death."

Rogers sucked a slow breath over her teeth. "It's compelling. Maybe you're right. This is definitely our best lead so far. But there's one question that remains. Maybe enough to lock it down."

"What's that?"

"Ownership of the farm and land. Why didn't the state claim it?"

"It's tied up in probate."

"But why? As I understand it, probate implies a surviving heir. Have we got that information?"

Wren swiped back to the joint doc, still filtered for land deeds. "It's in here somewhere."

Rogers leaned in and they both scanned the documents together, one after another, until they landed on a cream-colored scan of a legal filing. The top line read, 'Affidavit of Notice Regarding Estate'.

"Another delay request," Rogers muttered, zooming in and scrolling down, until at the bottom they saw a loopy signature matched by a name printed in careful capitals.

Wren blew out air. Rogers cursed. Neither spoke as they stared at the proof.

"That's it," Rogers said.

"It's her."

Rogers took a deep breath. "OK, let's hammer this out. Mona Gebhart goes dark at age seven and doesn't reappear for nine years, five years ago, when her parents die in a house fire, though their bodies aren't ever found." Wren nodded along. "She then somehow blocks probate on the state taking possession of the farm, though she doesn't technically exist, by using this new ID, Clara Baxter."

"Good so far."

"After that, at sixteen or seventeen years old, she starts flying around the country talking wealthy people into bankrolling her catfishing empire. She builds groups of likeminded people to hunt down and prosecute the sickest men in our society." Rogers paused for a moment before bulling on. "All that, and then two days ago she flies into Detroit and tries to snatch Charles DeVore, a perp who's actually the patsy in a Pinocchio trap, and they make their snatch instead." She took a breath. "That about it?"

"That's it. Exactly that."

Rogers frowned. "So where was she for those nine years?"

"Wherever her mother and father stowed her."

Rogers rubbed his chin. "OK. So ten years 'stowed' away, then she starts some 'grand revenge tour'?" Her eyes fixed on Wren. "I don't care how much of an outlier she might be. How does she do it?"

Wren just smiled. He could feel it, now. "She's Mozart."

Rogers snorted. "Mozart?"

"An extreme talent. A savant."

"Mozart. OK. But even Mozart wasn't just raw talent. He

worked countless hours since he was five years old, playing piano 'til his fingers bled. This girl would have to do even more than that, mastering a dozen skills and assets in just a year or two. Financial. Legal. Manipulation."

"Doubtless she can hack, too," Wren went on, putting another piece of the puzzle together. "There's no way she'd be able to wipe out the Idaho online records if she couldn't do that."

Rogers raised one eyebrow slightly. "You think she erased the records, now? Not the Blue Fairy?"

"I do. She'd know what the Pinocchios are capable of online, and she would definitely want to prevent them tracking her down."

Rogers rocked back a little. "Huh. That makes sense. With the online records gone, they could still try to get real-world access to one or two records facilities, but there's no way they could get into all the records we just unsealed. We only put this together with Humphreys' clout, and very little of it would be subject to a Freedom of Information request. So maybe the Pinocchios never knew where she was."

"So they set a trap."

Rogers took a heavy breath. "This is some crazy secret war bullshit, Boss. I can hardly believe it, but it's all there."

Wren said nothing. He was thinking of the parallel to his own life. He'd suffered as a child in the fake town, then done everything he could to erase all records it had ever existed. He'd tried to keep it invisible while letting it remain standing, like a testament to his suffering, or a way to regain control by just letting it rot. It wasn't his home anymore, but maybe it was the same kind of place for him as the farm was for Clara Baxter.

Maybe she was like him. A vigilante, out seeking her own form of justice.

Now the Pinocchios had her.

He swiped back to the photo of Mona Gebhart as a child. The intensity in those eyes made more sense now. She was a kindred spirit, and with that angry, intense glare she was sending out a call for help.

Nobody had ever helped her. Nobody had come to save her.

It sent a fresh burst of adrenaline into Wren's system.

He swiped back to the land deed, copied the address then pasted it into Google maps. The screen zoomed into a remote stretch of forest, valleys and barren land in the east of Idaho, sandwiched between Yellowstone and Salmon-Challis National Forest.

"Fifty miles north of Ririe," Rogers said, locating the nearest town. "We're almost there already. No airports, though."

Wren stabbed the snaking ribbon of Interstate 15. "We'll put down there. I'll tell the pilot. You get onto Humphreys and have him redirect our team. We'll be on site in less than two hours."

32

IDAHO

With I-15 as their target, the Cessna came in on an arc north of Ririe.

"4 a.m.," Wren said to Rogers. "Let's hope there's no traffic on the Interstate."

She snorted. Her eyes were still bloodshot and her cheeks were wan; maybe the lack of sleep was catching up with her. "You ever landed on a highway before?"

"No. I've landed on desert scrub before, working undercover with Qotl cartel, but that was in smaller propeller planes. How much difference can there be?"

Rogers managed a laugh this time. "About three times the speed and ten times the mass, I'd imagine."

"Speed is good. Time matters. Hold tight and think of mom's apple pie."

She nodded and strapped in. Wren looked out over the landscape as the plane began its descent. Countless tight constellations of light sparked in the distance; tiny towns like nodes in a nervous system of interweaving roads. I-15 swooped ahead to the west, flatlining against the massive darkness of Yellowstone.

America looked innocent from above. Its people had no

idea what kind of black dawn was coming. The Blue Fairy was ascendant and Wren could feel it in the air, their real-world attack clamping down like a blinding mask.

The plane rattled. The pilot's voice came through the intercom. "Brace for landing."

The Cessna tipped into a dive, and the lights of distant towns blinked out as the plane dropped, swallowed by the dark woods of the Salmon-Challis National Forest.

"You mentioned my nephews," Rogers said. "I didn't think you knew they existed. Either way, I wanted you to know that I'm all in for this. Whether we bend the law or have to break it, I'm sold. No mercy for the Blue Fairy."

Wren saw the familiar hard-charging certainty back in her eyes. "Dominic and Tom," he said. "Six and nine, your sister's boys. Last summer you all went fishing together."

Rogers looked stunned. "How do you know that? We never talked about them once."

"Usual order of business, I never would. That's your affair, Sally. But you're on my team, you better believe I know everything that matters."

She nodded firmly. "OK. Good. And your kids are Jake and Quinn. You had any word?"

"MacAuley's got a team watching them. They're home. That's all I can do for now."

"We're going to save her. Baxter."

"Final descent," came the pilot's voice.

The red and white lights of cars on the highway below raced closer, trees loomed up and the landing gear engaged, the wheels clunked into position then they hit the blacktop with an explosive kick.

The craft shuddered, the front gear touched down, the engines air braked with a roar then it was over and they rocked to a standstill.

Wren's ears popped, catching a beeping sound nearby; an

SUV swerved by on their left, horn sounding madly. The driver gave them the finger.

"Only in America, right?" Rogers asked.

"Exercising his First Amendment right."

Rogers laughed, then the door to the cockpit opened. The pilot stood there, sweat-drenched and as pale as Tom Solent. "That's me done," she said.

"Thank you," Wren said. "That was flawless."

"I hope it's worth it. I can't take off on this road. They'll have to send a semi and a crane."

"It'll be worth it," Rogers said, rising to her feet and heading for the exit door. "Boss?"

"Let's go."

Rogers popped the door and it deployed down to the blacktop as a four-step exit. The air was cold, dry and smelled of pine and woodsmoke. She led the way and Wren followed, placing a call to summon the Ririe squad car.

In five minutes it pulled up beside them.

"Saw you coming in," said the driver, a man in his fifties with a thick gray mustache and a severe gaze. "Sergeant Scott, Ririe PD."

"Thanks for coming out," Wren said, dropping into the passenger side. Rogers took the middle rear.

"Welcome." Scott took the car up to seventy in ten seconds flat, racing away from the blinking red lights of the Cessna and plunging into darkness.

"What do you know about this place?" Rogers asked the sergeant.

"Pig farm," Scott answered in laconic Midwestern tones, catching her eyes in the rearview mirror. "It's a bad place."

"Why do you say that?"

"Several people died there. I've heard its haunted."

"How so?"

"Some punk kids said so." Scott took a moment, like he

was settling in for a story. "I picked them up out that way a couple years back. Terrified. They were spray-canning or shooting up or something, thought it might be a good place to get high and screw. They said there were noises, a banging sound that wouldn't stop. That kept getting louder."

"Did you check it out?" Wren asked.

The sergeant chuckled. "Haunted pig farm? You bet. There ain't much else going on out here."

"And?"

"And nothing. It's a wreck. Not a good feel to the air, though. Smells like Hades' hog trough. Y'all be careful."

"You aren't going to stick around?" Rogers asked.

The sergeant shook his head. "No way. Once was enough for me. I'm your taxi and that's it. I'll wait ten minutes down the access road. You call when you need your route out."

Rogers shot Wren a look.

"And the Gebharts? You ever cross paths with them?"

Another moment passed as Scott mulled that over. "Think I did. The old man with his little girl, once at a hard goods store in Ririe, must've been when I was starting out. She was cute as a button in a bowtie, I'll tell ya. Kept themselves to themselves, though, you know? Mountain folk are like that; God-fearing, but in their own way. The hills are their church, the livestock their congregation."

Rogers said nothing more. Wren's skin crawled.

"Y'all mind some music?" Scott asked.

"Your car," Wren said.

Scott switched on the radio and tuned until he caught a sad country song, fading in and out of signal range. After perhaps a minute he switched it off.

"Better without, I figure," he said.

Soon after, he made the turn off the Interstate onto 287, passing the silent village of Three Forks. Now the only light came from their headlights, sending cones out over the dusty blacktop. The vehicle climbed into barren clay mountains scarred by centuries of acid run-off from copper mining.

Nobody spoke. Trees grew tall around them; Ponderosa pine needling the stars.

A few miles on they descended into a sparse valley, like a broad, bare gouge in the dead red rock. Steep cliffs rose to either side. The turn onto the access road followed, then Rogers pointed.

To the left ran a decaying wooden fence. Scott stopped by the gate, buckled on its hinges and seesawed at an angle. Moonlight illuminated the empty pig enclosures beyond; hundreds of small fenced sections, largely collapsed. At the end of a long and weedy gravel drive sat the farmhouse's fire-bitten husk.

A shudder passed up Wren's spine.

On the day the Gebharts died, their pigs must have begun to starve. He imagined them frantic in their pens, ramming their bodies against the wood and biting each other in desperation. The first would die and the others would eat, until there was only one left.

"This is it," Scott said.

Wren brought up his phone and checked the bars. He had one.

"You've got a signal, Sergeant?"

"Yes, Sir."

"All right then. We'll call."

Wren opened the door and strode out. The air felt colder here than on I-15. He touched his hip holster, still armed with the Beretta M9 he hadn't yet fired. He vaulted the gate to the gravel beyond. Rogers followed, and behind them Sergeant Scott drove away.

The gravel crunched underfoot as they walked along the track. A rhythmic flapping sound came from the old farmhouse.

"You think that's what the kids heard?" Rogers asked.

"I doubt it," Wren said. "That's probably a loose air conditioning fan catching the wind."

The air smelled clean; not a hint left of the corruption that must have hung over the farm after the pig die-off began. Flies would have buzzed thickly for months.

The farmhouse loomed tall as they drew near. There was a swing set out front with the chains rusted away, and an old Chevy up on blocks. Dense graffiti covered the facade, and scattered cans and bottles lay among pierced fly screens and rotten window shutters on the porch.

Wren surveyed the farmhouse's silhouette. The fire had ravaged it like a drunk wielding a boxcutter, slicing the first floor away at a diagonal on the northeast corner, leaving roof rafters poking through like desiccated ribs.

"There can't be anything left here," Rogers said quietly, as if standing at a wake. "More than a few punk kids have passed through. It'll be rotten. Any evidence will have been looted or burned."

Wren shuddered. This place had the same feel as the fake town; no neighbors within miles, and pigs to dispose of any organic evidence, just like the Pyramid had used the desert sands to bury its bodies. He peered down the side of the house and saw what he was looking for: an oversized, freestanding satellite dish in the back. He pointed.

"That thing's huge," Rogers said.

"And Gebhart had it at least five years ago. He could pull down gigabits a second with that. The mountains would scramble any attempt at detection, with no IP address to route through. It's a perfect hiding place for a Pinocchio."

Rogers shone her flashlight on the dish. It was a tarnished, graffiti-tagged moon on a metal frame, clearly swung out of place by vandals, but too well-secured to rip free.

"Pull data down or send it back up," Rogers said.

Wren walked up to the front entrance. The porch boards creaked under his weight. The nearest beer cans were cracked and rusted. Nobody had been by for years. Like Sergeant Scott had said, the place felt haunted. The fog of that dead family and all their hundreds of dead pigs still hung in the air.

The door stood ajar. Wren pushed and it swung in on groaning hinges.

33

VENT

Wren strode into the smoke-blackened dark of the hallway, his flashlight casting a narrow beam over shriveled family photos in cracked frames underfoot. The wooden walls had bent and flexed. The flapping of the AC grew louder, like a fist rapping on a door.

He turned right through an open doorframe and Rogers followed. The air was musty here. Damp had gotten into everything. There was a thick fur of moss on the walls where rainwater had run down. The den was obliterated, with holes bashed through the outer walls. The broken wooden frame of a sofa lay crumpled like a carcass at the edge, its bones mummified by their own upholstered leather skin. The TV was shattered glass and wood in the corner. A coffee table was kindling, the floor was strewn with papers and weeds grew up in a damp patch at the center.

"Creepy as hell," Rogers said.

Wren stood in the middle looking out through large holes to the desolate yard outside. Pipes, cables and vents dangled in the gaps. Vandals had done much of this, not the fire. It helped give the lie to the official story.

"Anything?" Rogers asked.

"Maybe," Wren said.

He walked into the adjoining dining room. A rustic farmhouse tabletop lay on its belly with its legs splayed. The back door was missing, so an open rectangle led down steps into an overgrown yard. Spikes of plastic toys lay in the long grass.

If Mona Gebhart really had gone missing fourteen years ago, then that was how long these toys had lain there. Either that, or someone else had been playing with them..

Wren passed through the kitchen and circled around to climb the stairs. The boards creaked. The upper floor landing was bare and black. To his right the walls shimmered silver where rain had glossed the soot, stretching away into empty air. A doorframe alone stood, last remnant of the master bedroom, with the walls and roof burned away. Graffiti cans lay at the edges of the hall. Through holes in the boards he saw down into the den below.

He paced the other way, stopping to inspect a tangle of wiring high on the left wall, matched by a shattered plastic box on the floor. He tipped it with his foot; it was stenciled with 'HomeSafe'. Some kind of alarm.

Beyond that another bedroom lay on the right. It had a child-sized bed frame with tangled bedding, a bookshelf and a rack of cubbyholes for teddy bears, a chest of drawers and a sooty mirror. It was clearly a little girl's room, with faded cartoons on the walls. Rogers' flashlight beam fell on the image of Pinocchio and she let out a cry.

It was a cartoon of the little wooden boy.

Wren bit his lip and leaned in, ignoring his ratcheting heart rate to pass his flashlight beam over more scenes from the Pinocchio tale shown on the wallpaper: images of the Blue Fairy, Geppetto, the whale, even the children turned to donkeys on Pleasure Island.

"This is disgusting," Rogers said, the contempt rising strongly in her voice. "These Gebharts were sick."

Wren said nothing. He scanned the shelves, the walls, the bedding. Everything about it said seven years old, a room cast in amber and left unchanged, but there were gaps that couldn't be explained by the fire. A whole section of the bookshelf was empty. Half the cubbyholes for dolls were vacant.

"She was here," he said. "Mona. Clara."

"It's not burned at all."

"It wouldn't be. This was the last place she was happy."

Rogers turned to him. "What does that mean?"

Wren took a tight breath. "Let me check one more thing.

In the master bathroom there was a metal frame embedded in the wall, peeking through holes torn by vandals. It looked like a brace for a heavy load, suggesting an unusually large water tank.

"What?" Rogers asked, looking from Wren to the brace. "That's structural."

"In a nineteenth-century homestead? Come on."

Rogers followed him back down. Into the living room, Wren imagined Gebhart's routine. As a mountain farmer, he'd want to keep his eyes on his livestock at all times. Stay close. He envisaged the plumbing map, coming down from the water tank in the attic. At the wall he kicked away the remains of the sofa, then he looked at Rogers.

"The Gebharts didn't die in the fire," he said.

"What? How do you know that?"

Wren pointed up through the gaps in the boards above. "Smoke's the biggest killer in a night fire. You asphyxiate long before you burn. But this," Wren approached one of the trenches in the wall and reached in, pulling out a large silver duct, "is an industrial-grade venting system. Factories have them in the event of an airborne contamination. Unless this was purposefully turned off, the smoke wouldn't have killed anyone. Rather, the system would've set off alarms, and you'd have to try very hard to burn to death on the second floor with those alarms wailing, especially when their master bedroom was the only badly damaged part of the house."

Rogers screwed up her features in thought. She looked at the vent. "Why'd they have that vent if it belongs in a factory?"

"Good question," Wren said. "The next question is, why have all these pipes?" He tapped one of them, clad in new-looking insulating foam. "This is an external wall with no easy access to the kitchen or bathroom, and no reason to run a pipe from the attic to here."

Rogers considered. "You're a plumber now?"

"I'm reading the patterns, Sally."

"And what do the patterns say?"

"They say she did this," he said bluntly. "Clara Baxter."

"She set the fire?"

"Yes."

Rogers was clearly unconvinced but listening. "OK. Walk me through it."

"It starts with her room. At seven years old, like you said, the Gebharts took her. They took some of her possessions and put her in a cell. That lasts for nine years, presumed dead by anyone who cared, which was nobody, until at sixteen years old she escapes. She incapacitates her parents and sets the fire as a cover story. Local sheriffs never found her parents' bodies, remember."

Rogers nodded along. "OK. It's supposition, but it has legs. So where are the bodies?"

"Here."

"Where?"

Wren looked down. Rogers tracked his gaze to a stretch of plain pine floorboards. It took her a second.

"Wait, you mean right here? You think we'll find a trapdoor?"

"We will." He pointed at the hole in the wall. "All those pipes, cables and vents go somewhere. One of those outbuildings probably covers a sump pump and an outlet for venting the underground structure."

Rogers studied the boards as if they might give up their secrets through deeper contemplation. "You think there was some kind of 'dungeon' down here?"

"I'm saying there still is," Wren said, and kneeled. He felt like he knew Clara Baxter, now. She'd been careful not to burn this spot, because it was a memorial for her, a way of stamping back control, just like the fake town was for him.

He dug his fingernails into a crack in the boards. Closely seamed. He prized, but there was no give. Good workmanship. He scanned the skirting board. Neat and flush. He tapped it, but it was even all round. No signs at all, but the pipes wouldn't lie.

He turned in a circle, casting light around the living room. On the second pass he saw it, a small divot by the baseboard in the corner, recessed into a natural knothole in the wood. He strode over and stuck his finger into the hole. His fingernail tickled metal.

"What?" Rogers asked.

"Hand me your belt."

Rogers stared, then unspooled her belt. The buckle was narrow enough to slot into the gap. It caught on the catch inside like a hook, and Wren stepped back and pulled, carefully at first then harder, until there was a crack like a gunshot, startling them both, and a large patch of the floor shifted.

"What the..." Rogers muttered.

Wren pulled harder, and the trapdoor rose. It was easily five feet on a side, itself as big as a small room. It rose until

Wren caught it and took the weight. A metal frame supported the boards on a squealing hinge. Six inches beneath that lay a broad oblong of raw concrete, with a metal hatch tucked flush inside it as big as a refrigerator door.

"This is where they stowed Clara," Wren said, then twisted the handle and pulled. The hatch cover lifted easily and harsh white light spilled up from within, illuminating cement steps leading down.

34

STILL

Wren's heart thudded and his mouth went dry. Rogers cursed under her breath.

For a second they both stared. Working lights? Wren counted the steps. Ten. Dribbles of oil stained them. Maybe blood. Seven feet underground, really just below the surface. The light came from industrial strip lights on the sides. That explained the cabling. Pipes ran above the wires. The air was warm and dry. There was also a menacing mechanical thumping sound.

"That's it," Rogers said. "The sound."

"There's power."

"How is that possible?"

"It means she was coming back."

Rogers looked at him.

"Clara Baxter," he went on. "Mona Gebhart. Back to the source of her suffering. It's common behavior for survivors of childhood trauma. Revisit the scene, like she can overcome it somehow." He didn't mention his visits to the fake town. He didn't need to.

"So she comes here," Rogers said. "Regularly. I get that. But why keep the power running at all times?"

"Let's find out."

Wren started down. The opening was big enough. The stairs dropped sharply. It would be easy to descend with a burden, like a child over the shoulder. A slight duck, leaning back as he hit the seventh step to avoid his head grazing the opening, then he was at the bottom.

Raw, dry concrete walls stretched to the west for maybe eight yards. It was a narrow passageway, barely tall enough for him to stand, sealed with a metal door at the far end. There was no smell at all, except maybe the dry fuzz of ozone, caused by electrical equipment drying out the air.

"Come on down."

Rogers followed. The sound was louder already. A piston, maybe, pumping endlessly. This was Clara Baxter's handiwork, Wren felt certain. He was beginning to understand her. She was more like him than he'd thought: darkness as a child followed by vengeance as an adult. She'd picked up catfishing, he'd become a special ops Marine. He'd built the Foundation, she'd single-handedly framed a catfishing empire.

"I don't want to know what's on the other side of that door," Rogers said.

"Let's hope she left it open." Wren advanced. Eight paces only, out from under the footprint of the house and into the dirt of the yard.

"Gebhart must have used an earthmover to clear all this," Rogers said. "Working alone, including drainage canals, foundational rebars and concrete pours, it would have taken months of work and thousands of dollars."

"And who would have known?" Wren replied. "Out here in rural Idaho, surrounded by the pigs, the works would only have been visible from above. A dungeon in his backyard."

The door was metal, with three large pneumatic bolts. On the wall to the right was a screen showing white static, a keypad with nine digits. No way to know how many numbers in the passcode. No way to guess. Would she have left it open?

Wren pushed the door and it moved. He said a silent prayer to Clara Baxter and pushed it the rest of the way. Eight more yards of concrete corridor lay beyond, ending in a dark wooden board with glints of silver. The back of a mirror? It was narrower here.

"I've seen similar designs before," Wren said, "in homemade dungeons from plans circulated on the darknet." He pointed. "This narrow, long corridor offers no room for the captive to struggle, no place to lie in wait and no way to charge or swing back a makeshift weapon."

Rogers pointed at a camera over the heads, bolted above the metal door. "Then add this on? Gebhart could order his victim to retreat to the end of the corridor when he was coming down. It would make escape attempts impossible."

Wren whistled low. "One way in, one way out, with the camera to confirm."

The piston-like sound was so loud now that Wren could feel the vibrations through the floor.

"This place is sick," Rogers said.

Wren advanced to push on the wooden board. It opened on oiled hinges, and the hammering sound grew cacophonous, hitting Wren like a jackhammer as he gazed into a red-walled hall.

Baxter had arranged a horrific tableau. It took Wren several moments to take it in. The room was a square space maybe eight yards by eight, with rich mahogany boards on the floor and lush orange light glowing from subtle wall sconces. Mirrors covered several walls, while others were decked with padded red leather.

Equipment was spread around the sides. Frames. Tools.

Several large wooden chests no doubt contained more, but none of that was what drew his eye.

There were six cameras in the middle of the space, red lights blinking to signify a live feed, pointing at two figures in the tableau. Slightly to the left sat a mangy, withered corpse in a chair bolted to the floor. It was dressed in a white nightgown, yellowed in places, with skeletal arms lashed to the chair and white hair stringing down a sunken, mottled face.

"Oh no," said Rogers, pushing past Wren. She covered her ears against the terrible hammering.

"Cindy Gebhart," Wren said.

Rogers gagged. Her corpse had decayed in an air-conditioned, clinical environment, making for more of an evaporation than a rotting. Moisture had sucked out of her pores, tightening her skin like a mummy. Still, she'd watched. Her chair was angled to face the companion piece in this dark installation.

Lance Gebhart. The sound drilled in Wren's ears.

His desiccated corpse was held upright in a large metal frame, draped in a kind of white ceremonial tunic. His mummified lips were curled back tightly in a silent, permanent scream.

Before him lay the machine making all the noise: a single long piston that pumped backward and forward with powerful force. A blade on the end stabbed a well-worn groove through his leathery chest, into the place his heart should have been.

Wren felt his own gorge rise.

Three motors sat neatly on the floor, attached to the piston mechanism. Each had some kind of breaker switch. Redundancies, Wren figured, just like the cameras. If a fuse blew or if part of one mechanism failed, the next in line would pick up the slack. Endlessly filming. Endlessly stabbing.

So Gebhart had died in his own dungeon. Nine years now and counting. All while he was violated, all of it filmed.

Suddenly Wren understood.

"This is why they hated her so much. Why that Pinocchio whispered Lance Gebhart's name in her ear. She's been live streaming this feed for them to see for nine years, and they haven't been able to stop it yet."

Rogers looked nauseated. Another revelation followed.

"The Blue Fairy," Wren whispered.

Rogers was already there. "It was his fascination," she said. "The wallpaper in Baxter's room."

"Pinocchios," Wren continued. "Pleasure Island, the Fairy herself. He's the source!"

"It all started here."

They were both left speechless.

Fifteen years ago, with a setup like this, with the will to lock his own daughter in place and who knew how many more, Lance Gebhart would have been the idol to an army of depraved monsters on the dark Internet. One of the first to run a livestream, delivering foul delights to a growing cabal of monstrous men. One of the first to bring them together under a single banner.

"This is the birthplace of the Blue Fairy," Wren said.

"But she broke free," Rogers said, so pale now that her freckles stood in sharp relief. "Clara Baxter did this. She strapped her father down. She made her mother watch. She turned the cameras on and made them all watch."

The cameras blinked. No doubt the satellite uplink was live.

She was making them all watch, still.

35

DEVIL

Rogers was first to stride over to the pneumatic piston. It was only a handful of paces, but Wren grasped her arm before she could reach it, holding up a silencing finger to his lips.

She swung back to him, her face flushed a blotchy red with outrage: at this room, at what it meant, and now at him for stopping her. The sound was intolerable, Wren understood that, but there were dangers here they hadn't yet fully understood.

He kneeled and carefully unplugged the cameras. The red lights died.

"Now go ahead," he said.

Rogers shook free, a tear spilling down her cheek, and ripped out the plugs for the piston. The thudding machine slowed, the racket stilled and the chamber fell into an uneasy silence, perhaps for the first time in nine years. Rogers turned back and nodded, unashamed by the tears running down her cheeks.

"Thank you."

Neither needed to voice what he'd just saved her from: her

face on the Gebhart livestream, transmitted into the darknet and recorded for posterity, logged by every Pinocchio in existence.

"This is what Clara Baxter survived," Rogers said.

"This is what she might be surviving right now."

Rogers bit her lip so hard the skin went white. Wren felt the same way, tamped down inside. You could use anger, he told himself. You had to burn it like fuel.

"We're going to bring these sick bastards down," Rogers said. "Every last one."

"WE NEED TO KNOW WHERE," Wren said. His voice sounded strange after the barrage of the machine, almost shallow and insufficient to fill the space. Clara Baxter's revenge still owned these four walls more than anything he could say or do. "If Gebhart was the Blue Fairy's architect, there's a chance they're following his blueprint still. There has to be something here about his plans. About Pleasure Island."

Rogers nodded, smearing the tears away with her sleeves. "Agreed. There's more to it than this room. Where did Baxter sleep?"

Wren scanned the walls again. There was a tall, narrow mirror on each wall, one behind the tableau and one to either side. He strode over the tangle of camera wires, passed between the frail cadavers of Mr. and Mrs. Gebhart and kicked the mirror.

The ball of his foot struck and smashed the silvered glass, buckling the board behind it and carrying through into empty space. Wren tore it away at the hinges.

Another narrow tunnel lay beyond, fading into darkness. There was a switch on the wall and Wren hit it. Harsh lights down the length chugged to life, ending some eight yards away at a metal grille door. Wren pushed his broad shoulders into the slim corridor and advanced. From behind came more sounds of crashing glass as Rogers took out another mirror.

The grille door was unlocked and opened easily, revealing a room barely three yards by three, almost identical to Mona Gebhart's bedroom in the farmhouse above. A single bed lay on one side, with a small tunnel TV on a nightstand, a range of books lined neatly in a bookshelf, with another set of teddy cubbyholes, along with a desk, papers and pens. A toilet, tiny sink and bucket to wash in had been crammed in at the far end.

This was where the missing books and dolls from above had gone, following Mona Gebhart in her one-way trip into the ground.

Some of those faded dolls lay on the threadbare bed, one of them blue with fairy wings. The same Pinocchio characters paraded on the wallpaper. Wren barely made it to the toilet before he vomited.

There were no words to express the disgust he felt. The betrayal. The rage.

He flushed the toilet. A flop sweat coated his face. He looked around, but there was no reprieve here. A few worn board games rested on top of a cupboard, documenting moments of play snatched from the horror, and all preserved just as it had been, like a museum exhibit.

Like his fake town.

A place for Clara Baxter to come back and listen to the machine in the room next door as her revenge endlessly played itself out, reliving the dreams she must once have poured her whole soul into, longing to be free.

As if she could bring comfort to the poor little girl she'd once been.

Wren staggered out and squeezed back down the corridor

like he was escaping his own prison, only to find himself back in the red room, cameras pointing directly in his direction.

The Pyramid had been bad, but never like this. Before he could stop himself, he charged the cameras. He hurled one across the room so hard it shattered in three places. One he smashed into bits on the floor. One beat off the ceiling, one flew into the corpses and knocked Mrs. Gebhart askew in her chair, one he tore apart with his bare hands, prizing the extendable view screen away, until he had the last in his hands and Rogers was there, one hand firm on his shoulder.

"Boss," she shouted, and not for the first time, he realized. He blinked and focused on her.

"Boss," she said again, giving him a moment to come back. "You have to see this."

He snapped out of it and let her lead him toward the wall on the left, where another broken mirror opened into a room crammed with computer servers. Thick slates of motherboards, CPUs and circuitry were slotted into dozens of racks that began at the floor and carried on up to the ceiling, each blinking with red and green lights. Hardware filled every inch of space except that taken by a desk with one chair, three large screens, a keyboard and a mouse.

Fans hummed but did nothing for the wave of dry heat that washed over Wren, stinking of ozone. Thick data trunk cables snaked across the floor, into a heavy-duty routing box bolted to the wall behind the screens, then up through the ceiling.

"Dear God," Wren whispered.

"More like the devil," Rogers said. "I think we found the heart of Lance Gebhart's Blue Fairy network; at least until Clara Baxter co-opted it."

Wren's gaze swept over the servers. There were hundreds of them. It was like Minsk all over again. There had to be enough intelligence here to keep a twenty-strong squad of forensic data analysts busy for a year.

This was it. But they didn't have a year. Wren checked the countdown on his phone.

9:58:32

They had just under ten hours.

36

BREAKER

"**I**t's a supercomputer," Wren said.

"The power drain alone must be immense," Rogers said, touching one of the server racks then pulling her hand back swiftly. "It's burning up in here. How did Gebhart conceal it?"

Wren had no answer. These were skills they hadn't accounted for. "He was far more than a pig farmer, that seems clear."

"No kidding."

"We searched for months. We scoured the darknet. We never even heard of this livestream. We never even heard of the Gebharts."

"I think it's fair to say the current crop of Pinocchios don't know about this place, either. If they did, they'd have shut down the feed already."

Wren advanced. He stood before the screens, laid out flush alongside each other to frame a single long panorama of black. With this much computing power, there wasn't much you couldn't do.

Only one screen seemed to be live, though; the central

one. It displayed a flashing character at the top left, a simple dollar sign that served as a command prompt: $.

"Linux," Wren said. "Open source operating system. Gebhart was a hacker."

"Looks that way."

"Probably an engineer, too," Wren went on, working it through. "That satellite dish, and this power draw, and wiring and plumbing this whole dungeon? On top of that, he kept it all secret for longer than a decade."

"And now his daughter followed in his footsteps."

Wren grimaced, picturing how it might have played out. "She captured him somehow, put him on the rack then made him teach her."

"He taught all this from the rack?" Rogers looked doubtful. "This is more than a few hours' of knowledge, Boss. We could try to break in, guess a password, maybe, but I don't like our chances."

"So it took longer. Days. Weeks, maybe. She could've learned everything she needed to know. Keep her parents in a state of semi-starvation, and she could control them. She could've milked Gebhart for months."

Rogers shuddered. "But it wasn't enough, was it? Whatever she learned from his system, it didn't break the Blue Fairy. Why else would she set up all those catfishing groups?"

"The whole thing must be anonymized," Wren said, pulling back the chair and sitting down at the desk. "The Pinocchios couldn't track Gebhart and he couldn't track them. But there's something here, that's for certain." He looked at the keys. "Getting a directory list on Linux, what's the command?"

Rogers just stared. "I'm not a hacker, Boss. I barely know how to control-alt-delete, and the clue's right there in the name. You want the darknet team, but you're not going to get them in here anytime soon. Operating protocol says we flag this to Humphreys and call in data forensics right now, let them pick it clean."

Wren shook his head. "Too slow."

"So try anything. Ask for a directory."

Wren pointed at the overlarge junction box on the wall, through which all the cables ran before shooting up through the roof. "You recognize that?"

Rogers peered. "It looks like a power box, maybe combo-ed with the data line?"

Wren shook his head. "Worse. I've seen something like it before, in the bodycam feed from Minsk before the building came down. It's an explosive breaker." Rogers's eyes widened. "Another Blue Fairy booby trap, like the deadman's switch in Redford. One wrong move and it goes boom."

Rogers took a moment to absorb that. "Seriously?" She looked around. "You think one breaker could bring all this down?"

"Maybe. Who knows how many more like it it's wired to? At the least, it'd destroy every server board in this room along with whoever was sitting at the desk. And the trigger? Who knows? Maybe I touch a single key, the wrong key to start with, and it all blows. Maybe I enter the wrong password three times. Maybe we try to disconnect a single cable and it blows."

Rogers opened her mouth, then blew out air and a curse.

"Yeah."

They sat for a second.

"How long you think, to get data forensics out here?" Wren asked.

Rogers snorted. "From Washington? Door-to-door? Eight hours, maybe."

"We've got ten; that's cutting it too fine. What about local assets in Idaho?"

"There's nothing in Idaho, Boss, just trees and fertilizer."

Seconds ticked by.

"We need another way."

"We can't just start tapping randomly until we get blown up," Rogers answered.

Wren looked at her. "You're right. We can't."

Rogers' eyes narrowed. "I don't like the way you just said, 'we', Boss."

"I don't see an alternative."

She shook her head. "No."

"I already drove you into one bomb blast. I can't do it again."

"You don't even know the command for the directory list."

No," Wren allowed. "But I know some people who might."

Rogers peered at him. "You're not talking about the darknet team, are you?"

"They'd never break protocol."

"You're talking about your Foundation, aren't you? You must have some hackers in that. Who've you got?"

Wren answered softly. "Better you head up now, Sally."

"Not a chance."

Wren ignored that. "This thing's a bomb either way. If I tell you who I'm working with, either you stop me or you don't, and that's your career shot in either case. Go up top. Let me do this alone."

Rogers said nothing for a long moment. "Chris."

"That's an order, Agent Rogers," he said firmly.

Her gaze strayed to the junction box. "The whole team died in Minsk."

"Everybody died. Go up."

"It's not worth it. Your career. Maybe your life."

"If Clara Baxter's not worth it, then who is?"

There was nothing to say to that. She simply nodded. "Then good luck, Chris."

"To you too. And clear the building, Sally, in case there are secondary explosives." He turned back to the screens. Behind him her footfalls padded away, until the server room was silent bar the humming of Lance Gebhart's supercomputer.

Wren brought up his phone. Still one bar. He tapped a number into his phone; a long shot but at least a shot.

Their names were Hellion and B4cksl4cker, two of the world's greatest black-hat hackers. They were volatile, anarchic and fickle, and they'd once brought nations to their knees. They might just laugh in his face then watch while he blew himself to bits.

9:47:13

He called the number.

37

HELLION & B4CKSL4CKER

B4cksl4cker was a twenty-nine-year-old Armenian who waged 'ransomware' hacks through his enormous 'botnet'; a network of half-a-billion hijacked devices across the globe, including computers, phones, watches and tablets.

He used that botnet to infiltrate corporate networks, then automatically encrypt all the contents, using unbreakable codes. He then ransomed the key to decrypt the contents back to the corporation, sometimes for millions of dollars.

Usually, they didn't even call the authorities. They simply paid the fee as a part of doing business.

B4cksl4cker was notorious in the hacker space, with an operation worth hundreds of millions of dollars, and he was impossible to pin down. Rumors suggested he lived in a multiple-coach convoy that constantly moved throughout Europe, wielding his botnets like a virtuoso conductor, erasing his trail of legendary exploits behind him.

Hellion was an eighteen-year-old Belgian wunderkind who'd cut her teeth on the e-sports strategy game StarCraft. In that game 'APM', or Actions Per Minute, was a vital determiner of success. Speed on the keys mattered just as much as tactics and strategy; the best players at pro-levels were capable of 300+ APM, equating to at least five keystroke decisions per second.

In StarCraft the player used those staggering APMs to control a squad of fighters in pitted, top-down open warfare against another squad. At her peak at the age of twelve, Hellion had averaged a stunning 400 APM, with an armada of strategies that saw her undefeated on the semi-pro boards. She could have gone pro, but that hadn't seemed like fun. More fun were the amazing opportunities her APM offered as a professional hacker.

Three years earlier, she'd initiated open warfare on B4cksl4cker. He counter-attacked, and for seven days and nights they fought a war of attrition to bring each other's virtual identities down. Hellion was at her parent's home, going deep on single techniques with an intuitive grasp of tactics and speed on the keys, while B4cksl4cker was in his convoy leveraging his entire botnet at once.

Ultimately, Hellion won. A blisteringly original, lightning-fast gambit disrupted B4cksl4cker's network of control, peeling off his hacked computers one by one until he was left without any defense capability. Hellion ran rings around him, ultimately locking him out of his own network with a repurposed version of one of his own ransom hacks.

When it was done, she sent him the unlock code and message.

THAT WAS FUN LET'S DO AGAIN SOMETIME

There was no ransom; she didn't take his money, only his reputation.

B4cksl4cker could have gone after her in the real world. His hack had worked too, just more slowly. He had her physical location by then, and knew how unprotected she was; just a school girl waging a secret war from her parent's attic. He could have handed her to her own government, the Russians or the Chinese. They all would have been glad to have her.

Instead he went to see her. Outside her school one day he introduced himself. She laughed at how old he was, then offered to teach him a thing or two.

It became a friendship. They saw something in each other that they couldn't get in any other way: the understanding and respect of a peer. He taught her about ransomware and botnets. She worked on his APM and ability to adapt.

Two years later, from that blooming platonic partnership came their first joint hack, a new approach to ransomware that dealt billions in damage globally. They used a 'cryptoworm', a type of ransomware program capable of seeking out soft targets on its own, then proliferating to any and every computer even remotely connected. They called this the 'HugginTime' hack.

It proved to be immense, swallowing thousands of companies into its encryption embrace, and prompting a massed response from the US government to hunt down its perpetrators.

Wren spearheaded that hunt.

Using his newly-formed darknet squad in the CIA, he acted swiftly in the hours after HugginTime first struck, infiltrating a likely target corporation and lying in wait for Hellion and B4cksl4cker to strike. When they did, he sent a message from the CEO requesting an in-person meet

By that point, they almost certainly realized he was a government plant, but they agreed anyway, but on their terms.

For twenty-four hours they ran Wren around western Europe, laundering him of any possible bugs, tails or oversight. By the end he was exhausted, sitting alone in a hut in the Belgian Blue Forest.

They were both there.

Hellion was slim but tall, dressed in black with a Betty Boop face on her t-shirt. B4cksl4cker was a shambling bear of a man in a navy cashmere sweater, as tall as Wren but thicker still.

"We know you," B4cksl4cker had rumbled. "You are not CEO. You are CIA."

"I'm not here to try and arrest you," Wren said. "I need your help,"

Hellion had laughed.

"Have you heard of the Blue Fairy?"

The laughter stopped.

"We are leaving," Hellion said, standing immediately.

"Aren't you tired of playing games for money, Hellion? Why did you even come today if you didn't want to listen?"

"To waste your time," Hellion answered. "Games are fun."

"You don't believe that," Wren answered. "Not really. Hacking corporates is dull. Beating overpaid idiots in software security isn't the rush it once was. This HugginTime hack is beneath you. The Blue Fairy, though?" He paused. "That would be epic."

"Not interested. B4cksl4cker."

The big man gave Wren a half-smile and a shrug and stood up.

"I'm talking about bringing down the largest cabal of evil people on the darknet," Wren said. "With the best cryptography and hackers in existence. You don't want to take that on?"

Hellion snorted. "Evil? Who is America to lecture on evil people?"

"You're not dealing with America right now," Wren countered. "You're dealing with me."

"And who are you?" she snapped back. "A liar. A cultist. A manipulator."

He smiled. "So you have done your research on me."

"This isn't as fun as I thought," she said, and spun to go.

"You don't want fun," he called after her. "You don't even want money, or fame, or any of that." She paused at the door. "I can give you what you want."

She turned with a laugh. "And what do we want, Christopher Wren?"

"Purpose and belonging, like everyone. The same reason you took this meeting and the same thing you glimpse in each other. B4cksl4cker, it's the reason you lost to a fifteen-year-old but didn't have her assassinated. Hellion, it's the same reason you didn't take all his money. You saw something worthwhile in each other, and that felt good. I can help you live in that place all the time, alongside a hundred other people." He took a breath. "You already know I've got a group called the Foundation, made up of people fighting their way back from the edge of bad decisions. Just like the two of you. I offer the exact same thing to all of them, purpose and belonging, and nobody's quit on me yet."

Hellion stared a moment longer. "Nobody has yet," she said, then left and B4cksl4cker followed.

By that night, all Wren's social media feeds went down. By the morning, his bank accounts were drained, even the hidden ones. By the afternoon, the Foundation darknet site had been scrubbed out of digital existence.

He didn't do anything in response. He didn't go after them again, though they had to know he could. A week passed, during which he began hearing reports of strange occurrences happening to Foundation members. Their computers locked up. Their credit cards stopped working. Some were even approached online and asked questions directly, about Wren and his role in the Foundation.

He understood what it meant. Hellion and B4cksl4cker were vetting him.

A week later, it all ended when he got access to his accounts and the Foundation back, along with a report card. It was on pink paper, waiting in a manila envelope at his home.

B MINUS

He opened his darknet site to find new security protocols in place. The Foundation had been transformed into a digital fortress. Impregnable, unbreakable, unlike anything he'd seen before.

In a new chat board under the name 'B-', he found them waiting.

YOUR PEOPLE ARE REAL. FOUNDATION MAY BE GOOD.

He tapped out a response. I'M GLAD YOU THINK SO.

IS ALL VERY LOOSE NOW. They replied. PERHAPS WE CAN HELP. PERHAPS WE CAN JOIN THIS GROUP OF MISFITS.

YOU'LL BE VERY WELCOME.

OF COURSE WE WILL. NOW, WHERE SHOULD WE BEGIN?

Wren flexed his fingers and typed the challenge he'd been facing for months. I NEED A LOCATION FOR THE BLUE FAIRY.

LOL, they'd responded. BLUE FAIRY HAS NO PHYSICAL LOCATION. THEY ARE RAW DARKNET.

SO SQUEEZE THE DARKNET UNTIL IT BLEEDS. DO WHATEVER IT TAKES. ARE YOU THE BEST OR NOT?

Moments passed.

WE WILL SEE.

Within a month of hunting, they discovered the Minsk facility, prompting Wren's raid. Then it had blown up, taking his whole squad with it.

He hadn't been able to contact the hackers since.

Now, the phone answered.

"Christopher, you are in Idaho." It was Hellion's voice, young but sharp, strongly accented by her Bulgarian background. "Why?"

38

BACKDOOR

"I'm chasing a lead on the Blue Fairy," Wren explained, getting right into the meat of it. "I'm in a server room in a dungeon, looking at a junction box just like Minsk. It's gotta be wired to explode if I touch anything."

A few seconds passed. "So touch nothing. What is problem? Just walk out of room, yes?"

That was these hackers all over. Wren shook his head, though they wouldn't see it. "No. I need to get into this server, Hellion, but I don't want to die. Can you help me?"

A few seconds passed. "Most probably we can. Will we? I do not know. Minsk was very disappointing, Christopher."

"It was my squad that died."

"Yes, very disappointing outcome. We do not wish to be disappointed again."

Hellion could be infuriating. "They threatened my kids, Hellion. I don't have a choice."

She sighed, like children at risk was tiresome. "One moment. I will ask B4cksl4cker."

The line muted. Wren listened to the hum of the servers' cooling fans around him. Somewhere very far away, two child-like, god-like hackers were deciding his fate.

"Christopher!" came the deep burr of B4cksl4cker's voice, sounding every bit like the giant bear of a man he was. "What pleasure this is."

"Thanks, B4cksl4cker. I'm on the clock here."

"Ah yes, Blue Fairy." He tutted. "Very dark. We do not wish to see you explode." A moment passed. "This would be very disappointing."

"That's what Hellion said. I don't want to explode either. So help me."

"I suppose we will," Hellion came back in. "Save conversion of Christopher Wren to pink mist until there is 4K camera nearby."

Wren grunted. To Hellion and B4cksl4cker, life and death issues were very distant, almost unreal. The only thing that consistently worked with them was a tone of cynical disinterest.

"Nice to know you care."

"I do not. B4cksl4cker may, but he is gentle soul. Now, do you have hard-link access to servers?"

"Like via a cable? I'm afraid I left my hacker kit in my other pants."

"Always underprepared," Hellion said, sounding bored. "Then we will do this wirelessly. I am taking control of your phone." Wren looked at the screen and saw a band of color rippling across it. Hellion had pulled this trick several times before; hacking his devices while he watched. "Done. Activating Bluetooth and near-field radio frequencies. Scanning. Hmm. There are no open nodes."

"So you can't get in?"

"Not without open node. Perhaps one of servers has switch for wireless access."

"Hellion!" chastised B4cksl4cker. "This could trigger explosion."

"Many things are possible," Hellion allowed.

"Do not risk this, Christopher. Better option is to find wireless backdoor, could be additional device, perhaps hardwired to current network, with open or accessible wireless Bluetooth node. Could be earbud headphones, speaker, fitness watch, keyboard, many things. We can enter system through this."

"There's nothing here," Wren said, looking around again. "Just the servers. There's cables, but-"

He froze as a thought struck him.

"What is it?"

"One moment," he said, then tucked the phone into his pocket and squeezed back out of the server room, re-entering the red room. The diorama remained, only slightly disturbed by his fit of rage earlier. Smashed cameras lay around the space. He sped from one to the next, picking them up then putting them down.

There were six in total, and five he'd destroyed completely. Their screens were blank, but all remained attached to black power and data cables which led back along the corridor to the server room.

The last camera was operational. He handled it gingerly, like unexploded ordnance.

"I think we are in pocket," came Hellion's voice, muted from his phone. "Sounds like very stuffy, very stupid pocket."

Wren brought up the camera's settings, scrolled through swiftly, and found what he was looking for. He pulled out the phone.

"I'm holding a camera that's hard-linked to the computer system."

"Camera?" came Hellion's voice. "Why camera?"

"The Pinocchios here were streaming video through the computer and up via a satellite scoop. It has Bluetooth. Shall I enable it?"

"This will allow us access," Hellion said. "Also may

trigger explosive junction box. Are you near bomb, Christopher?"

"Not so near."

"Shame. B4cksl4cker, are you ready?"

"Yes."

"We are ready. Push button, Christopher."

"It's really more of an icon," he said, then tapped it.

No explosion came, other than Wren's heart slamming hard inside his chest.

"Ahah!" came B4cksl4cker's voice. "Yes."

"You're in?"

"We are in. Most excellent backdoor, Christopher. Working. Routing around encryption. Locating livestream line to satellite scoop. Claiming. Beginning upload of material."

"Ah," came Hellion's voice.

"What is it?"

"Seems we have triggered latent security system. Servers are now auto-wiping. Timer has begun. Junction box will explode in ten seconds or less. Advise you get out immediately, Christopher."

Wren was already running.

He was halfway down the final narrow corridor when the bomb blew, smashing him forward into the concrete steps on a blast wave of fire, force and shrapnel. The explosion was ear-splitting and the impact stunning, but Wren scrabbled up into the den just as a second wave of detonations began; each deeper and altogether more disturbing than the last.

He found his feet beside the ruined couch, charged at one of the shattered windows and dived through it just as the house collapsed around him, dropping into the hellish crater Lance Gebhart had gouged into the earth.

39

SHALLOW GRAVE

Wren and Rogers stood side-by-side on the scrubby gravel looking over the wreckage of the Gebharts' farmhouse, sunk into its own shallow grave.

Shards of wood spiked upward from the debris heap, amidst mangled lines of pipe, ducting and electrical cable. Wiring sparked and water sprayed in several places like a tumbledown fountain.

Rogers cursed.

"I'm fine, thanks," Wren said.

She turned to look at him. "You cut it close. Your forearm's bleeding, by the way."

Wren brought up his right arm. There was a gash across the outside edge where he'd caught his own weight against the stairs. "It's OK."

"So what happened?"

"Let me find out." He brought up the phone and held it to his ear. "Tell me you got something."

"You are alive," said Hellion flatly, sounding almost disappointed.

Wren looked at Rogers then away. "B4cksl4cker?"

"We are assessing, Christopher," came the big man's bass voice. "Uplink was very strong. In brief time, we have retrieved over three hundred gigabytes of data. Of course, all is encrypted. We are beginning decryption, but this may prove impossible. At minimum, will take time."

Wren breathed out. They'd gotten something, at least. "Why impossible? And how long?"

"Many factors come into encryption. Good code is impossible to crack. Is this good code? I do not know. One hour, maybe, to crack? One year? We cannot say. We are best, of course. No one will do this faster, if can be done."

"I believe it. Thank you. Let me know the instant you have something."

"We have something now," B4cksl4cker said. "Single image, perhaps this was screensaver or desktop background. Un-encrypted, at surface level of digital storage."

"Let me see it."

"Sending."

Wren's phone chimed and an image appeared and auto-full-screened itself.

It was a map.

It showed a flattened globe with hundreds of fine lines arcing across the oceans in a scratchy, riotous rainbow; a layout Wren recognized at once.

Rogers leaned over to look at his screen.

"Shipping routes," he said. "But what does it mean?"

"I do not know," B4cksl4cker replied. "Hellion?"

"Also unclear. But image like this, peeking head through encryption like last survivor of shipwreck? It is important. Screensaver is something you wish to see many times, again and again."

Wren zoomed in on the map. There were hundreds of curving lines. "Maybe smuggling routes," he muttered. "Human traffickers often use giant freight ships, stowing their cargo in large metal container boxes." He looked at Rogers. "Maybe Gebhart was shipping in containers full of children?"

Rogers brow pulled tight. "Was or is, via the Blue Fairy?"

That reality thudded hard into Wren's chest. "Maybe is."

"From where?"

Wren scanned the map. No one route or set of routes stood out. "Could be any of these. Refugees from wars in Africa or the Middle East. Families displaced by escalating gang violence in South America. Young people fleeing religious persecution in China. It could be all of them."

"To sell in America? So Pleasure Island's the habitation facility once they land? Maybe the auction site?"

The cool simplicity of that hit Wren like a punch in the lip. "Maybe. Yes."

"And taking Clara Baxter there is, what, a way to drum up business?"

Wren nodded. "Yeah. The Pinocchios despise her more than anything. Killing her on their livestream would be like ringing the bell at the New York Stock Exchange. Maybe bigger. Like the ball drop at New Year's in New York. It would change everything, signal a sea change in the order of global child trafficking, with the Blue Fairy planting themselves firmly above all competitors."

Rogers cursed. "You already said this is a celebration. Now with dozens of catfishers dead, they just made America safer than ever for Pinocchios to operate. They're really coming out into the light."

Wren nodded, working through that. Gebhart's system had outlived him by far, becoming an unstoppable juggernaut made up of members constantly driving themselves to greater depths of depravity: more pics, more gifs and more video.

"That's his vision," he said. "Gebhart. He designed the Blue Fairy to take on a life of its own. The Pinocchios who feed his beast rise up. The moderates get left behind. I've seen this kind of thing before, Sally, and it only ends in one way."

"It's a death cult," she whispered. "Spiraling toward an implosion."

"And it'll damn us all if we don't stop it now."

For a long moment neither spoke. Wren looked again at the map. Then he swiped sideways to the timer.

8:05:26.

Just over eight hours left.

"This has got to be what the countdown celebrates," he said. "A new shipment of children. Maybe a new facility to auction them in."

"A container ship could bring in hundreds. Thousands."

Wren's mouth ran dry. "And thousands of ships to choose from. Tens of thousands, I expect, at any one time on the ocean. We-"

"This is matter we will look into," Hellion interrupted sharply, clearly bored with the conversation. "Encryption may give answers. We will be in touch, Christopher."

"Wait," B4cksl4cker said. "Christopher, will we receive additional coins for this?"

Wren couldn't stop a small smile. His Foundation worked on a coin system, like AA, except higher coin rankings led to benefits such as greater access to Wren himself, as well as membership in higher coin circles.

"I could possibly-"

"I do not care about coins," Hellion interrupted again.

"Coins will buy prizes," B4cksl4cker countered.

"We have half billion dollars," Hellion snapped back. "We can buy prizes."

"Christopher?"

"Yes! It's possible. Get me usable intel on Gebhart's specific shipping route and you'll get a coin each."

"Sold!" said B4cksl4cker enthusiastically, then more quietly. "Half billion dollars cannot buy coins, Isabel."

"Coins are joint figment of your imagination," Hellion spat and cut the line.

Wren let the phone drop by his side.

The after-effect of adrenaline was setting in now, leaving him drained and weary. A hot trickle down his back made him think he'd pulled some stitches loose. Ahead, across the mountain flanks a pale sliver of sun was rising, sending streamers of light through the cold dawn fog. They looked oddly beautiful in that dark place.

He looked back at Rogers. She wore a mixed expression.

"B4cksl4cker," she said. "Hellion. I recognize those names."

Wren said nothing. She already had enough to court-martial him.

"We wanted them for the Blue Fairy task force," she went on. "It led nowhere, you said."

Wren's lips tightened. "I may have recruited them directly, after all other approaches failed."

Rogers scowled. "With coins? For your Foundation?"

"They were never going to work for the CIA, Sally."

"So now they work for you?"

He squinted. "I think calling them employees would be stretching it."

Rogers looked like she wanted to say more, but bit it back with a sigh, and returned her gaze to the collapsed house. Something shifted, and a swathe of tiles on a portion of roofing lost their grip, cascading in a ceramic waterfall to drum into unseen metal dregs below.

"It's good it blew up," she said

Wren took a deep breath and let it out slowly. "Yeah."

For a moment they just stood. The sun rose a little higher

in the sky, casting their fuzzy shadows across the crumbled structure; the location of so much misery for Clara Baxter.

"We need to call this in," she said. "Start putting together matrices of global container ships on these routes. Humphreys is going to want to know the source of the intel, but we can finesse that. We can also-"

She kept talking, but Wren's mind wandered as he looked over the collapsed house and decrepit pig enclosures. With the sun rising higher, the bleached-white bones of pigs emerged from the shadows, lying half-coated in mud and interleaved with bright green weeds.

It was strange, like the tombstones laid out in the Arizona desert. So many dark secrets, hidden in plain sight.

Then it hit him.

"Pleasure Island," he said abruptly.

Rogers stopped whatever she was saying. "What about it?"

Wren caught her eyes. It was perfect. The kind of thing you'd never look twice at, buried in paperwork and global shell companies; able to appear then disappear just like the Blue Fairy on the darknet, never questioned, never nailed down, always in motion.

"Pleasure Island is the ship."

40

SHIP

Rogers' jaw dropped slightly. "Pleasure Island's the container ship? I suppose with the shipping lines, it could be..."

"It's more than that," Wren raced on, trying to catch up with the thought. "It's the Blue Fairy all over, it's Lance Gebhart right down to his DNA. He built a network on the darknet that no one could find, and a dungeon in his backyard no one even knew existed, but all along he was dreaming of a way to bring it all into the light."

"On a ship?"

Now Wren saw it stretching ahead clearly. "Out there in international waters, cruising unseen, unwatched, they could do anything, Sally. No law, no police, no FBI, no government. He uses the ocean as the darknet of the world. A freight ship can pop up then disappear at will, dump the used-up bodies of kids at sea, host as many Pinocchios as they want and nobody would ever know."

Rogers' jaw dropped a little further, matched by the light of mounting rage in her eyes. "Gebhart would've loved that. All his sick Pinocchio freaks would."

"A place where they could act out their sickest fantasies,

without fear of being caught. Pleasure Island, alone on the dark ocean. This is it, Sally."

She nodded with increasing vigor. "Yeah. I buy it. I'm sold, Boss."

"And these container ships, they're vast. Tens of thousands of containers, like a small city, enough room to store all the kids they could ever want, to host countless Pinocchios. This is Gebhart's ultimate dream, finally coming to fruition."

"Then that's what it's all for," Rogers said, picking up the thread and running with it. "The celebration, the recruitment of fresh Pinocchios, even killing the catfishers!" Her eyes widened. "And most of all, the capture of Clara Baxter."

Wren nodded along. It was all coming together now. "When you launch a new ship, you smash a bottle on the hull." He paused a moment. "Clara Baxter is that bottle."

Wren felt like he was in free-fall on the far side of a long drop, but Rogers was right there with him, her eyes flaring with the thrill of the hunt.

"She's the bottle," she confirmed.

"Her death starts a new age of impunity, christening their launch at 5 p.m. sharp. That's in," he checked the countdown timer on his phone. "Eight hours. Around five years to the day that Gebhart would've died."

"It's their anniversary," Rogers snarled. "Their July 4th."

"We can't let it happen."

They both fell silent as this new information settled over them.

"We need to find that ship," Rogers said.

Wren nodded firmly then brought up his phone. "You call MacAuley, have her start scouring every cargo record and ship manifest we have at the state and federal level. Get the rest from Interpol or wherever, along with sites of origin and lists of every single container aboard. We'll want satellite overwatch at harbors, off coastal waters, plus any movement DeVore's made toward a major port." He stopped sharply then, and turned to look at her. "Wait. DeVore's the key. He's got to be their highest-profile recruit. If any of these new Pinocchios are going to Pleasure Island, it's him. He was headed for the East Coast; where is he now?"

Rogers checked the GPS app. It took agonizing seconds to load, then she looked wide-eyed up at Wren. "Philadelphia. All three Micro Hornet trackers have been stationary for the last forty-five minutes."

"That's it!" Wren barked. "A container ship off Philadelphia. Find it, Sally."

"On it, Boss. What about you?"

"I'll get us there."

He called Humphreys' direct line and this time the Director answered swiftly.

"Christopher, at last," he said, his deep voice sounding strained. "I just heard that your plane put down on a highway in Idaho. What did we say about regular updates? Where have you been?"

"In Lance Gebhart's underground dungeon getting blown up. We're both fine. But listen, Gerald, I need you to redirect that squad of Marines to Philadelphia, and send a chopper out to fetch us and jet us the same way."

A few seconds passed. "Philadelphia?"

"Yes. We've just uncovered evidence that Clara Baxter was born as Mona Gebhart, and her father was the originator of the Blue Fairy. She killed him then went after his network; that's why they wanted her. Our working theory is that Pleasure Island is a container ship headed for, or already moored off, Philadelphia, because that's where Charles DeVore is now. We've got eight hours before they launch us into a new era of unprecedented, unaccountable abuse on the darknet of the world's oceans, beginning with the livestreamed death of Clara Baxter."

A moment passed as Humphreys absorbed that. "What is all this based on, Christopher? It sounds like supposition."

"It's based on a map, a hunch and a deep understanding of how these bastards think. If that's not enough, my team also uplifted a vast amount of intel off Gebhart's computers before the place came down like Minsk. Set everything up and I'll have solid evidence for you before the strike hits. We'll nail this thing down; we just need presidential authorization to strike the ship with extreme prejudice."

Another second passed. "You're talking about a kill order."

"Anybody on that ship deserves to die."

Humphreys did not sound impressed. "Only if you're right. Only if all these guesses ring true. There's a lot of hope in that plan, Agent Wren."

"It springs eternal, Gerald. Within eight hours, that's all it'll take; that's all I'm asking for. Get me on board before the time counts down and we'll end this for good."

Humphreys took a shuddery breath. "Eight hours. All right, maybe I can do that. But I need proof. I can't get the President to sign off on a kill order without it."

"You'll have it."

Keys clacked in the background. "Very well. Resolve this, Wren. Do you even know how many more catfishers have died while you were playing farm out in Idaho?"

Wren's heart sank. "How many?"

"It's close to a hundred now. A hundred citizens tortured to death, with almost a dozen law enforcement officers lost in three separate suicide blasts. Three! All that, and we haven't got a single Pinocchio in custody. Turn that around or we're all going to pay. I'm sending a helo for you from Yellowstone

Airport. You'll be on a jet in fifteen minutes. Get me that evidence."

The line died. Wren looked at Rogers.

"MacAuley's working up a list of container ships in and around Philadelphia," she said. "It's in the hundreds."

Wren nodded numbly, looking at the Gebhart farmhouse for a final time. As if on cue, a sparking cable finally caught fire. The flames licked hungrily over the house's exposed innards, dried out after five years exposed to the mountain winds of Idaho, finishing the job Gebhart's daughter had begun.

Within minutes the whole tinderbox was an inferno.

"Payback for Redford," Rogers said, beside him. "So the Gebharts burn in their own private hell."

"There's no payback big enough for what they did," Wren said, feeling the adrenaline come on again, pumping him full of fury. He was done with Lance Gebhart and his grotesque dream of the Blue Fairy. It was time to rip it all down.

41

HACKERS

The helo came and the jet was waiting on the airstrip at Yellowstone Airport. The Marines from California were there already, fully kitted up with rifles and a crate of gear.

Wren shook hands with their captain, Brick Callahan; a wiry, rugged man in his mid-thirties with a weathered face and steel-gray eyes.

"Six hours," Wren said, leading the way on board the jet, a Gulfstream G280, capable of three and a half thousand nautical miles on one fueling, easily enough to take them to Philadelphia. "Thanks for coming."

"The nation's under attack," Callahan said simply, like that explained everything.

The G280 was bigger than the Cessna and decked out for luxury, but with Callahan's six-strong squad, their packs and their gear crate, it felt tight.

Wren sat in the back across from Rogers, listening to Hellion and B4cksl4cker chatter in his earpiece as they worked to crack Lance Gebhart's encryption. The jet took off and reached cruising altitude in minutes.

"DeVore's still static," Rogers said. "We're down to two blips, though."

"Show me."

Rogers held out her phone. Two trackers blipped at the edge of the Delaware River, and Wren zoomed in. They were on what looked to be derelict industrial land near Philaport, the Port of Philadelphia.

"That's got to be his Firebird," Wren said. "I dotted it with two Micro Hornets, one in the scoops, one in the wheel well. The third one's in him, but he's got to be out of range."

Rogers cursed. "I'll send local forces to check it. Maybe we can-"

"Belay that," Wren said. "We can't do anything to tip our hand. If even one Pinocchio is left watching his vehicle, they'll know we're coming. They'll get spooked and run. We'll never find Pleasure Island again."

Rogers cursed louder. "So we just let him go?"

"He's already gone. We can narrow this down with what we've got. Get onto CCTV overlooking the river, all remotely. Maybe we can find his route, his transport craft, something. There's no way they'd bring the ship up to the port."

"They're in the open ocean."

"Definitely. Work on satellite oversight, add drones where they'll go unobserved. I want a silent flock in the air scouring every inch of the Philly coast."

"On it."

Wren looked out the window as the G280 roared east. The sun beamed down over a new dawn. Across America, millions were waking up to the chaos wrought upon them in the night: the most vicious series of murders in modern history.

And it wasn't over yet.

Wren brought up the shipping map and stared at it. He brought up everything he had, every scrap of evidence they'd gathered over the past two days, and sifted through it looking for the one clue they needed to nail down Pleasure Island.

After three hours in the air, with the jet somewhere over Indiana and his eyes blurring from reading and re-reading every intel report he could get, the constant low chatter from Hellion and B4cksl4cker in Wren's ear sharpened.

He immediately tuned in, but they were talking too fast in Russian for him to follow, though the urgent tones were clear.

"What's happening, B4cksl4cker?" he asked.

Rogers turned at the name, and Wren hit speakerphone, allowing B4cksl4cker's voice to bark from the speakers.

"Christopher, apologies, I am most occupied. Speak with Hellion."

"Hellion, give me a report," Wren said.

Hellion's audio clicked in louder, backed by the rapid-fire blattering of keys. "We took leaf from Gebhart's book, Christopher, or his daughter's." She sounded energized, clearly caught in the adrenaline throes of an epic hack. "Cryptography is too difficult to break, so we have taken sideways step into metadata."

"Metadata?"

"Uplink analytics, Christopher. Gebhart had satellite scoop that fed into darknet in way we have never seen before. Very clever. Metadata, data describing bandwidth used, router ID, timestamps; this cannot be so easily encrypted, so we are searching here. Details are unclear, but wider records suggest fifteen years ago Gebhart hacked weather satellites."

Wren looked over at Rogers. "Weather satellites?"

"Yes. There are thousands in orbit, run by NASA over North America, with capability to take high-resolution images of cloud cover, track storms, many other things, but typically not connected to Internet. From this metadata, it seems Gebhart wired in genius backdoor to Internet. Very high level of sophistication. I do not believe he could do this himself. This data signature, access required, it looks like he had considerable help."

"Helped by who?"

"Impossible to say. If I guess, based on similar code we saw from Order of the Saints, you will jump to conclusions."

Wren's stomach went cold. "You're suggesting Gebhart knew my father. Apex of the Pyramid?"

Silence for a moment. "Or they used same hackers. Very professional, many assets in place. Many millions spent to achieve this."

Wren stared at the gray wall of clouds outside the window, momentarily floored. All this time he'd pushed aside the potential link to his father; the fact that the Blue Fairy image itself may not have originated with Gebhart. At the outset of this odyssey to take them down, he'd learned that his father had once carved that marker into the bunks of children, back in the fake town over twenty-five years ago.

"My father's dead," he said flatly. "At best, you're talking about his copy cat's infrastructure."

"Don't care," Hellion answered. "Could also be nation-state, such as Russia, China, North Korea. Many have resources to fund this, along with access to satellite systems. Dark money and darknet ability."

Wren grunted. "Does it help us locate Pleasure Island?"

"Perhaps. I do not know. This hack is most elegant, Christopher. Beautiful, even, but should have been discovered in one of numerous updates to 'weathernet' since, but we believe Clara Baxter has taken responsibility. She has been upgrading. So, Gebhart's private darknet network stayed invisible, with only one access route."

"Gebhart's supercomputer."

"Now destroyed. All we have is partial record with no decryption key, but there is still more to learn."

Wren's heart rate was climbing. "Tell me it's the location."

"Possibly location, yes!" She sounded annoyed. "Metadata may also tie into existing Blue Fairy servers. They would not know it, as Gebhart built many backdoors. B4cksl4cker, are we..."

She trailed off.

"What?" Wren prompted.

"There," said Hellion, distracted. "Things are happening fast, Christopher. I am going to-"

"Don't cut me off, Isabel! Tell me everything you see."

Hellion said nothing for several seconds then began a disjointed running commentary over the racing of her keys. "We are hacking into Blue Fairy, Christopher. Encryption remains, but they may know we are here. They are back-tracing. I am running reverse cryptoworm. We should..."

"Hellion, don't let them know-"

"Running analysis on their data streams," she bulled on, "I have something. B4cksl4cker thinks it is first piece in Blue Fairy re-routing algorithm!" A pause as keys rattled manically, prosecuting invisible espionage. "We could never find them before. This is why; they learned tricks from Gebhart, but it looks like he did not give them his weathernet. Instead..."

"Hellion, stop what you're doing if it'll compromise our-"

"Here!" she shouted. "OK, I am seeing … there are countless information streams … they should not be able to carry this kind of data. Webs … like weathernet: I see earthquake warning systems … networked buoys … GPS satellites … even piggy-backed signals on radio and television. We never thought to look for it before because..."

She trailed off again. Wren looked up to find Rogers and the Marine squad all listening rapt.

"Routing is astounding," Hellion barked. "We have never seen something like this. I have outline of Blue Fairy's organization, Christopher! I see self-reinforcing authority systems ... democratic gamification long before it was popular ... like and dislike voting systems with unbreakable anonymity. He had all this fifteen years ago! I think Gebhart was truly genius, Christopher, to create this system! He died nine years ago and his system is still in operation."

Wren tried to make sense of that. Self-reinforcing authority? Democratic gamification? "What does any of that mean? How does it help us find-"

"It is crowd-sourced," Hellion interrupted, clearly delighted with her discovery and high on the battle. "Like social media algorithm. People enter his system and vote with likes. These votes raise up influencers, powerful people in Blue Fairy system. These influencers then carry more weight than others; they get deeper access and greater powers. This is gamification, makes competitive game of media content. So system builds and refreshes leadership cabal constantly, based on contribution and voting." A pause. "It means there is no single or fixed leader for entire Blue Fairy. Just members fighting for influence, with all decisions crowd-sourced to masses in votes. This is kind of meritocratic democracy; more votes per person weighted to value."

Wren blinked. He was familiar with such structures, primarily from social media, and Hellion's enthusiasm had his attention now.

"What determines value in this system?"

"Video and photographic files," Hellion answered. "I cannot see actual content now, only outlines, but I can see ranks and shifts."

Wren knew what that meant. They'd known for years that PICS, GIFS and VIDEO were the lifeblood of the Blue Fairy. A strong PIC had been enough to get DeVore invited into the inner circle.

"Does any of it lead to Pleasure Island? We need a location."

232

"I cannot say this yet. We are not close enough. They are fighting back."

Wren weighed the risks. After three hours of scouring, he had nothing; no way to identify Pleasure Island from the air, from its records, from anything. If he let the hackers keep up their attack, would it tip off the Blue Fairy that he was coming?

"Can you find it through this system?"

"Working."

"That's all that matters, Hellion." Wren's mind raced ahead, darting to the worst case scenario. "If you can't find that, I'm going to need you to drop a ransomware bomb, enough to scramble the Blue Fairy beyond comprehension."

"Scramble it?" Hellion shot back, sounding exhilarated. "This system is thing of beauty! Truly incredible resource, Christopher. We can learn-"

"It's a poisoned chalice, Hellion," Wren snapped. "All that matters is finding them, and if we can't find them, then we drain the names of any Pinocchios you can then destroy their network."

"Not possible!" She sounded dismayed.

"Break them, blind them and rip them apart. I don't care how beautiful their system is. B4cksl4cker, I know you're listening too. You get a location and names then burn these bastards to the ground."

Neither Hellion or B4cksl4cker replied, and a pause stretched out. Wren felt the hackers' gears turning.

"You do not command us, Christopher Wren," Hellion said, her voice turning deadly calm but with deep anger bubbling beneath the surface. "You should know this by now."

Wren gritted his teeth, fully aware where this rebellion could lead. Hellion was fickle to begin with, and had always taken more convincing than B4cksl4cker. Perhaps the draw of

Gebhart's weathernet and the Blue Fairy's gamification would make her pull the plug on him forever.

"You don't care about coins, I get that," he said, trying to head her off. "You're a god on the Internet, and this weathernet would make you invincible. I understand the appeal, but the cost is too high, Isabel. It's a deal with the devil, a power that will only corrupt. It's why the coin system exists, because temptations like this are very real."

She scoffed. "Coin system is for control. For you. Not for us."

Wren opened his mouth to argue, but nothing came out. She was almost completely wrong, but it would do no good to argue that, because on some level she was also right. It was why Humphreys called Wren a cult leader, and why the hackers had called him a cultist, and why he kept the Foundation a secret from his CIA handlers.

A group like the Foundation required one hand at the tiller, somebody to steer them according to a guiding principle, and that person was Wren. He made the judgments. He brought new members in, and handed out the coins, and took away coins when necessary. He guided his members because he felt he knew what was best for them, but that was undoubtedly a form of control.

"What do you want?" he asked.

"What do I want?" She sounded surprised.

"Let's talk turkey. What will it take for you to work with me on this?"

A second passed. "With you. This is key, Christopher. Not for you."

Wren shot Rogers a glance, but she shook her head; she had no answers. He strained for a way forward, considering ideas then dismissing them rapidly, until finally he saw it; the thing that would get them through this, and a bizarre thing to learn from the 'genius' Lance Gebhart and his gamified system.

"So put me on a coin," he said. "Make the Foundation more like the Blue Fairy; no central authority, just a driving principle. Build influencers in the Foundation who help determine our direction, but reward something better than pics and video. It's got to have growth, integrity and responsibility at the core. "

No answer came. Wren wasn't quite sure what he'd just suggested, but he felt the ramifications stretching out ominously.

"Hellion?"

"Deal," she said at last, sealing the covenant. "We will do this. You will be on coin like all else in Foundation. Authority will be earned, not granted."

"And you'll break the Blue Fairy, when we're done hunting for Pleasure Island?"

"If we can inject cryptoworm, we will. Changes will come swiftly, Christopher. Be prepared."

42

A WAY IN

The Gulfstream jet soared through blue skies over rural Indiana, and for thirty minutes Wren hadn't taken his eyes off the weathernet connection.

Still there was nothing. No breakthrough from Hellion and B4cksl4cker. No answers from CCTV along the Delaware River. His eyes were blurry from scanning countless darknet feeder boards, the kind of places Pinocchio-wannabes gathered hoping for their invite to the Blue Fairy. He felt numb from the images he'd seen, not least among them being the fake PIC he'd produced using DeVore's family.

It was everywhere now, doubtless cementing DeVore's place as an influencer aboard Pleasure Island, but there wasn't a single thread leading deeper.

He checked the countdown timer. Barely five hours remained until Clara Baxter shattered against the hull of a container ship on the open ocean, after which Pleasure Island would be gone.

The trail would be filled with cold, dead catfishers.

He put his phone down and looked at Rogers. "Where are we on ship records?"

She turned to him and dropped her phone from her ear. She hadn't stopped calling and coordinating with Robin MacAuley and their team for hours.

"We're down to twenty-five potentials, Boss. Big freighters, tankers or container ships in the waters off Philly with records we can't fully trust. There's hundreds out there in range of a small transport boat, but most of them check out. We know exactly where they came from, exactly what they have on board; some we've even spoken with their captains and had them run tours of their cargo holds."

"What?"

"It's OK," Rogers said, holding up a hand, "apparently that's standard operating procedure for the Port Authority and the Coastguard, it happens all the time, not enough to tip anyone's hand, and entirely voluntary. Every one we checked was clean."

Wren let out a heavy breath. "Leaving twenty-five. What do we know?"

Rogers brought her phone back up and checked it. "Functionally they're identical. Big ships, ranging from a thousand containers to twenty thousand to tankers holding two million barrels of oil. With ships like these, they're never done with their trawling. Some come from east, some west, they drop some goods off at Philly, they pick some up, but they never stop."

"What kind of freight?"

"Everything from black gold to Iowa beets. Doubtless some are covers for smuggling; could be drugs, unrelated human trafficking, even exotic animals, but there's no way to know. All of the twenty-five have records that don't quite pass muster, or they jump through the hoops of too many shell companies, obscuring their controlling interest. So which one is Pleasure Island?"

Wren cursed. "Can we start rolling up to them one by one? Would the others know?"

"Some are in eye-shot of others. Others are talking to each other all the time. There's a loose criminal cabal out there, a smugglers' code, if you will. We could start on-the-spot inspections, like we did with the others, but the risk rises that we'll tip them off. We want to avoid that, right?"

"Right. So..." Wren thought, but nothing occurred. "Twenty five."

"Twenty five," Rogers repeated.

"How do we narrow that down?"

"Short of getting Charles DeVore to call us on a satellite phone and tell us his coordinates? Or the hackers breaking through and sending up a digital flare? I don't know."

Wren churned that over. There had to be a way in. Maybe there was something they hadn't tried.

"Good work. Keep checking the records. Maybe we can trim the number further."

"On it."

Wren tuned into the constant ebb and flow of conversation between Hellion and B4cksl4cker. "Where are we up to, B4cksl4cker?"

"Cryptoworm is ready, Christopher," B4cksl4cker replied smartly. "Tailored perfectly for Blue Fairy. We know their structure. We can crack them, own them, locate them, destroy them, but we need entrance point."

"There's no way in through the weathernet?"

"Not through this cryptography. Not inside. We need internal attack vector."

"What about phishing access?"

"Not possible; we have tried. Only things allowed into Blue Fairy are brought in by members. Influencers have higher rating. We cannot fake our way, Christopher. They also know we are watching them. They are being careful."

"So how? Do you have any ideas?"

"Asset on board," Hellion answered flatly. "Ravenous6. Use him."

Wren shook his head. "DeVore's a full convert, and he's out of reach. I don't have-"

Then Wren stopped as something occurred to him, something he couldn't quite grasp but that felt real.

"Christopher?" Hellion asked, but he barely heard, too focused on building out the thought. It grew out of his hours poring over chatboxes filled with men sharing PICS, GIFS and VIDEO, all hoping to climb the same mountain as Charles DeVore, producing content vile enough to earn them a place on-

Then he had it.

It hit like a car wreck, clashing and raucous and bloody, but it brought everything full circle. Back to catfishing, back to PICS, back to the Blue Fairy and to Charles DeVore.

But it could work. It could be the key that cracked open Pleasure Island.

"Video," he said.

"What about video, Christopher?" Hellion answered.

"It's better than pics, better than gifs, right? Video tops the Blue Fairy popularity listings."

"Of course, yes. This is obvious. Why-"

"And you can embed a cryptoworm in video, right? Make it switch on if it plays on a certain network?"

"Yes, of course, but we have tried this before. Blue Fairy has safeguards. Videos are screened intensively, we cannot get virus in this way, we-"

"What if it's the hottest video on the darknet? Unmissable and pre-approved. It only takes one Pinocchio to stream it without running every check, right?"

"Hmm. Is this possible? Perhaps. High popularity, past

approval, these may lead to human error, bypassing security protocols. Do you have such video, Christopher?"

"Not yet. But hold tight. I think I know how to get it."

He turned to Rogers, who was looking at him now. "What is it?"

"Ready for another re-enactment?"

She frowned. "Of what?"

"You're not going to like it. It's ugly. I'm going to need the number of the safe house holding DeVore's wife."

43

RE-ENACTMENT

Thirty minutes later, an FBI witness protection agent walked up the driveway to Amanda DeVore's safe house, carrying a videoscreen tablet streaming footage of Wren on the jet.

The agent knocked. Amanda DeVore answered.

Standing in the doorway of an unfamiliar home, she looked distraught, pale and worn. Her brown hair hung in lank curtains, her eyes were sunken and dark. Probably she hadn't slept. She'd barely had a chance to process what had happened to her or her girls. The mental scars would take a long time to heal.

"You," she said, when she saw Wren's face on the tablet screen. Her disheveled features warped into a defensive snarl, looking from the agent's face and back to Wren's. "What is this? What do you want?"

"I'm sorry to disturb you, Mrs. DeVore," Wren said, keeping one eye on Rogers, sitting beside him on the jet. He'd been right that she wouldn't like this; she'd encouraged him to proceed as softly as he could. "I need your help."

DeVore stared back at him. "My help? I thought you were calling to apologize."

"I do apologize," he said, and Rogers nodded approvingly. "What you went through yesterday was every parent's worst nightmare, and I know I made it worse. But the situation is changing rapidly. If you could listen-"

"Listen to you?" she barked. "The last time I listened to you, you traumatized my girls! They already thought they were going to die, and then..."

Wren listened as her rage and frustration spilled out. Time was counting down, only three hours remained on the clock with his jet was already over western Pennsylvania, but there was no choice but to wait.

Everything was already in motion.

B4cksl4cker was paving the way to use his entire botnet for a mammoth task of data crunching. Hellion was tapping up her contact list for the precise skillset required. Robin MacAuley was prepping the studio and gear they'd need.

All that remained was Amanda DeVore.

"We're done here," she finished. "I never want to speak to-"

"Your husband isn't alone," Wren interrupted, cutting her off before she could end the call. "He's part of a group called the Pinocchios; very sick and dangerous men. Perhaps you've seen their work on the news."

Perhaps ten seconds passed by. "I am not responsible for him or what he does," she said, her voice now sounding cold and dangerous.

"No, you're not, but you do have the power to stop him."

She shook her head. "No. I can't do any more. We're finis-"

"Clara Baxter was only seven years old when her father locked her in his backyard dungeon."

He said it fast enough to forestall her hanging up. Her eyes widened as the words entered her brain, giving Wren an opening.

"That's the same age as your daughters. The same as my daughter, Quinn." He studied her eyes. "I went to that dungeon, Amanda. I've seen it. Six cameras. All manner of vile equipment. This little girl lived there for nine years. Nine years. Neither of us can imagine the suffering and humiliation she endured in that time, but we don't need to, because her father recorded every second of it. He shared that with his Pinocchio friends. Men like your husband." He watched as her expression shifted toward anger. "But somehow, that little girl survived. At sixteen years old, she broke free, killed her father and started hunting men like him. Two nights ago your husband was her target."

Amanda DeVore took a sharp breath.

"Witting or not, he helped them take her, Amanda. Now she's in their dungeon again, and your husband is the big Pinocchio hero headed for the biggest party they ever held. If we don't do something, they're going to put that little girl back on camera and torture her in ways I don't want to think about, then kill her in the worst way possible, for all the world to see." He took a breath. "And that's just the beginning. Her death is just a starting gun for these people, trying to out-compete themselves with greater atrocities, in places we will never be able to find them." He searched her eyes. "I'm sorry to put this on you. You are not responsible for your husband, but right now we have the power to stop him. I need your help to do that, Amanda. I need your daughters' help."

Her mounting outrage dead-ended as surely as if she'd been slapped. "You need my daughters?"

Wren braced himself. Rogers was glaring at him; he'd gone way off-script already. "We need to take high-resolution photographs of all your faces. It'll be in a clean, bright studio, near where you are. It'll take moments only, and they need never know what it's for."

"What is it for?" she demanded.

"It's better if you don't know."

"It's my face," she shot back, beginning to slip back into the frantic terror of the basement. "It's my daughters' faces! I have a right to know."

Wren glanced at Rogers, who gave a slight shake of her head, but he couldn't stop now. He needed her trust, and that meant telling the truth.

"We'll construct deepfake versions of your faces in a computer," he began, "then we'll attach them digitally to actors in a studio that's rendered to look just like your basement. Like a Hollywood special effect. We'll put an actor playing your husband into that scene wearing a Pinocchio mask and set him loose. We'll film it, and use that footage to locate the Pinocchios' base, a huge container ship on the open ocean. We'll capture all the Pinocchios and rescue Clara Baxter, along with any other children on board."

Amanda DeVore's eyes shone and widened. She looked to either side like she was no longer safe, and a tear leaked down her right cheek. "Other children?"

"There could be hundreds on board, Amanda. All ages. Like your daughters. Like mine."

DeVore wiped her cheek but more tears followed in a stream. It was too much to take, Wren knew that, but there was no choice.

"'Set him loose'," DeVore whispered, her voice cracking. "What does that mean? What was he going to do?"

He shook his head. "I think you already know that. I think you've been reliving it all night. So please, don't ask for the details. They're bad things. A list of bad things these monsters wanted Charles to do. Things no one should ever do or see, that ends with all three of you dead in the basement of your home."

Amanda DeVore began to shake.

'Stop,' mouthed Sally Rogers, but Wren couldn't. This was the critical moment, and he focused on Amanda DeVore as tears streamed down her cheeks, hoping she would pull through it.

Perhaps half a minute passed in fraught silence.

Then something shifted. It reminded Wren of the way her husband had altered once he'd believed his family were dead, like he was becoming a new person. She straightened, the tears stopped coming, and she stared at the screen.

"And he'll be there?" Her voice was as brittle and cold as ice. "On this ship of monsters?"

"Charles DeVore. Yes."

She mustered herself, leaning into some new source of strength. She rubbed her eyes dry and stood tall. "Then I'll do it. But on one condition."

Wren was ready for this. Victims of abuse often went back to their abuser. "I can protect him, if that's what you want."

"I don't want you to protect him, Agent Wren. I want that man to never come home again. Not to any home, not to anywhere. Do you understand what I'm telling you?"

Wren did. He was surprised. It was a promise he wasn't authorized to make, absent the kill order Humphreys was still trying to obtain, but that didn't matter.

All that mattered was justice.

"Done," he said. "Charles DeVore does not leave that ship."

Rogers gritted her teeth. Amanda DeVore nodded. "I'll wake the girls. Take your photographs."

44

CRYPTOWORM

I t went quickly after that.

The studio was five minutes from the safe house, with twin rooms already prepared: one that was bright and airy, as promised, for headshots which took only another five minutes to complete; another with a green screen background to serve as the Canton basement.

DeVore and her daughters were in and out swiftly.

"We have received digital models," B4cksl4cker said. "Sending to deepfake render team to begin prep."

While they worked on making 3D models, a jury-rigged team of four volunteers drawn from local FBI and CIA agents were brought in as actors wearing green masks, upon which the digital faces of the DeVore family would be transplanted.

"Basement was dark," Hellion said in Wren's ear as the shoot began. "Will make digital effects easier. Also, camera does not move, with DeVore's body blocking visual much of time. Will be fast."

"How fast?"

"Once footage is complete? To render digital faces and fix digital background in convincing way? On normal computer this will take weeks."

"And you've got B4cksl4cker's botnet. How long?"

"One hour, maybe."

Wren shuddered. They were down to two and a half hours on the timer.

"And then to upload?"

"Upload is instant. We already have Charles DeVore's computer from FBI team, access to his darknet accounts, including Ravenous6. Video will seed on lesser known chat box. We expect, based on first photograph, viewership will explode. VIDEO is better than PIC, yes? Sequel is much better than original. Soon, it will be everywhere, even Pleasure Island. Perhaps thirty minutes, one hour to make this spread."

Wren sucked in a sharp breath. That gave them barely thirty minutes to play with.

"And you're confident it'll open the door to the Blue Fairy?"

"Cryptoworm code is embedded in video, Christopher. When first Pinocchio on Pleasure Island allows video in and streams playback, we will be inside. Cryptoworm will act instantly, sending up digital flare. We will receive this and geolocate, then follow protocol: drain Blue Fairy for names, break with cryptography, blind weathernet and destroy all darknet assets, leaving warm bodies in place for you to capture/kill."

Wren grunted. Thirty minutes.

"Now stop distracting me. I am prepping as your operator."

Wren didn't follow. "My operator?"

"You will need best. I am best."

It took Wren a few more moments to catch on. She was talking about being the voice in his ear, guiding him via intel and satellite and interpreting his bodycam footage.

"Wait, you're actually serious? You're a hacker, Hellion! Maybe you're great at video games, but this is the real world."

"Real world is easy. Video games are hard. I am operator, you will wear bodycam and earpiece, this is deal, yes?"

This was unprecedented. It was worse than demanding he enter the coin system, himself.

"Or what, you won't complete the hack?"

"That is my current feeling."

Wren gritted his teeth. She'd left this kicker until the last moment, until there was no way he could argue. It pissed him off, but if getting this done meant having Hellion in his ear, he could live with that. "Fine. But do not walk me into a death trap, Isabel."

"Whole ship is death trap. This is appeal of CIA, no?"

He almost laughed.

"Now I will work," she said.

The line died. Wren was left looking at Sally Rogers, who stared back at him intensely.

"You blew right through everything," she said. "Every guideline we talked about."

Wren took a breath. "I know. It seemed necessary."

"There's that choice again," Rogers said. "How far to push."

"Into the gray zone," Wren agreed. "How far we go to achieve our goal."

Rogers just looked at him. "It's like in Detroit. You manipulated Amanda DeVore like you manipulated the witness at the People Mover."

"I did."

"You pumped her up and made her feel responsible for her husband, even though you said she wasn't. You went for her emotionally. She was code for you to rewire."

Wren nodded. "Like I said, Sally. These are the tricks I've

got. Maybe I shouldn't use them. Maybe I'm going to pay. But right now, here we are."

"On track for Pleasure Island."

He nodded.

"Except we don't have the kill order."

Wren's jaw set. "You heard from Humphreys?"

"Yes. It came direct from the President. She doesn't want a massacre off the Philly coast, based off fruit of the poisonous tree."

"Fruit of the poisonous tree?"

"Evidence that would never stand up in court. This whole idea, the rigged-up deepfake video as a kind of catfish? It's morally deplorable, she said. It's a honeypot. It implicates all of us, and the President doesn't want that stink on her."

Wren studied Rogers. "You sound like you've taken a position."

"I have. I'll drop onto that ship with you, Boss. I'll kill the Pinocchios, if it proves necessary, right by your side. But I will never be OK with doing it."

Wren nodded, then reached out to put one hand on her shoulder. "That's why the zone's gray, Sally, not black. When we reach our hands into the darkness, it bites back. But we keep one eye on the light."

Rogers' eyes shone. "Now you're emotionally manipulating me."

"I'm just so good at it."

She snorted then laughed. "You're something, all right."

"So are you. We'll get this done for Clara Baxter, Sally, and if a boatload of creeps die along the way, I know I'll sleep better for it."

She shook her head. "No wholesale slaughter, Boss. No vigilante bullshit. This is not the time to go rogue."

"OK," Wren said. "Agreed."

"Swear to it. Only the ones who have to die, die. The rest go to jail and get their day in court."

Wren looked in her eyes and lied. "I swear."

45

FALL

Two hours later, Wren stood at the open door of the Gulfstream, fifteen thousand feet above the border shallows of the Atlantic Ocean, scouring for glimpses of the surface far below, fleetingly visible through drifting mists.

Weather fronts had collided east of Philadelphia; hot from the south, cold from the north, thickening into a wet fog that hung over the ocean and coast, obscuring the line where land met sea and making any kind of visual identification impossible. As ever, Pleasure Island sailed in a sea of uncertainty.

"You're sure it's down there," Wren said to Hellion, his voice carrying clearly through the flat mic strapped to his throat, despite the roar of the wind and the engines.

"We believe so," came her calm reply in his earpiece. "DeVore video has gone platinum aboard Blue Fairy. It is everywhere, and cryptoworm is rooting and spreading. We have their rough location, currently working on taking their servers. Soon we will drain, blind and break them."

Wren brought up his wristwatch. There was just less than

thirty minutes on the countdown timer. "Soon isn't soon enough."

"It will be. Once you are on board, we will use your phone to hijack local nodes on network. It will go faster then."

Wren grunted and looked down. Fifteen thousand feet to fall was a long way. Water was like cement, if you hit it from more than two hundred feet high. It didn't compress. It shattered anything coming in hard.

Wren squeezed the walls of the plane, leaning further out to graze the buffeting, freezing jet stream. Wind ripped at his clothing and tried to tug the air from his lungs. Free-fall for a minute thirty. The chute deployed for five seconds, ten at the outside, then release. He'd have to judge the height by eye; too low and he'd die on impact, too high and every second longer increased the chances of his deployed chute being seen, if anyone was there to see it.

Call it seven seconds under the parachute, followed by icy cold water.

His mouth was dry. He'd skydived many times before, tactical insertions with his Force Recon squad out of USSOCOM. Each time he'd come through unharmed, but never in mist, never with a mere seven-second deployment, never from fifteen thousand feet, without oxygen, into water.

He'd already checked the waterproof pack and gear three times, all supplied by local FBI and picked up at Philadelphia Airport; tactical knife, twin Sig Sauer P226 handguns with spare magazines, Twaron bulletproof vest, sat phone linked direct to the weathernet, magnetic clamp boots, dart gun, front and back body cams, throat-mic. One-man insertion was notoriously challenging. Only one pair of eyes on board had to raise the alarm for his chance to be lost, but his chance alone was better than a full squad of Marines dropping out of the sky.

His job was to take Pleasure Island's deck and clear the way.

He took a deep breath. Behind him Rogers and the Marines were waiting.

"Why not send in Marines in fast boats?" Rogers had argued an hour earlier. "We could lead the attack at the head of an army."

"Because of what they've done every other time we got close," Wren had said. "I don't think they'll wait around to be captured, do you?"

Her eyes had widened. "You think they'll kamikaze Pleasure Island? Blow the whole thing up just to stop us getting in?"

"If the alternative is being made to pay for their crimes? I believe it. You should too, Sally. We just have to move faster than they can. Blinding comms will help, but this is all about speed and silence."

Rogers had crossed herself. "Then God help us."

"It is here," came Hellion's voice in his ear. "Directly below, or as close as we can triangulate."

"I can't see anything," Wren said.

"Neither can satellites, but Pleasure Island is there, location confirmed two hours ago, when last mist cleared."

Wren took a breath. Every second now was wasting time. He turned, gave a thumbs up to Rogers in back, then leaned further out into the biting wind. Fifteen minutes in icy water and he'd be dead. If there was no ship down there, he'd hit that boundary fast. If the chute deployed a second out of place. If the Pinocchios saw him coming down. If Clara Baxter wasn't even there…

The engines screamed. After ten seconds he'd hit terminal velocity and gain maneuverability, be able to cover a mile or two horizontally in the minute remaining.

A hand came on his back. "You've got this, Boss." Rogers shouted over the wind.

He didn't turn. She was right, and there was nothing more to say. He pressed his goggles tight, stepped out into air and the wind yanked him away like a kite in a storm.

He tumbled and soared, counting the seconds as mist streamed over his cheeks, cutting and chilling. Nine seconds, ten, then he hit terminal velocity. He threw his arms back and his legs out and felt the wind catch him like he'd hit a steep slope on a sled, stabilizing his fall and propelling him forward like a loosed arrow.

Still there was nothing visible through the fog.

"Fifteen seconds," came Hellion's voice in his ear.

"Nothing yet."

"Scanning thermals. It is too thick. Get closer look."

Wren couldn't laugh for the icy wind buffeting his face.

"Twenty seconds."

Still nothing. Falling out of the sky like an avenging angel. A memory came to him; a girl he'd played with as a child in the Pyramid. Maybe eight years old behind the fake town, dancing together in the dust. A few captured pure moments of joy from all of that horror.

"Thirty seconds."

She'd been so pretty to him then. Not because of her face, but because of her smile. The way she'd laughed; to think that any kind of true, joyful happiness could exist in that place. The Apex had put her in a pit soon afterward, and she hadn't come back up again.

He hadn't thought of her for a long time. His eyes streamed in the goggles. Had his father marked her bunk with the Blue Fairy symbol? He'd never know. What had her name been? Grace, that was it. Just a child, trying to be a child. Maybe Maggie in the fake town had found her bird-like bones by now. Laid them to rest, trying to build something good from her death.

Wren couldn't feel anything but terrible rage.

"Forty seconds. Christopher, I think I see something through bodycam."

Wren felt like he was being guided by the hand of God. If only vengeance brought justice and peace. It had never brought either to Wren. Better to build than to burn, Maggie would say, but how did you let go?

"It is there, Christopher!"

He saw nothing. He yanked at the goggles, rubbing his eyes to clear them. The movement sent him into a slight roll but he corrected quickly.

"Where?"

"On thermal imaging, northeast at one mile distant, Pleasure Island."

Wren lowered his right arm slightly, lifted his left and felt the wind resistance drag him in a sweeping arc. Still he could see nothing. Fifty seconds? Almost there. Somewhere far off he heard the first explosions ring out.

Fireworks, blowing low in the mist several nautical miles away after they'd been tossed out of the jet, loud enough to drag all eyes in that direction.

"How far now?"

No answer came.

"Hellion?"

The wind roared. The signal must have cut out. Wren had forgotten the count. How high was he? How far to the ship? His hand swept to the parachute release; a modified skydive chute, cut for a more explosive deployment.

He had to be at more than a minute now, but still there was nothing. Still he coasted the fog like a skipped stone, soaring into gray with nothing to see but-

The mist parted like a fading dream, unveiling the ocean

below in a sudden blast of information: Pleasure Island hulking low in the water ahead, with a faded red and black hull and container boxes stacked ten high above the deck. Around it the choppy gray Atlantic breakers frothed with white, while black-clad figures with rifles spotted along the railing looked off to the left.

Just a few thousand feet now, thirty seconds until he hit; cut off ten for the chute to deploy, five to ride it, two more to drop, and he had thirteen seconds to work with.

One second gone already.

More fireworks blasted; rolling through the deadening fog, they sounded like distant thunder. Two seconds.

He threw his body into a sharp, arching twist and the wind responded, spinning him into a back-breaking curve. He had to get closer before putting down in the water.

Five seconds more and the wind raked at his belly and arms, threatening to toss him any second into a roll. The turn was too sharp. To tumble at this altitude was a death sentence; he'd deploy his chute in a tangle, get caught up in the lines and splatter across the water below.

But there were white breakers on the wave tips. Frothy water could compress better than flat; maybe enough to buy him a higher entry speed. He cut seconds off the chute deployment. The ship soared closer and he plummeted down in a dizzying corkscrew, around the stern where the great engines loomed silently, arching until his spine creaked under the pressure. He let out a scream, hit thirteen seconds, swept right up to the blind side of the ship's aft corner and ripped the release cord.

The chute ejected, caught the wind with an enormous whomp on its shortened lines, and nearly yanked Wren's shoulders out of joint. The ship was so close now; he saw the spinning radar vanes a set of huge upstreaming satellite scoops.

Six seconds of float time, no eyes on him that he could see, then he pulled the release to cut the chute's left tether. It yanked away and the wind fell out of his chute, then there were two seconds left with the ocean charging up toward him and his legs slightly bent, toes tilted down, aiming his body like a pro diver at the frothy tip of those breakers, until-

The ocean hit him like a truck; straight up into the bowl of his gut followed by a heavyweight uppercut in the chin and off the pack on his back, then he was under and blacking out.

"Christopher."

He was back underground, buried alive by his own father, and-

"Christopher."

He blinked in the black, feeling loose and disconnected, like a Pinocchio doll with its strings cut. Damage, his body said. Maybe his ankle, but he couldn't be sure which side. He'd be lucky if it wasn't pulverized by that rough landing.

He looked up to the ocean surface, some twenty feet away, cut the chute's right tether, safely buried underwater now, and kicked upward. His left foot screamed in pain but he kept kicking. His lungs burned. Hellion was chattering away in his ear, or was that static? At the surface he pushed through violent waves, sucked in a gulp of air and reoriented.

The ship was right there, barely fifty yards away. He'd come in perfectly.

"You are clear," came Hellion's voice, sharply reconnecting. "I have reviewed footage from bodycam. They did not see."

That was a relief. Already the cold was spreading through his body; he had thirteen minutes yet before hypothermia. Fifty yards would only take him one. He began to swim toward the sheer metal wall of the ship.

Pleasure Island. At last.

46

PLEASURE ISLAND

After three minutes of front crawl, he hit the ship's flank. Up close it loomed like an overhanging cliff face, towering and sheer. Touching the rough, barnacle-scarred metal, he felt the low thrum of the engine reverberating like a pulse.

From his pack he dug out the first clamp, an oblong high-powered magnet fixed at the end of a wrist-mounted frame; specialist oil rig-repair equipment MacAuley had been proud to source in time. He touched it to the hull and it clamped on hard. He tethered a cable, linked himself in, then leaned back in the freezing water to get the foot braces on.

They looked like chunky black snowboard boots, with large magnetic plates mounted vertically in front of the toes. He tightened the plastic catch on his right foot then tried to slide his left foot in. The pain of his ankle almost blacked him out.

"What's taking so long?" Hellion asked in his ear.

Wren grunted as he tugged the boot on. "I might have broken my ankle."

Hellion said nothing. Not shocked, Wren figured, but

hopefully re-working. A good operator would compensate for the injury in his route to clear the ship. Footage from his spiral descent should have given her a clear view of the guards on patrol; now she'd be mapping them atop the ship's schematic.

"Can you walk at all?"

"Let's find out," Wren said, and heaved at the boot again. His left foot slid in and the blackness rose up, but he gritted his teeth and willed it back. Pain was just weakness leaving the body. He tightened the plastic strap; it hurt, but the boot functioned like a splint. He touched the front plate to the hull and it clamped noisily.

He leaned in and stood up, lifting his body out of the water. The pain came like a mantrap around his ankle, stars spun before his eyes and he felt nauseous, but the clamps held and so did Wren.

"Well?"

"Maybe a stress fracture, could be just an ankle sprain. I'll manage."

"Then manage. I'll talk you through the route."

Wren attached the right hand clamp then began to climb, shifting his hands up one at a time, shifting the foot clamps, bracing his weight on his right leg and arms as much as he could. His ankle grated on every step, but he gritted his teeth and kept moving.

"There are ten guards on walkway around container stacks," Hellion said. "Each spread three hundred feet apart, plus four more on top of stacks. Best spot for insertion remains aft-port corner, where you are."

Wren worked that through as he climbed, . "How long between sweeps?"

"Working … calculating pace … looks like three-hundred feet per minute, take out two, this would give you five minute lead time to enter main ship body."

"Any idea where the children are? Where Clara Baxter is?"

"We have nothing on thermal imagining. Too many layers of container metal to see through."

That made sense. Three quarters of the way up now. They could be anywhere on board, hidden in more floor space than a dozen city blocks, deep inside the belly of the whale.

"Christopher?"

"In position," he whispered back, reaching the top of the ship's flank and squatting on his magnets just under the railing. The ship groaned, the ocean lapped far below and the sour tang of cigarette smoke curled in the mist.

A sentry. Wren strained to hear. Sounded like footsteps clanking closer. The scent of smoke grew stronger. He waited until it felt right, silently drawing his dart gun, until he heard voices, and realized this wasn't a solo patrol.

There were three of them.

It was time.

Wren peeled his right foot off the hull, pulled it back and kicked the metal hard.

A deep, ringing bong thrummed out.

The footsteps stopped. Wren aimed, guessing, to his right at the railing twenty yards away. Not a good angle for them to use their rifles. Not an easy angle to see him. For him a straight shot up into their eyes.

The first leaned over. Wren saw only his silhouette, like a paper target on the range, and loosed three darts with three fizzing whips of air. Two thunked home, eye and cheek. The man's mouth opened wide and then he tipped over the railing and tumbled to the sea.

Wren didn't wait.

A second face appeared almost directly above Wren, too soon after the first to react well. He fired three more fizzing darts and they all hit, face face neck, and the man, a ruddy-cheeked giant, sagged instantly.

"What the-" came a voice from above, but Wren was already moving. He sprang over the railing, landed awkwardly and in pain, but used that pain to fuel his anger.

The third man had his rifle up and ready, fifteen yards away, but Wren fired first. Two darts remained, one missed and one hit in the guy's right arm and it sagged off the trigger, but not enough to take him down. Signals were still getting to his brain and back again with the message to swap arms and pull the trigger.

Wren flung his knife, a sweeping cross body toss from the holster on his left hip like he was sending a Frisbee for the distance. The knife shot out, end over end closing the gap in half a second, to take the guard in his open mouth.

His head rocked back and he dropped without a further sound.

Wren stood unevenly, looking left and right along the perimeter walkway.

Two bodies. The railing lay ahead, the huge iron mass of the stacks stood at his back, containers rising in rust-patched red and yellow and blue. He had no sight line to the aft, the castle, or the nearest guard in either direction.

"Three down," he said, and retrieved his knife. Two bodies went over the rail. A clean sweep, and no time to waste. "How long?"

"Fourteen minutes remain," Hellion answered.

He was going to need every second. "Send the team. I'm going in."

47

PYRAMID

W ren padded along to the three-deck-tall castle, the only portion of the ship with a door, and tried it. It swung open. Inside was the guards' quarters: a wide, dimly lit space with a low metal ceiling; two desks stood to the side with old tower computers; several beds lay along the far wall behind a partially-drawn curtain, with a rec. area and modest kitchen in the middle. No stairs led up or down, though, and there was no door leading deeper.

"It's not this," Hellion said, watching through his body cam. "You're only seeing half the width of the castle. Access must be on the other side."

Wren strode further in.

"Where are you going?"

Near the desk he looked up. There was a hatch in the ceiling and one in the floor, welded over. There had been stairs here. It put the guards on their own loop, completely separated from the Pinocchios. Layers within layers, like multiple VPNs built into reality.

"Go around," Hellion said. "Two more guards on the

walkway, will waste time but this is only choice. Marine team yet to make insertion."

"No time for that," Wren whispered back, and strode toward the curtain, hung from rivet holes in the deck beams above. He stepped through into the dark rear section. It smelled of stale sweat and musty clothes, like a locker room. Standing in the hot, humid dark, Wren's eyes adjusted. The far wall that partitioned the castle didn't match the sides; it wasn't metal, more like plasterboard painted to look like metal. He scanned the beds; four of them with two figures asleep. Pinocchio wannabes, Wren figured. Hoping to prove themselves and one day be admitted.

Their bad luck.

"What is it?" Hellion whispered.

Wren strode to the first man. There was no time to be kind. Every Pinocchio left here was a man he'd have to fight later or his team would face coming in. He leaned in quietly, cradled the man's head in his hands then twisted.

His neck broke with a crack like a dry stick. Dead in his sleep, instantly. No thrashing, no mess. The second went just the same.

"Christopher," said Hellion, sounding disapproving.

"It's a false wall," Wren said, already moving on. "Plasterboard. It'll come away."

He moved to the edge, where damp had turned the plaster black, pushed against it, and the softened material gave way. He pushed harder, tearing the boards from bolts fastened to the bulkhead.

On the other side lay a dark, cold cavity space, five feet wide and bordered to the right with another wall; this one was inset with wide windows and a door. Cameras were set up in the darkness, blinking red and pointing through the glass to a very different world.

The space beyond was opulent, with dark mahogany

flooring and red leather paneled walls fitted with sconces releasing an orange glow. It was like the lobby of a five-star hotel, but modeled after Gebhart's Idaho dungeon. Lush-looking armchairs were set out with ashtrays, potted jungle plants bloomed in the corners, fresh flowers sprayed outward on a central table, and a reception desk was manned by a young blond woman in a pert blue cap. On the left an ornate gilt door was built into a marble-effect wall.

Bingo.

"That door leads into the containers," Wren whispered.

"Perhaps some structure hidden within," Hellion answered. "Excellent concealment. I am 3D modeling possible outline. But why cameras here?"

"Insurance," Wren said, striding toward the door. How much trust could there be in a society shaped by daily votes for popularity? Given their gamified system of control, the Pinocchios would be constantly vying with each other. This was the elites keeping tabs on each other, stacking up blackmail material for future leverage.

He strode behind the cameras, switched off the last on the left that overlooked the marble wall, then opened the door leading through.

Instantly the atmosphere was different. Underfoot the wood flexed like ancient boards in a grand Southern home. The warm air smelled of jasmine and lemongrass. To the right the girl at the reception desk stared.

"Don't you move," Wren said.

She didn't move. There was no way she was a Pinocchio. Maybe she was someone's favorite, graduated to an above-decks role.

"Keep quiet and you'll be free soon," Wren said, then opened the door leading through the marble wall. Beyond it lay a corridor that passed seamlessly through the outer skin of the castle and into where the containers should be.

It felt like stepping through the looking glass.

Wren couldn't help but admire the workmanship to cover up the welds where this five-star corridor cut through the containers. It extended for some fifteen yards: carpeted in red and gold, framed with elegant dark baseboards, wallpapered in taupe and hung with scenes of ancient Greek temples. In reality it was a tunnel bored through metal container boxes, a tube hanging in carved hollows, but it didn't look like that.

Gebhart would have loved it; a secret realm hiding in plain sight, like the dance of the Blue Fairy through the darknet, like his dungeon beneath the Idaho dirt.

Wren turned at the corner. Ten yards further on stood an elevator; a classic brass frame with a safety grille concertina and a guard either side. These were not the same caliber as the men outside. These were clearly Pinocchio elites, with better gear, greater alertness and their hands already on their weapons.

Wren fired, dual-wielding his twin P226s so four shots rang out in fast succession. They took one each in the head and chest in the midst of two enormous combined blasts. Echoes rang around Wren as he advanced, and the guards thumped to the floor with ringing metallic bongs.

"Couldn't have done it better myself," Hellion said. "Team is on your six, about to insert."

Wren entered the elevator, feeling the flow state of his black-ops days descending upon him. The walls were fringed with gold, mirrors and carvings of depraved sexual deeds. The pain in his ankle felt very far away. He yanked the concertina grille across and pulled the brass lever set in its attractive casement.

The carriage began to descend.

48

BELLY OF THE WHALE

T he elevator stopped some four stories down, the door opened, and a luxurious corridor extended ahead through the concertina grille, stretching at least a hundred yards away.

Wren took it all in: plush beige carpeting, soft-glow wall-lamps, wood-paneled walls, and men in cream terrycloth gowns walking, talking and smoking.

Pinocchios.

The warm, balmy smell of vanilla cigar smoke on the air, barely masking the earthy undercurrent of sweat and the tang of blood.

And there were children.

All ages, boys and girls, waiting outside doors, dressed in uniform blue tunics with eyes that were either wide and terrified or dull and numb.

Wren's breath failed him, like he'd been hit with a hammer in the gut. The belly of the whale. Tactics went out the window and strategy failed him as he battled an overwhelming surge of rage, disbelief and disgust. For five seconds, ten, he just stood behind the grille and stared, feeling the red mist descend and push everything else aside.

This was it. Pleasure Island. It was real.

A guard broke the gridlock by leaning in from the side to peer through the concertina.

Both Wren's Sig P226s fired at once, the hollow-point bullets expanding on impact and obliterating the man's head.

So it began.

Wren raked the concertina aside and strode into the corridor, shooting the guard to his left then firing into the rich hunting ground ahead; unleashing twelve bullets from each Sig in less than ten seconds, striking twelve targets each. Heads rocked back as the hollow-points flattened and tumbled through to targets beyond, high above the height of the children and stamping gaping holes into their tormentors.

Screams pealed out and the chaos of blood and gunpowder became a scrabbling, desperate roar as the Pinocchios panicked and ran; some toward Wren, some away, some into their rooms.

Wren smoothly reloaded from the bandolier around his chest and continued his rain of fire, gliding forward in a transcendent haze, bringing retribution for unspeakable crimes. The President's capture order didn't matter. Innocent until proven guilty did not matter.

There could be no mercy for these men. Pleasure Island was an abomination and so was every Pinocchio aboard; no sympathy for them, no coin status or way back to the light, only the cold certainty of the grave.

He reloaded again and advanced. He shot a thick man with yellowish skin and a large liverwort exposed on his chest. He shot a tall man as thin as a cadaver, standing in a cluster with two others. He shot the men running toward him and the men running away, he shot those cowering on the blood-soaked carpet, and those pretending to be dead amongst the bodies of their fellows.

A minute. Two.

How many reloads? He didn't know.

His arms moved independently of his mind, finding targets one after another as he flowed over freshly-fallen corpses, cutting the Pinocchios' strings, and the hail of gunfire built into a storm in the corridor, thunderous with the pealing of screams and the endless ricochet of bullets.

Children stared wide-eyed as he passed, unable to comprehend what they were seeing. A man on the floor tried to shield himself with one palm and Wren shot him in the head through his fingers.

Doors slammed to all sides as Pinocchios took refuge, but Wren didn't care. They couldn't hide from this.

"Christopher!" came a voice in his ear, but he didn't hear it. It didn't matter.

He kicked in a door on the left. It looked like a five-star hotel room, with a luxurious bed, furniture, lights, trimmings. A powerfully muscled man held two glass-eyed little girls in red tunics before him as a human shield, trying to shout out some kind of negotiation. Wren fired through a gap into his groin. He shrieked, his blood spuming out over the sheets like a burst catheter. Wren shot him in the head then moved on.

"Christopher!" came the voice again.

He came back to himself in the center of the corridor, looking at the P226s in his hands. Spattered blood smoked and baked dry on the hot barrels. A trail of bodies lay behind him and a trail of bodies lay in front, like the streets of the fake town, back when he'd burned them all. They were burning still, and it was all his work. He felt his father's hand at his back even now, guiding him on, gleeful with his dedication to devastation, but this was not his father's work.

This belonged to him alone.

"Christopher, think of Clara Baxter, you must-"

A shot rang out. He looked at his guns, momentarily perplexed, then another came, and this one he felt. It hit his lower back, left side, and reeled him sideways. He lurched into the wall, staggering on his bad ankle. His back bloomed cold; hopefully the bulletproof Twaron vest had taken the worst of it.

He turned to see a man in a Pinocchio mask standing in the middle of the corridor, holding up a gun.

"Charles?" Wren asked.

The man fired in a frenzy now, spraying the walls and floor. Wren holstered his empty guns and advanced, pulling his knife.

"Shh," he said, "it's OK."

The man fired only once more, arm shaking so badly that he hit the ceiling, then he dropped the weapon as if it had bit him and turned to run, but stumbled on the bodies.

Wren caught him on his knees.

"Please, please, I didn't-" the man began frantically, but Wren simply brought the knife around and pushed it into his throat in one smooth movement. The man pawed up at him. Begging for mercy, but Wren had none to give.

He sagged. Wren lifted the mask and looked at his face. It wasn't DeVore, though. He touched his lower back and his hand came back clean and unbloodied. The vest had done its job.

"Christopher Wren, get on point right now!"

He blinked and turned. The voice was familiar. Coming from very far away, nearly tuned out by the mass of metal above. Probably she'd found a way into the Fairy's wireless network. His very own Jiminy Cricket.

"Hellion."

"Yes, Hellion! What happened, you went crazy."

"I-"

"There is no time. We have their livestream, Clara Baxter is on altar with blade over her head. Go now!"

It came back to him. He wasn't here just to kill

Pinocchios. He needed to save Clara Baxter, or they'd get their moment of revenge, and every dead man here would become another martyr to their cause.

He looked to the elevator. The concertina grille still hung open, perhaps the only unsullied part of the corridor. The mirrors within reflected the world back at him. Children moved amongst them now, some escaping, some taking their revenge. Here a little girl punched a dead man in the face again and again.

Good. Anger was the only bandage that had ever helped Wren.

He found one man amidst the dying, struggling to breathe with what looked to be a sucking chest wound from a ricochet, and kneeled beside him. Wren descended across his field of vision and he tried to jerk away, but Wren held him firmly.

"Where is Clara Baxter?"

The man sucked air like a bellows.

"I- I- who?"

Wren pressed the muzzle of the gun against his forehead. "Clara Baxter. Mona Gebhart. Lance Gebhart's daughter. Where is she?"

The man's eyes flared wider. "Uh, you mean, Girl Zero?"

Wren blinked. "Zero?"

"The first. The first girl. The foundation?"

Wren had heard none of those names, and right now didn't care.

"Where?" he roared in the man's face.

"The temple! In the temple!"

"Where's the temple?"

"Down there!" The guy pointed with one flailing hand. "Please, don't-"

Wren put the knife in his throat, swiftly reloaded his Sigs and ran.

"Mapping this," said Hellion, but Wren didn't need it. The corridor went in only one direction.

Wren burst through the doors at the end of the corridor, into a space that took his breath away. The 'temple'.

It was a cavernous, conical pit that plunged deep into the bowels of the ship, easily forty yards across at the top but only five or so at the base, sinking maybe thirty deep through carved-out container boxes. A vaulted iron ceiling hung overhead, supported on five giant girders rising to a peak, beneath which the space dropped away in narrowing concentric rings of tiered seating. At the very bottom lay a spotlit circular stage, within which stood a metal block altar.

Wren stood in the upper circle, mind boggling at the mechanics of this negative space, dug out like the tunnels in an Egyptian pyramid and decked everywhere in raw, corroded metal edges.

The fake, bullshit luxury of Pleasure Island ended here.

This was grimy and harsh, the brutal, primitive heart of Gebhart's Blue Fairy, beating in time with the thrum of the engines.

Cameras were spotted everywhere amongst the seating tiers, trained on the altar and blinking red with a live signal.

Pinocchios in their terrycloth robes scrabbled everywhere Wren looked, fleeing through several exits like termites blending back into wood.

Wren didn't care.

He only had eyes for one Pinocchio, a masked and naked man kneeling on the altar, skin shiny with streaky bronzer. He saw Wren arrive and reared back, raising a knife high in both fists, straddling the thrashing, naked figure of Clara Baxter.

Wren knew this man: the Pinocchios' new hero, the influencer who'd 'sacrificed' his family on the Blue Fairy's command.

Ravenous6. Charles DeVore.

The knife came down and Wren fired.

The hollow-point bullet struck DeVore in the shoulder and blew out through his upper arm, the force slinging him off the altar to crack face-first on the metal floor. The knife dropped, DeVore shrieked and Wren sprinted down the stairs toward him, clouded by a red mist.

DeVore struggled to get his legs and ruined arm beneath him, but Wren dropped across him and punched him in the throat, then flipped him on his back like a landed fish and ripped his mask away.

Blood was everywhere already, spraying from DeVore's gouged arm and his smashed face. His features had been wrecked by the fall, lips smashed and teeth cracked, but Wren ignored that and looked into his eyes.

They were the same as they'd been in his den a day ago, filled with terror and uncertainty.

"Y-you," DeVore spluttered through his seizing throat, spraying blood and flecks of teeth. "You s-said ... I could ..."

"There's no permission for this," Wren said, barely able to speak for the fury pulsing through his system. "There's no mercy for this."

Tears sprang from DeVore's eyes and leaked through the

blood on his cheeks. He struggled to breathe. His hands patted Wren's face feebly, like he was seeking something. "Please," he mumbled. "Please."

"No-" Wren began, then something struck him in the back of the head like a ten-pound hammer.

Lights exploded across his vision as he jerked forward, his body tumbling numbly across DeVore's. Instantly he felt weak as blackness chased the lights and the echo of the strike rang around the metallic temple, allowing one stray thought to twist a path through: 'So that's what a wooden bat to the back of a skull sounds like.'

He tried to roll off DeVore but his body didn't listen, and he barely managed a feeble shrug as a second blow came down. It thumped across his broad back, cracking ribs and driving the air from his lungs.

"How dare you?" roared a furious, deep voice from above, then a third blow landed, striking Wren's right upper arm in a burst of agony. Numbness spread instantly down to his fingers and the Sig dropped from his fist.

"How dare you enter this place with your filth and your violence?"

Wren used the momentum of the strike to roll left, finally getting onto his back and taking a look up at his attacker.

It wasn't just one.

There were four, maybe five, men dressed in jeans and check shirts, wearing grotesque, cragged Pinocchio masks and wielding wooden baseball bats. The same view Malton Bruce would have seen. The same view countless catfishers across the country had seen as they were battered, mutilated and bled out.

The fourth blow came and Wren just managed to duck his head close to his chest, taking only a portion of the blow on his left temple. Still the strike bounced his skull off the floor and upturned his thinking.

"This is our sacred place!" the Pinocchio boomed, already swinging the bat back for the fifth strike. "This is our day for glory."

The bat came down and Wren was helpless to avoid it, but managed to get his left arm up. The impact was crushing, pummeling into the muscle of his forearm and through to the bone, crumpling his arm inward. His own fist smashed back into his face, drawing blood across his teeth and slamming his head once more off the floor.

Wren sagged limp, feeling consciousness ebbing away. Perhaps this was how it ended, on a livestream for all the Pinocchios to see. He couldn't tell if his arm was broken, but the pain was all-consuming.

The other Pinocchios gathered around him. Four, five, maybe more of them now. Their masks leered down, their bats raised in the air over his head, then they fell.

50

ZERO

None landed.

A bloodcurdling shriek pealed out, high and piercing like the wail of a banshee, dragging all eyes to the side.

Wren could scarcely believe what he was seeing.

Clara Baxter stood atop the iron altar, naked and fearsome with her arms spread and DeVore's knife in her fist. Blood ran in streams from the torn zip-tie bracelets on her wrists. Wren's brain spun in circles as the Pinocchios swung their bats in her direction. She'd caught the knife somehow. She'd cut her wrists to shreds to get free, but free she was.

A Pinocchio-killing savant.

Girl Zero.

She leaped onto the chest of the nearest man, plunging the blade perfectly into his left eye socket.

Blood spurted from the wound and he dropped without a sound. Zero fell with him, hit the ground and rolled, surging up beside Wren with the knife shooting out.

It stabbed it into the crotch of the nearest man, she raked it sideways across his femoral artery then plunged it into the next man's kidney. A bat swiped in and she swayed below it, but caught the man's arm and swiftly slit his wrist then backhanded the blade into his throat.

He gargled and fell, but Zero was already moving on to the next.

Wren watched entranced. Blurred by the gray waves of unconsciousness, Zero became a phantom, flowing between the falling bats like she could dance between raindrops, whipping out the blade like an asp's tongue.

Throats slit. Eyes cleaved. Blood rushed out.

Three more men fell as they struggled to bring their bats to bear in close quarters. Four.

Zero made them pay for every second of panic and confusion.

But more were coming.

Wren saw them through the crush of bodies, dozens of Pinocchios flooding down the tiered seating, bats raised, eyes burning.

Zero evaded a downward strike, spiked a large man through the heart, then finally a bat came down toward the back of her head. She didn't see it and couldn't stop it.

Wren caught it with his bare left hand.

The bat slammed into his palm but he buried the momentum and swallowed the phenomenal pain, then brought his right hand up and twisted, ripping the bat away. It came free and Wren swung it at the wielder in a dizzy blur.

It hit and bounced back bloody so he sent it out again. He became a whirlwind of massive, skull-crushing blows, flattening Pinocchios with single strikes, shattered their masks and their faces, while Girl Zero weaved a lethal trail in his wake.

The flood of Pinocchios reached Wren, but it didn't matter now. Their bats pounded off Wren's arms and legs like the pattering of butterflies' wings. He didn't feel them, lost in a flow state of violence, the bat just an extension of his body designed solely to hammer Pinocchios into the ground.

This was for Malton Bruce and Tom Solent, for Reince Jeffries and poor little Mona Gebhart, for all the dead catfishers and a ship full of forsaken children.

Then the bat cracked, split and separated. The flow state stopped.

Wren stood gasping by the altar, soaked with blood and streaming with sweat, the broken bat useless in his hands. The surge of Pinocchios had stopped, but not because there weren't any left.

They were massing at a dark rathole tunnel running up from the bowels of the ship, halfway up the tiers. Wren tried to count them but his vision was doubled and blurred. A dozen? Two dozen?

Too many.

The bat dropped from his shaking fists. He was drained beyond exhaustion. He looked at Zero. Her bare skin gleamed red like crimson armor, but she was pale and trembling. There was no fight left in either of them.

"You'll die slowly for this," one of the Pinocchios shouted. "We'll take everything from you. This is for Lance!"

The shout was answered and taken up by the others, swiftly morphing into a chant that swelled to fill that yawning space.

"Lance Gebhart, Lance Gebhart, LANCE GEBHART!"

Their pig eyes burned in their filthy masks.

Wren scanned the twitching bodies at his feet as the crowd amped themselves up to charge. None had guns, only masks and bats, which told him something. His mind raced for what that meant. A sign. A symbol, maybe, of what they'd done to earn their place.

They weren't here as security. They hadn't expected to fight.

Which meant...

"LANCE GEBHART, LANCE GEBHART, LANCE GEBHART!"

He spotted one of his Sigs lying a stride away, but kept looking: there were bodies convulsing, there was DeVore's bloody and tear-stained face, there were robes and zip-ties and finally he saw what he was looking for.

"LANCE GEBHART!"

The Pinocchios charged.

Wren strode to scoop up a dead body on the floor. One fist wrapped around the man's upper arm, the other snagged his belt, and Wren pulled. Every muscle in his body activated at once, from his calves to his thighs through his trunk to his chest and shoulders as he lifted and twisted with all his strength, accelerating the corpse upward into an arcing trajectory and released.

The body flew, directly toward the charging Pinocchios. They couldn't stop it. They didn't try.

After a second it reached the peak of its flight, five yards out and halfway toward the throng of Pinocchios. After two it was falling, on three it dropped into the midst of their clamor and fury, by which time Wren had snatched up his Sig.

He sighted in on the suicide vest strapped around the dead man's chest and fired.

The explosion bloomed like a brutal red flower, burning its crimson petals into Wren's retinas. Blood blew out in a pink mist, shrapnel chunks of body parts spattered and thumped against the tiers out and the altar. A severed hand slapped off Wren's shoulder, hot blood foamed across his face and a dart of sizzling metal embedded in his chest.

The chant was over. The echoes of the blast rang.

Wren stood alone, surveying the carnage.

Not a single Pinocchio remained intact. Their bodies were spread in a swamp of red at the heart of Lance Gebhart's vision. Pieces of them still fell from the air.

It was done.

51

FREE

The silence that followed was strange and incomplete. There was a voice talking in Wren's ear, but it sounded very far away.

He looked around the temple. Devastated bodies convulsed and died. Blood flowed and pooled around the metal altar.

"You need to get out of there, Christopher," came the voice again, clearer this time, bringing him back to the moment.

"Hellion?"

"Sally Rogers and team are entering ship. I do not think she will like what you have done here."

Wren grunted. That was an understatement. This was a massacre, exactly what she'd made him swear to avoid. He looked up at the vaulted ceiling of the temple, wheeling and fuzzing so far above. It was perhaps the only part of this great, bizarre hall unmarked by blood.

"I'll get out," he muttered, then dropped his gaze to the cameras on their tiers, to the red lights flashing that signaled a livestream, and felt the anger coming back. This is what Clara

Baxter, Girl Zero, had grown up with. They'd gulped down her suffering for years.

He gazed into the lenses and boomed out a message.

"You will never be this free again. You will never be this bold again. Turn yourselves in or die by my hand, because I am coming."

"Christopher, should I cut livestream?" Hellion asked in his ear. "We are gaining access to everything in Blue Fairy now. I am uplifting all data. I have control of cameras."

"Kill them."

The red lights started winking out around the tiers. Wren stared the last of them down, then turned to Clara Baxter.

Mona Gebhart. Girl Zero.

She stood naked still, bloodied and unbowed, astride the body of Charles DeVore. The fury blazing in her eyes was terrifying and wondrous. That rage had survived for nine long years in her father's dungeon. Maybe it was the reason he'd kept her alive for so long, fascinated by her strength.

"Where did you come from?" she asked, her voice husky and raw.

"Detroit," Wren answered, feeling like at any moment his legs might give out. "I've been hunting the Blue Fairy for months."

"Why?"

He saw no reason to lie. "Because they threatened my children."

That seemed to surprise her. "You have kids?"

He managed a half-smile. The weariness was descending, now, the post-adrenaline crash combining with the swirling pain and nausea in his head. "I do. It's possible, Clara. Mona. For people like us."

She shook her head fiercely. "Not for me."

There seemed to be nothing more to say. Both their gazes

fell to Charles DeVore, mewling and bleeding on the iron floor. She pointed at him with the blade.

"He's mine."

Wren studied this young woman. Most people who'd experienced what she just had would be reduced to sobbing heaps on the floor. Only a handful of the hardest operators Wren had ever known could handle themselves like this.

But she was special. A savant. Wren recognized a fellow traveler on the road out of pain. The only relief he'd ever found had come through justice. Through death.

She needed this, but it could cost Wren everything.

Sally Rogers would never understand. All the deaths up to now, perhaps they could be explained. The fog of war. Exigent circumstances.

Not this. DeVore was subdued. He was unarmed. Wren's role in any further punishment could end his career, even dump him in a black site for the rest of his life.

But it was what Clara Baxter needed.

He bent down to scoop up Charles DeVore. For a moment there was hope in his watery eyes, perhaps believing this was compassion, maybe even a rescue.

Then Wren set him down on the altar.

DeVore began screeching like a wounded animal.

Wren strapped his arms and legs down with zip-ties, like he was buckling the seatbelt of an unruly child. Zero joined him. DeVore tried to resist but was too weak. In moments he lay naked on the altar, spread-eagled and vulnerable, just like Lance Gebhart before him.

Zero stared at Wren. "Turn the cameras back on."

Wren met her gaze. If there was anyone in the world who came close to understanding how she felt now, it was Wren. If he'd had the chance, wouldn't he have done this to his own father?

"You heard the woman," he said to Hellion.

The red lights flickered back to life.

"He's all yours."

Zero set the blade down on Charles DeVore's body and began to cut.

His screams climbed an octave.

Wren walked away.

52

DEPTHS

Wren entered the rathole tunnel amongst the tiers, limping and breathing raggedly, while the world spun around him. He'd taken too much damage. He needed a hospital, but he couldn't stop now.

The rathole led deep into the dank innards of Pleasure Island.

"Hellion?" he murmured.

"We are here, Christopher," came her distracted reply in his ear. "Breaking Blue Fairy right now … Cryptoworm is active. I am seeing whole map: addresses, code, cryptography. B4cksl4cker is relaying it live, sending details of multiple VPN and IP addresses of Pinocchios now to law enforcement agencies internationally. .... Interpol, Germans, British, Japanese, Chinese, French … locations all around the world."

She was excited. She'd earned it.

"I need an exfiltration," he mumbled.

"Sally Rogers team are coming, no? They are," keys clacked furiously, "above you now. Clearing first corridor, it seems."

"They'll arrest me. Baxter too. You need to get us both out."

Seconds passed. "How do you suggest I do this?"

"You wanted to be my operator. Figure it out."

"Working. B4cksl4cker, handle breaking of Fairy."

"Breaking," came B4cksl4cker's response.

"Coast Guard are also inbound, Christopher. You must be fast."

He didn't feel fast. "Understood. Can you communicate with Baxter?"

"Yes. There is speaker system in temple."

"Let her know the exfil. We can't let Rogers have her."

"Understood. Working. Estimate you have ten minutes before Sally Rogers' team reach Temple."

The rathole opened into a wider hall, stretching into the distance along the keel of the ship. Wren felt dizziness swamp him and dropped to his hands and knee. The floor beneath his fingers was metal grille. He breathed slow and carefully, trying to avoid aggravate the cracked ribs in his back.

Slowly, he lifted his head. The walls around him were damp, all made of rusted container boxes. The hallway was lit by hanging strings of industrial strip lights, and seemed to stretch forever, far along the spine of the ship.

Everywhere was the sound of children crying.

Wren scanned the walls. There was stenciled writing in place, next to bolted doors and grille-windows. Cells. They detailed age, gender and ethnicity.

Different batches of children for different foul tastes.

The job was not done yet.

Wren pushed himself to his feet, bulling through the weakness and the nausea, to look through the nearest window grille. There were at least a dozen children inside clustered together at the back, dressed in red tunics. Their eyes darted right.

That was everything Wren needed to know.

He pushed the door open and lunged left. His knife buried in the neck of a thick Pinocchio hidden against the wall. The man looked surprised. There were two more behind him, clutching their robes as if they could protect them. Wren shot them through with one hollow-point bullet from his Sig, and they gasped like whistling reeds and dropped.

"They're yours," he mumbled to the children, echoing what he'd said to Zero, and moved on.

The next cell was much the same. These Pinocchios hadn't thought clearly, hiding in the cells of their victims. Again the children's darting eyes gave them away. The door opened, the Sig fired, the knife rose and fell. Some tried to fight, but these men were soft like DeVore. Pleasure Island's resistance was broken.

Wren killed this way from cell to cell.

Children ran in his wake, stamping, stabbing, raking with their fingernails. They taught each other how to get their revenge, and Wren made no effort to stop them. Like Zero, they needed this. The Pinocchios begged, but there could be no mercy now.

"Coast Guard will arrive in moments," came Hellion's voice in his ear. "Your team are in Temple."

"Baxter?"

"Gone. Found her own way."

Maybe that was for the best. Wren stood and weaved. Dead Pinocchios lay everywhere, again. Children ran madly, some drenched with the blood of their captors.

"Charles DeVore?"

"Not dead. Almost. He screamed very much. All wounds are sealed with zip ties."

"Like Tom Solent," Wren murmured, drifting on the blood haze. "You have my exfil?"

"Yes. I have back route to deck, away from Sally Rogers."

"Direct me."

At the end of the long hall of cells lay a spiral staircase which bored into a broad vent rising upward. It felt like he climbed forever. Wren finally emerged through a container box and out onto the frigid, foggy walkway encircling the ship.

The air was bracing, like he'd stepped out of a dream and back into reality. There were no guards left. Wren stood at the railing and looked out. Off to the right lights beamed through the mist and voices called on megaphones. Coast Guard.

A fine rain fell. Wren felt altered, as if his passage through Pleasure Island had left him as dozy as the boys turned into donkeys in the Pinocchio story. He didn't feel healed by what he'd done, nor did he feel broken. He felt nothing.

The sea below thrashed with white foam on gray waves. It would be good to go over the railing, drop into the cold water and sink. What could be better than that?

"Exfil is there," Hellion said. "Fishing vessel, lights off. Go now, Christopher."

Wren saw nothing through the mist. He thought about the children whose lives were forever scarred by this place. At least they weren't victims, now. Like Girl Zero, they were survivors, and he hoped that was a gift, not a burden.

"Boat is directly ahead of you," Hellion said. "Go, Christopher."

He couldn't see it. It didn't matter. He hoped he'd done enough to insulate Sally Rogers from blowback, then he rolled himself over the railing, dropped and splashed into the deep, smothering black.

53

HOME

Wren stood at the edge of the fake town in Arizona, looking out at the fire pits.

Children were clustered around them, toasting s'mores. Children from the ship, from around the world, who had probably never had a s'more before, who might not even know what a Graham cracker was. They seemed to be having a good time. There was only a small group of them, for now, but more would follow.

His back throbbed still. The Pinocchio's bullet had dug through the Twaron vest and bumped against his hip; a flesh wound and a bruised bone, extracted and sewn up three weeks ago. The cracked ribs hurt when he breathed in deeply, and he still had some nausea at night from the baseball bat concussion, but generally, he felt OK.

A lot of things had changed since Pleasure Island fell. His Foundation site was different, in line with the lessons Hellion and B4cksl4cker had learned from the Blue Fairy's system. They'd put voting systems in place for every member, with coin rankings linked to influence and visibility. The higher members had their comments and posts amplified; most of those so far were about the criteria used to drive future growth of the system.

Many members were contributing ideas. So far, it was proving an effective way to funnel new ideas up, and not merely descending into an ego-driven echo chamber. That was good to see.

His sprained ankle was healing, too, after a week in a cast. He'd probably broken records for that skydive, but he wasn't shouting it from the rooftops. After the fisherman had scooped him out of the cold water, he didn't really remember much. He hadn't checked in with Humphreys or Rogers since, but was aware no official charges had been laid publicly at his feet.

As for unofficial? Humphreys was probably glad Wren had disappeared. It allowed for a narrative where the Blue Fairy had self-combusted, the members turning against each other in an offshore bloodbath.

Better for the President. Better all around.

Now Rogers had been promoted and was leading her own intelligence team, freelance for the CIA, FBI, DHS, whoever needed her. That made Wren proud. She'd stayed on the lighter side of the gray, and that was for the best.

Hellion and B4cksl4cker had crushed the Blue Fairy, but managed to keep some of their hidden network, carried on Gebhart's weathernet. It expanded their covert power, which Wren hadn't shirked away from using.

Their first priority had been to ensure, via blackmail, bribery or other means, that every child trafficked to the United States by the Blue Fairy would be granted immediate asylum, with a trust fund set up in their name. No questions about it, no delays, just done, while keeping their existence off the front pages.

On every one of their new passports was Wren's name, alongside Clara Baxter's, both enshrined as legal guardians.

Wren hadn't confirmed that with Baxter, or 'Girl Zero', but he thought she'd be pleased. He'd been proud to see the first of the certificates, for something good to come from something so bad.

It was an enormous expansion to his Foundation, and a substantial shift of focus. Thanks to Hellion and B4cksl4cker draining the Blue Fairy's coffers, though, the Foundation had the funds, but it required a phenomenal degree of management.

Wren asked Maggie to host their recovery at the fake town, and she'd almost bit his hand off.

Now donations were pouring in. The fake town was coming back to life with new construction; dormitories, a library, a school, a gym and pool, a new oasis of life in the desert. That made Wren happy in the most complex way.

Stars tumbled overhead. His leased Jeep stood ticking at his side.

For the Pleasure Island children there'd be a hayride soon, and a tour of the desert without flashlights, giving them a chance to be kids again. He'd wanted to erase this place from the map, like Clara Baxter had memorialized the Idaho farm, but this felt better.

The site of his childhood trauma was being transformed and reclaimed, becoming a home to so many lost children.

The sound of laughter rose from below. Bobbing for apples in water barrels, it looked like, while some played with sparklers. A Roman Candle fizzed yellow and green. The smell of s'mores carried on the wind, along with hotdogs sizzling on a charcoal griddle.

"Here you are."

The soft, familiar voice took him by surprise. She knew the desert better than him, now.

He turned to face Maggie. She was standing by his truck, with a sad smile on her warm, ringlet-framed face. She wore a long, flowing gown in cozy shades of brown, with a tan sash hanging across her shoulders, wrapped up like a desert rose seed husk.

Wren smiled. "You got me."

She just gazed at him, and her eyes seemed to peel through his defensive shell, like she knew him. She stepped up beside him and they looked out at the reinvigorated town together.

"They look happy now," she said, "but they still cry at night."

Wren didn't know what to say to that. It was too close to his own experience. At night was when the terrors came.

"You're like a ghost, haunting this place," she said. "I've felt you watching us. I know you've been out here."

His throat felt dry. "I don't want to scare them."

Maggie put a hand on his arm. "You won't scare them. You're a good kind of ghost. I feel it, and the children feel it, too. They feel protected." She paused a moment, and a single shooting star streaked across the dark sky. "You were right before, when we first met. This is your town, Christopher Wren. It belongs to you and we are just guests within it. Thank you for letting us stay. I'm sorry our presence here is so hard for you."

He said nothing. He didn't trust himself to speak."

"I know pain," Maggie went on gently. "I've felt echoes of it all my life. The Pyramid scarred me, but now those ghosts are in the ground. You're not a ghost, Christopher, or a ghost. You can still come back to the living and join us. Maybe tonight, at least for a little while."

Her green eyes entranced him. He thought about his wife, Loralei, and his own kids back in Delaware. He'd gone to see them, but she'd stopped him at the door with a printed restraining order, saying she'd already called the police.

He'd left.

There was nothing else for him out there in the dark, now. Only the copycat Apex who'd ruined his life, and the long, endless search for justice.

But maybe justice could wait for one night.

"Come," Maggie said, taking his hand. "Join us."

Her touch was warm. Wren let her lead him down from the darkness, into the light of the town.

FROM THE AUTHOR

Thank you for reading No Mercy. I'd love to hear your thoughts on the Wren books so far - they're a labor of love, and all reviews are most welcome.

Now, are you ready to take Wren's mission forward, battling for his beloved United States?

In MAKE THEM PAY, the 3rd Chris Wren thriller, a mad director takes reality TV to the extreme - gladiatorial-style 'games' streamed live to the masses, featuring the most hated people in America - billionaires.

Wren's in bad shape, but when the FBI calls asking for a quiet end to this very noisy threat, he mobilizes at once.

Along with Sally Rogers, Wren will bring blind justice wherever he goes. Because rich or poor, all must pay for their crimes, no matter the cost.

- Mike

ALSO BY MIKE GRIST

Christopher Wren (thrillers)
Saint Justice
No Mercy
Make Them Pay
False Flag
Firestorm
Enemy of the People
Backlash
Never Forgive
War of Choice
Hammer of God

Girl Zero (thrillers)
Girl Zero
Zero Day
Kill Zero

The Last Mayor (post-apocalypse)
The Last
The Lost
The Least
The Loss
The List
The Laws
The Lash
The Lies
The Light